THE MEASURE OF ENOUGH

DEONNA KAY

YELLOW SHOES PRESS

THE MEASURE OF ENOUGH
Deonna Kay

For Hope

CONTENT GUIDANCE: This novel explores aspects of psychology and mental health and contains depictions of domestic abuse, eating disorders, sexual abuse, and substance abuse. Please read with care.

PROLOGUE

stare, unblinking, at the series of numbers Daddy lays before me.

2, 6. 10. 14. 18, __, 26.

Anticipation impregnates his voice; he always has faith in me to make him happy. "You've got this, baby girl." He pushes the paper so it's directly in my line of sight. My pigtails, pulled tight against my scalp, feel as if they are trying to squeeze an answer out of me as sweat droplets seep through their curly tension.

"Twenty-four!" I exclaim, fist pumping my hand in the air to prematurely congratulate myself on the correct answer.

"Not quiiite," Daddy relents, drawing out the last word, disappointment accidentally punctuating his voice. "Let's try another one. Your big test is coming up soon." He smiles. The mention of the dreaded Texas Assessment of Academic Skills makes my stomach churn. Daddy says giving the same test to all second graders in the whole state makes about as much sense as trying to tie a bow on a cow's tail. I agree, but Mrs. Edmiston says we have to do it anyway, so I keep studying. With a quick squeeze of my shoulders, he says, "You can do this, Kacee."

I guess since he's a doctor, it makes him more qualified to tutor me in math than Mom. She's just a nurse. Mom walks over to the pair of us, clutching a platter the color of sunshine holding grapes and tiny cheeses. She peers down at the paper. Mom fiddles with my hair, twisting each pigtail around her finger in a corkscrew, then letting it spring back to life. I inhale her scent, a mixture of strawberries and fresh soap.

"Hmmmmm…"

I hate it when she makes those sounds, letting me know she knows the answer. "Kacee…come *on*," she says, as if I'm purposefully withholding the answer to the math problem. She balances on one foot, bent so far over the page she blocks the numbers with her thin body.

"Don't you need to go to your meeting?" Daddy questions without raising his eyes to meet hers, annoyance rifling his voice.

She twists her wrist, checks her watch, and startles, kissing me atop my head as she announces she will be back, and just like that she's gone. Mom's always off to volunteer somewhere, usually at my school or the local library. That's okay with me because Daddy and I have a lot more fun together. Most of the time, anyway.

People think only children get all the time they want with their parents, but when you have one really important parent like my dad who is the town doctor at County General, he is gone a lot doing important things like saving lives. Although he's never too busy to help me with my math homework and to try and make it fun. I watch him as he scurries about the room placing number sequences in the form of a scavenger hunt. My eyes silently plot the pattern. I think I can nail this one.

I jump up from my chair, sending the high-backed antique clattering to the ground, then begin gathering the cards. I slap them all on the table as if a contestant on Supermarket Sweep and fill in the missing number.

"2, 8, 14, 20, 26, 32!"

I flop on the floor, face down in exhaustion, and Daddy piles on top of me, tickling, while I wail in laughter.

Daddy always says, "Math is the key to any worthwhile career, like medicine or law." I don't know what happens if I choose to be something other than a doctor or a lawyer when I grow up. But, let's face it, I'll probably want to be a doctor just like him. Then again, I am only eight.

We eat our snacks while Daddy makes his special drink in the short glass cup etched with a letter "R" for Richard. We plop down on the sofa, snuggling close together, and turn on "Pocahontas." She's one of my favorite Disney princesses, but Mom refuses to let me watch the movie, because she says it "sexualizes women and inaccurately depicts history." I'm not one hundred percent sure what all that means, but I've heard her say it so many times, I can quote her. I know she thinks it's not good for me. But it's just a *movie*, for goodness' sake.

Daddy lets me watch it over and over when Mom's gone. He has his own set of rules, and we have don't-tell-Mom understandings. Mom means well; she's just so stuffy. I like that Daddy and I can have secrets between us, and that he can trust me.

I'm not supposed to know people call my mom crazy, but I know that, too.

I'd say I know a lot of things most kids my age don't. I just don't tell, and I'm good at keeping secrets. Just ask my Daddy.

CHAPTER 1

Nobody ever expects to get the one phone call that will change their life. They expect it less to come from a crotchety old biddy regarded as the town gossip. Yet, sitting at my desk at TrueU, the non-profit agency I own, on a perfectly good November day in the perfectly good town of Glendale, Texas, my perfectly good life (okay that part is a lie), but my reasonably mundane life was disrupted by none other than the infamous Edna McIntyre.

Having already dealt with a domestic violence situation and spoken with child protective services over a custody battle—all prior to ten a.m.—I slumped behind my large mahogany desk in exhaustion, head buried in my hands and noted those same fingers to be in desperate need of a manicure. The southern drawl of my assistant Dottie broke through the intercom like the shattering of glass, tearing me out of concentration.

"I'm not sure I'm going to improve your morning." Her hesitant tone confirmed her words.

My hand searched the bottom of the right desk drawer housing my own personal in-office pharmacy to retrieve the orange bottle containing one of the last two remaining Xanax. I pulled it out, turning it over in my hands, and fighting against myself as my therapist Margaret's voice sounded thick in my head. I flipped the top to open the bottle and closed it again, dropping it back into the drawer.

"Why's that?" I asked, turning my attention back to Dottie's voice.

"You've got one of those callers who won't take no for an answer. She's holding on one. Said it's an emergency."

Three emergencies in one day might be more than I can bear. Three deep breaths and count to ten. 1, 2, 3,…

I lifted the receiver. My other hand reached to light the lavender candle on my desk, hoping its magical relaxation properties would work fast and wondering what fresh hell awaited me on the other end.

"Well, hello there, young lady." The familiar voice piped into my ear as my morning coffee swirled sour in my stomach. Edna McIntyre, my mother's best friend. At least she was the last time I talked to Mom about five years ago.

What could Edna possibly want from me?

For a brief moment I felt an unentitled sense of worry, wondering if Mom was okay.

"Your mother is being awarded the Glendale Lifetime Achievement Award for Community Service," she blurted.

The fact that *my* mother was receiving such an honor seemed laughable to me.

"Kacee," she pleaded. "What if you were the one givin' it to her?" Her words dredged up thoughts of a publicly sacrificial mother, doling out every bit of energy to others with *nothing* left for me. Sweat beaded along my forehead, and I pulled a tissue from the box on my desk to dab at the growing collection of perspiration.

Still hearing silence on my end, she continued. "You know that'd make your momma happier than a dog with two tails!" She paused as her cackle faded into a sincere tone, almost a whisper. "You know you're more like her than you want to admit."

I imagined Edna, sitting cross-legged with perfect posture. Her frosted football-helmet hair was teased to within an inch of its life. Her tangerine-hued foundation slathered ear to ear, ending abruptly as it met her neck, creating a perfect line of demarcation. She sported rings on every finger, and her bracelets jingled as she spoke, crawling up a dazzling sweater arm.

I opened my mouth to object, yet no sound escaped. She continued, "You're a servant to the people just like her. I hear you're down there savin' kids and mommas and spreadin' all kinda goodness in Plantation doing social work at that fancy agency of yours. Folks round here are expectin' you, tho. Now you don't want to disappoint them *again,* do you?"

I left for a reason, and everyone in that godforsaken town knew it.

By the time the guilt trip had stopped on the other end of the line, you could melt a double dip of mint chocolate chip by holding it too close to my face.

Why does she think she has any sort of authority sticking her nose where it doesn't belong in this long battle of resentment between me and Mom?

"I appreciate your call, Edna. I hope your family is well. I'll think on it," I said in my most polite and professional tone.

"But, you *need* to—"

"I said I'd give it some thought. Thank you for calling." I hung up the phone, hands trembling and jaw clenched. The obvious answer was to refuse the invitation to my estranged mother's event. A simple no. Yet, the idea niggled a little too long in my brain. The decision wouldn't be quite so easy.

CHAPTER 2

Boots echoed behind me on the concrete stairs leading to the bay of apartments where I'd lived since moving to the tiny town of Plantation. *Clomp, clomp, clomp.* Blood rushed through my ears, drowning out any rational thoughts, as I slid the pink-camouflage key into the front door and turned it to the left. No sound. No click.

I knew I locked the door. I *always* locked the door. The only problem with someone beating me home is that I lived alone. Well—just Barry and me. Tiny hairs stood against the nape of my neck like soldiers commanding attention. The footsteps approached faster and faster, their heft growing louder. I tried not to turn my head, so I cut my eyes sharply, frozen in place at the door jamb. A hunched figure approached at a quick clip, the clomping turning to shuffling of heavy feet.

The cobweb-shrouded single bulb hung from a low-slung dingy ceiling in the exterior hallway, making it difficult to see as my left hand furiously dug toward the bottom of my bottomless purse. I landed on the small can of Mace I'd purchased online, feeling silly at the time. Now my finger rested on the red button. One white-knuckled hand on the Mace, the other on the door-knob, both paralyzed by fear.

I kept my head down, heart thudding in my chest as the sound stopped close. I stole a quick glance, preparing to raise the cylinder of blinding chemicals. A closer look, and my eyes identified the figure as Jeb, my across-the-hall neighbor. My shoulders sunk in relief as I released the breath I'd been holding. In a shaky voice, I mustered, "Oh, hey, Jeb." He responded with the usual head nod.

Jeb was the strong silent type, with emphasis on the silent. He stood, brooding in heavy boots, worn out Levi's and a brown and white flannel shirt, and he smelled faintly of earth. I rarely saw him come in or out of his apartment. In the three years I'd lived here, I'd heard him say exactly five sentences and those were not directed toward me. I'd made it a personal mission to elicit a conversation out of him before I moved out one of these days, if I ever moved out of this place.

"You haven't seen anyone around my door by chance today while I was at work, have you?" I asked. He worked from home, one of those remote jobs that fit him well since people-ing was not his specialty.

"Nope," came the reply. And he disappeared into his apartment, cracking the door barely wide enough for him to slip in, single grocery bag in hand. I wondered what he did in that apartment all day.

I fixed my gaze back to the green door labeled 331, regretting not installing the little camera above my door Aunt Jackie sent me money for last Christmas. At the time, I thought my aunt was overreacting and being ridiculous, so I'd used the money to purchase some new shoes I had my eye on. She'd seen some news story about a girl my age being abducted in the parking lot of her apartment building and had panicked. Maybe she wasn't so far off the mark with her worry after all. I'd come to accept it was a rarity that Aunt Jackie was wrong in the long run.

A thought filled my brain, as unease filled my stomach. Barry. I hadn't heard a peep from him, and he was tucked inside all alone. I turned the knob and prepared for the worst.

My eyes dilated to the darkness, trying to soak in all available glimmers of light. I must have forgotten to leave a lamp on. I called out to him as I fumbled through the kitchen to flip the switch. My foot caught on something brushing against my leg and I screamed, bracing myself on the kitchen cabinet for stability. "Barry!" My eyes now adjusting to the dimmed light, I collapsed my body on top of his, thankful to bury my face in his fur, yet curious as to his stillness and silence.

My four-legged best friend stood at attention; his head tilted in a question mark. Waiting for my return—never quite the guard dog I'd hoped he'd be, yet eighty pounds of pure love. He'd stifled his typical "I'm so glad to see you" barks to nuzzles and whimpers.

"Hello?" I called out, feigning bravery as my heart hammered in my chest. "Is someone here?" My questions settled unanswered, echoing through the walls of the tiny apartment. Stepping over my stockpile of Converse and Hey Dudes in colors ranging from navy blue to drab khaki to oh-my-goodness-here-she-comes neon green, I bent down to squish Barry's midnight-streaked face in my hands and cooed, "How's my favorite boy? What happened here?"

He proffered Ted, his saliva-ridden purple fuzzy monkey, in place of an answer, which I pitched across the living room for him. *Three deep breaths and count to ten.* In my best effort to tamp down the panic, I practiced logical reasoning just as my therapist Margaret and I had rehearsed during many sessions. It was somehow easier within the confines of *her* four walls than mine.

I tossed my impressive collection of keys on the smooth golden countertop, noting the half-eaten tub of macaroni salad still sitting in the sink from Sunday afternoon and its sister, a chipped, floral-printed cereal bowl complete with a healthy dose of souring milk beside it. One of the few benefits of living alone. Nobody criticized my poor food choices or housekeeping. I crossed the room, cluttered with file folders, applications, and one half-read novel lying face down on the sofa to turn on the large floor lamp as the room illuminated bright the detritus that had become my life.

No broken glass. No smashed windows. Perhaps I forgot to lock the door. Just this once? No. No. No.

Perched on the edge of the sofa, my knee bobbed up and down, planning my next move.

Let me calm down and think.

As I stared at the popcorn white ceiling, deep in thought, Barry hopped up beside me. An old photo caught my eye. Looming in a small, black metal frame, perched atop the mantle, A snapshot of Mom and me was positioned to the left of my treasured Von Nessen bookends—Christmas gifts from Mammi. The last before she died. The picture is one of the few of the two of us that I keep around. The photo, snapped from much earlier days, serves as a reminder that I still have a mother. I didn't exactly like her back then either, but at least she hadn't been full-blown crazy---yet. We stood arm-in-arm, surrounded by several of her fellow nurses at one of her work Christmas parties held at the fancy hibachi grill in town. Never having met a stranger, she didn't hesitate to ask a waiter to snap the photo. Mom's blonde curls were cut in a new bob she detested, even though she knew it wasn't doing any favors for her skeleton-thin face.

She could have been the spokesperson for the term, "skin and bones." Of course, that's not why she didn't like the cut. I stood beside her, grinning like I was first in line for opening day at the amusement park, wearing a purply-blue dress with obnoxious flowers that didn't quite fit right and did nothing for my oversized bubble butt. It wasn't an exceptional photo of either of us, but I had framed it and fancied it for the pure memory of the evening. Those few hours had gone by with no arguments, no discussions of Daddy, no critiques. It was damn near a Christmas miracle.

The odd placement of the photo is what struck my attention. I knew I was exhausted, but I could have sworn that the picture had always been in the wooden frame and the one of me and

Aunt Jackie had always been in the black metal frame. They were reversed, and upon further inspection, shifted from the right of those bookends to the left.

Apprehension filled the room. And my growling stomach.

"Hello? Hello? Is someone here?" I called out again, panic impregnating my voice.

A siren sounded in the distance outside, and I paused, just in case it came closer. Another joined the emergency orchestra, yet the noise receded, leaving behind only the sound of my own heartbeat thrumming in my ears. I latched onto Barry's collar as I guided him through each room with me. We tiptoed like two twitchy detectives, jumping every time a car door slammed outside or someone upstairs turned on a shower. Room by room, we snuck. I rubbed my own anxiety-seized shoulders, hugged myself for reassurance.

Woof. Woof. Woof. The sudden and incessant baritone barking startled me, as Barry darted through the meager bedroom and toward the French doors leading out to the small apartment patio door, a string of saliva lagging a few inches behind.

"Settle down, buddy. What is it?" Barry remained wide-eyed with ears perked as he nuzzled the gauzy red curtain hung over the glass panels of the doors, pushing it out of the way with his sizable inky snout as he gazed into the blackness of the balcony. I followed behind, praying he was overreacting and ruffling his velvety ears. Barking and anxiety deafened mine.

I slid my hand across the paneled doors to unlatch the deadbolt. Unlocked. I clenched my hand around my cellphone, my brain pleading with me to press the emergency 9-1-1 button, the only sensible course of action being to call the police and report the incident. Yet my past stopped me cold, terrified the nice policeman would end up whisking me away and I'd be stuffed into a white coat and whisked away for *rehabilitation* like my mother.

"Is someone here?" I called out again, louder than the other times, as though an intruder hiding in the lower kitchen cabinet would jump out like a jack-in-the-box and yell, "Surprise!"

Opening the exterior door with caution, I leaned into my arm and eased my head out ever so slowly to peer toward Barry's lead. He dashed past me, fur on high alert and nose pointed toward the pot of dying Rhododendron. Mom always said I couldn't take care of my own self, let alone keep so much as a pet rock alive. That's why we never had real pets or plants in the house.

As we stood gazing out into seeming nothingness, I could tell Barry smelled something aside from the fresh rain hanging heavy in the air. Or someone. I heard a crash and leapt to the left, squealing like a five-year-old girl barefooting a slippery snake. Barking and yelping, Barry turned in circles, bidding my attention. Shattered porcelain and potting soil lay splayed across the porch—so much for my new flowerpot. Yet nothing else seemed out of place–the small chairs, the tiny table, the citronella candle. Even my leftover Diet Coke and bent issue of *Psychology Today* sat atop the table where I last left them. Barely enough room on the tiny two-story square of a patio for both of us to spread out, I squatted near the small wooden table and ran my hand along the cold iron railing. All I felt was moisture and one stray nail.

"Was somebody inside our house, buddy? Is that what happened to my picture?" My mind wondered about all the possibilities–someone related to the agency. I thought of Mary Hernandez. The look on her face, or rather the bruises on her face, yesterday as she strode through the doors of TrueU Agency asking to speak to me.

"I think he might try to kill me this time," she'd whispered, as she spoke of her dangerous husband. Her left eye, bloodied. Her cheekbone, blackened and swollen the exact size and shape of a man's fist. She not only feared for her own life but the lives of her children—those three precious children. When Mary first stepped through the glass doors of TrueU, shaken and nervous, seeking references for shelters to escape her abusive husband of fifteen years, she'd done all the right things. She'd applied for restraining orders, protective orders, and ultimately tried to divorce her husband, Robert, to keep herself and her children safe. With each attempt, he found her, intimidated her and beat her mercilessly. He'd started similar tactics with the kids, too. Her requests for restraining orders were denied, and he refused to sign divorce papers. She met with me, revealing her belief he had an informal connection to authorities, rendering him untouchable. Her suspicions and mine centered around a long-standing drug ring in the area—one involving some dirty cops as well as a few out-of-town pariahs willing to play the part for a little extra cash and an acquittal of their misgivings. In Robert's case, that would include the repetitive color-changing beating of his wife and kids. I was in no position to confirm or deny Mary's suspicion that Robert was involved at this point yet planned to use my resources to dig further. I kept her casefile open and handy in the top drawer of my filing cabinet, as something told me I may need it one day. I had a feeling this would be an ongoing case and one not easily settled.

Even yesterday, I'd said all the right things—make a report, go to the police. But she'd tried all those things before. She was asking *me* for help. Not help from the non-profit agency I own. She knew it and I knew it. She needed help relocating her family. Somewhere he couldn't find them. She only wanted her life back. The photos of cuts and bruises, bloodied lips, and broken bones weren't good enough for the police. So she was doing the only thing a reasonable mother could do—taking her children on the run. Wasn't she?

She followed up with an email from the assumed name written on her note—Marianne—and asked if I'd help find her a place to live—in Arkansas of all places. I encouraged her, out of pure obligation, to contact the authorities. Of course, she didn't, and why would she? Police failed to provide any protection or any help thus far. In fact, the Plantation Police Department continued reuniting her with Robert, dragging her and her children right back into the lion's den of harm.

As she squeezed my hand, walking out the door, she told me, "Just think about if you can help me or not, my friend. It's a lot to consider. It's a lot to risk, for both of us." Is this what she meant? Did she know Robert Hernandez would try to intimidate me? To invade my privacy, my home. To threaten me and my safety?

My mind began reeling as to whether there had even been a break-in at all. It was running away from me. I needed to clear my head. *Do not give in to Krazy Kacee.* I rubbed the old scars on my arms, looking down at the raised evidence of past days filled with anguish, humiliation, and fear. They also represent victory, my therapist Margaret had told me. I'm still here. I pulled my sleeves down, not wanting to think of those days anymore. Yet another reason I don't want to return to that godforsaken Glendale.

Barry's all-knowing large brown eyes stared back at me, and I begged him to divulge information held sacred beneath those worriless peepers. Whatever—or whomever—had been here was gone now. Or were they? I should keep watch tonight. Kissing goodbye to my good night's sleep, I stumbled into the kitchen and made myself a nightcap. I opened all the cabinet doors, as if an intruder may be hiding in wait, folded like an omelet into a tiny overhead cabinet. I subsequently made my way through the apartment and opened all the closet doors, yelling, "I've got you!" as I jerked open each door and stamped my slippered feet hard, I'm sure much to the displeasure of my downstairs neighbors. Only four empty closets answered. No need for the police. It's my mind playing tricks on me…oh God! My mind!

Allowing a generous pour over ice into a glass, I gulped the spiced drink in two swallows. I was overreacting, as Mom frequently accused. My mind needed to relax from the stressful day at the agency. Tomorrow morning would be better. Two more finger pours and things would look brighter.

I patted Barry on the backside, and he padded behind me to the solitary bedroom, Ted dangling from his mouth. The rhythmic click clicks of his nails against the bathroom tile comforted me.

Removing my pink fuzzy slippers but keeping my socks, I hoisted myself onto the high mattress and pulled my covers up tight, hoping for at least a little shut eye and knowing it'd never come. Even less tonight than the normal five hours I had come to enjoy. My insides quivered with uneasiness and questions. I laid in the darkness, watching the hours tick by, until the last time I blinked at 3:17 a.m.

CHAPTER 3

y whole body shook stiff as I sat up in bed, clock declaring 4:03 a.m. in big blocky red numbers. I missed something. Clearly, I missed something. *We* missed something. I glanced at Barry, though he did not appear as disturbed as me by my sudden revelation—demonstrated by his soft snoring. My feet hit the floor, and my stomach seared from acid climbing into my throat, stealing my breath. The soft lump of fur beside me remained undisturbed until I illuminated the room with the bedside lamp, cinching up my terrycloth robe. Barry flipped over on his stomach to offer me the opportunity for a belly rub. Despite my unease, I obliged. He then righted himself and sat up straight—ready to help after a noisy yawn. The hardwood floor felt cold under my sock feet, as I floated in silence across the room.

The opposing wall to my bed featured a five-foot tall maple jewelry box adorned with tiny red stained-glass inserts etched with winding vines culminating in clusters of flowers. The doors to the jewelry box opened with a high-pitched squeak as I searched the top velvet lined trays, finding nothing but cheap imitation jewelry. Everything in its place. But, then again, who would steal my $14.99 Target earrings? Then my eyes and palms frantically scanned for Mammi's jewelry.

A short time before Mammi died, she bequeathed much of her jewelry to me. Daddy and I went for a visit about a month before she passed. Mammi may have been Mom's biological mother, but Daddy was her favorite. It had been quite some time since my last visit, and memories of Sunday lunches came rushing back. The smell of pot roast and lemon pies permeated my senses, made at the hands of Mammi's finest servants and doted on as her own handiwork.

I perched on the side of her makeshift hospital bed, now sitting in place of the nineteenth century cherry wood four-poster which once stood as the focal point of the matriarch's bedroom. I siphoned a deep breath and silenced my shock, inhaling the sharp stench of urine and bleach mixing to fill the room. I gawked at my grandmother's pristine hair piled atop her head. Cancer had slowly sucked her like a kid melts a popsicle. Eyelids coated with the same mystic blue eyeshadow she'd worn for years. Her high cheekbones highlighted the soft pink rouge on her pasty thin skin caked in a deep layer of cream beige foundation, now sagging at the jaw. She'd inevitably asked–or demanded—one of her helpers to apply makeup and fix her hair.

"Your momma won't ever wear these jewels," she blurted, as she plopped fistfuls of diamonds and pearls in my lap. Mine and Dad's eyes grew wide. "God knows she don't put a stitch of effort into her appearance these days, save that gaudy red lipstick she won't quit wearing, and she sure ain't going to any fancy parties."

Dad expelled a confirmatory chuckle.

"She's not interested in my jewelry, doll." Her eyes turned downward, and I wasn't sure if she was hurt or angry. I could relate to Mammi at that moment. "I want to give this jewelry to someone who'll take care of it. Some of these pieces have been in our family for dang-near a hundred years. It's worth a pretty penny, is what it is. I don't believe in cheap things. I hope I've taught you that—despite your momma." She paused, and I was unsure if her monologue was complete. After a ragged breath, she continued. "And I hope you always remember that about me. The finer things in life are expensive, as is sacrifice, my darling child. You must make your statement and mark on life. If you don't do it, nobody does it for you. I've made mistakes in my life, Kacee. Lots of 'em. But talk is cheap, and that includes apologies. Don't apologize- shows frailty. You make your mistakes, and you don't look back. Especially as a proper young lady. T'aint no reason to show weakness. Never. Do you understand me?" Crimson spread across her cheeks, ruddy as a youngster's after playing in the snow. Mammi launched into a violent coughing fit. I offered a tissue, but a portly looking lady of about fifty and donned in purple scrubs brushed by me. She affixed an oxygen concentrator with the quick turn of a metal tool, hidden at the side of the aging woman's bed, and began delivering the air in one swift motion via a clear mask over my grandmother's nose and mouth. Mammi's coughing subsided, and her breathing steadied.

She waved it away and tried resuming the conversation, but it only sent her back into a symphony of sputters. I placed my index finger in the air indicating she should wait and laid a flat palm on her left shoulder for comfort, leaning into the edge of her bed.

Her breathing became rhythmical with the whir of the concentrator, and she could no longer fight sleep. Her eyeballs moved under lids like those of a dreaming dog. I sat on the bed and stared out the window at her and Pappi's expansive property, the peacefulness of it stolen by sad solitude. I wondered if Mammi felt lonely also. She tried so hard, it seemed, to make Mom perfect. Yet, Mom pushed her away and never wanted to talk to me about the reasons. She'd simply say, "Mammi was tougher on me than she was on Aunt Jackie and especially on you, Sweetie. She's a whole new woman when it comes to being a grandma!" I don't know what that meant, but she sure favored Dad. Mom tolerated her but kept a safe distance. Once Mammi drifted off, Dad and I recused ourselves from her bedside and drove back to his apartment. I would only see Mammi on one other brief occasion before she lost her battle with cancer.

I stared at the open chest, the moisture from my palms moistening my skin. I wiped them on my pajama pants, heart hammering in my chest. Some of Mammi's jewels were stored away in a safety deposit box at First Bank, though a considerable amount was laid in the case. I'd say a half a million dollars' worth, at least. One hooked index finger on each side of the burgundy velvet-lined compartment, I tugged at the first drawer to reveal its contents. South Sea Baroque Pearls. Tiffany and Company yellow gold camel pin. Fire Opal ring, 18K. Three carat triple diamond and triple band ring. The second contained the red ruby and diamond necklace I wore to the agency fundraiser last year along with another set of expensive pearls. Nothing seemed missing so far. The pattern continued, and familiar panic built up. Every piece of jewelry appeared accounted for, yet that same feeling from last night came back, even stronger. The last pieces laid atop the bottom compartment. My palms moistened as I pulled up the lining, where I kept the letters Mom had written me over the years, mostly remaining unopened to this day. She began sending them over the years after I left Glendale. I'd only ever unsealed two, though I contemplated many times ripping open the rest. Dad convinced me it would be too damaging, and they'd all be full of lies, just like the first ones. Words from a "psycho," he would say. I don't know why I never went back and opened up the rest of the thick stack tied with twine after he and I got crossways. I suppose I really forgot about them. And now—they were gone. They were all gone.

I closed the drawers and performed a fifty-foot visual inspection of the remainder of the bedroom. Not so much as a pillow overturned on the black leather chaise pushed against the window and used as my reading nook.

I floated from the bedroom back toward the front of the apartment. My robe caught underfoot, and I tripped forward, landing splayed across the espresso carpet with a thud, Barry rushing to lick my face in comfort. After catching my wits about me and pushing myself up on my elbow, my eyes fixated on the eight-foot mahogany bookshelf centered on the back wall of the dining area. When I moved into the apartment, I reasoned I read way more than I dined. It only made sense for me to transform the would-be dining room into a personal library. In this, my favorite room, stands two five-foot walnut shelves flanking my grand eight-foot mahogany bookshelf, books neatly and alphabetically ordered by author. Well, they *were* neatly ordered. The center case now displayed an entire shelf of ransacked books. I didn't notice it last night, as the door opens into the cases, and I was too focused on Barry as I walked in. Then my worries soon became consumed with imaginary people hiding in cabinets.

This wasn't a random break-in. I pulled my iPhone from the front pocket of my ivory terry cloth robe and snapped pictures for proof—of what I wasn't yet sure. This is what they always do on shows like 20/20 and Dateline, and I watched an obscene amount of true crime television and documentaries. Dottie has told me multiple times I should try and socialize more, and with more people than just Barry. That I'm "too young and pretty" to not go out with friends or try and meet someone. At the age of thirty-four, the last thing I felt these days was young. Or pretty. My brain was much more comfortable with Barry and my books. And my vodka. My vodka never failed me like the others.

Classics section, by author. *Don Quixote* by Miguel De Cervantes, *Robinson Crusoe* by Daniel Defoe, *Sybil* by Benjamin Disraeli, *David Copperfield* by Charles Dickens, *Madame Bovary* by

Gustave Flaubert...wait! Where was *The Count of Monte Cristo*? If there's one thing I know, it's books. Growing up, books were revered as rightly as a second religion. I could hear Mom's voice. "Don't fold those pages; be careful with that one." She'd screw up her lightly freckled nose that looked as if she'd been perfectly pixie-dusted with the right amount of stippling, take a deep breath, and squint her eyes. Her red lips outlined every word as she spoke in her soft southern voice. "The answer to every question we have now and will ever have in the future can be found at the hands of these skilled authors," she'd begin. "Starting with the Bible, books have provided ways for people to record their thoughts and have allowed others to learn from their experiences. Even works of fiction have lines of truth buried in them, for those who dare to look..." Every now and then, she made a valid point.

I must have loaned *Monte Cristo* out, or it possibly became misfiled in all this chaos. Justifying in my head yet unable to think of anyone requesting to borrow the book, my brain worked overtime to tamp down the panic. Who would rummage through all of this and take a single title?

I stopped and thought about Mom dropping me off from school and hurrying back out the door to a PTA meeting where she was in charge of Library Friends. She also served on the Glendale Library Board. Always prioritizing time for other people's kids but not her own. I supposed that's exactly why Edna McIntyre wants to give her this award.

I plopped at the kitchen table, wooden legs screeching against the cheap linoleum floor. I popped up and began frantically rearranging, as if getting them back on the shelves in the right order would make all of this vanish. I could pretend it never happened. Nobody was watching or following me or even interested in my actions. My hands shook so violently that I split a couple of the books' pages apart trying to force them into their rightful slots. The pages wrinkled forever. I continued. All the while, the skin on my back prickled. Someone *was* watching.

They had to be. Or maybe they weren't. Maybe it was all in my mind. Maybe this was the beginning of the craziness. I tried recounting my steps that day and day before for any plausible reason I would have rummaged through my own bookshelf. I came up short.

CHAPTER 4

Therapy and I have a love/hate relationship. The battle runs way down deep, growing in the pit of my stomach like some putrid, perverse fungus. After each session I'd tell myself it was useless and that it wasn't going anywhere, yet some unknown magnetic force drew me back for the following week's opportunity to pick apart my pitiful life and "get to the bottom" of the bane of my misery.

The answers to my own questions—those which have thrown me into therapy for half of my life—just might be hidden in Glendale. The thought turned over in my mind after Edna's phone call—even before I spoke it aloud to Margaret.

Margaret's lobby walls were bare, save for the single faded watercolor painting of a man holding a young girl's hand and wading through an empty wheat field. You'd think she'd opt for something a bit livelier. After all, most folks come to visit her trying to find a recipe for that life goulash they managed to dang near destroy on their own.

I remember tiptoeing into a hospital visit with Mom when she was sick, and I was barely ten—a room not quite so large as this yet brimming with a similar stale chill. The walls gleaned pristine white, and the room stank of bleach and conformity.

"No, Mrs. Robinson. You cannot have visitors today. That's the price you pay for resisting treatment," I'd heard the stern-faced nurse bark at Mom. Dressed in starched maroon scrubs and clunky white shoes stained with rust-colored dirt, the same woman clopped out to the waiting room to tell me and Daddy we had wasted our time. I began to whimper, but Daddy tugged at my arm and said there was nothing we could do. Mom had made her choice. I processed that moment on replay in my mind, like a record with a scratch stuck on the skip—and not only in therapy—wondering why she hadn't chosen me. Once they let her come home, I'd shower her with kisses. I'd do the dishes every night. I'd keep my room spotless clean. That would surely make her want to choose me. It all made sense to my ten-year-old brain, but my actions never panned out. They weren't enough. They never made her choose me, and I couldn't figure out how to measure what *was* enough to make her choose me. I'd asked both Mom and Daddy about the incident years later. Exactly what ailed her, and why was the nurse so mean.

"Your mom is just crazy, and can't make decisions for herself," is all Daddy would tell me. Mom sat with pursed lips and a crooked smile. She looked as if air could escape her mouth at any moment, yet she must hold it in with all her might. Deferring any medical decisions to Daddy was the rule. He was a doctor, so he should know best. Daddy held me and comforted me, let me cry into his scrub top that smelled of fire and woodsy soap, then took me down to Harold's and let me pick out my favorite treat from the barrels.

Peeking her head around the corner from the hallway, Margaret startled me out of my memory. I jumped at the sound of my name. "Kacee? You ready, dear?" She made a summoning motion with her hand, pretending not to notice my jump scare.

"How are things?" Margaret inquired, once seated into her brown leather armchair. Her jovial voice fileted wide the office walls.

"Been a rough week," I sighed, surprising myself with my openness.

"Why so rough?" She cut her eyes upward, tilting both of her chins in a strange juxtaposition of her neck.

"A confusing week, I guess you could say. Been engrossed at work, getting ready for the agency fundraiser and all. Barry thinks I've darned near abandoned him as much as I've been away from the house lately, I'm sure."

"So, what's *really* bothering you, Kacee?" A white sandal dangled from my therapist's foot and her gaze alone willed me to submit an answer. The right answer.

Picking dog fur off my black pants with more care than necessary, I answered her question with another question, an act considered reprehensible to my late grandmother, and I thought how Mammi would have chastised her for wearing white shoes after Labor Day. "Why do you ask?"

She leveled eyes framed by mascara-laden lashes at me. "Since you walked into my office, you haven't stopped fidgeting. You've rearranged your hair five times, crossed and uncrossed your legs more times than I can count, and you keep checking and rechecking you've turned off that dang phone. Your butt's not even been in that seat long enough to make it lukewarm. And, if I'm laying it all out here, it doesn't look like you've eaten in days."

She leaned back in her chair, tightly compressed into the confined space and spilling over the edges. "So, my dear…tell me what's bothering you."

I could always count on Margaret to be a straight shooter. After all, this *was* why I was paying her. Airing my dirty laundry, opening it up for discussion. My chest tightened, pressed against my buttoned tunic, and my mind wandered to places it dare only tread within the confines of these walls. Fingers of thoughts crawling out like players in the game of the Itsy Bitsy Spider. The anchor necklace lay heavy against my collarbone.

"There's something strange that happened in my apartment a

couple nights ago. Picture frames have been switched on two of my photos. And random letters have gone missing as well as a book. A single book." My eyes probed the top of my brain to make sense of the situation, knowing I sounded like a complete idiot. "Problem is, I can't prove it, but I swear it's true. Barry felt off kilter, too. I'm not sure how else to describe it other than eerie. I don't know whether my next call should be to the police… or the loony bin." Uncertainty hummed through my veins as my mouth set in a hard line. My biggest fear ate away at me from the inside out. I'm losing my mind—like Mom.

Margaret seemed to fumble for her next words. "Perhaps we should explore this a bit before we jump to extremes. Let's stay in this space. Maybe —"

"There's more." I cut her off mid-sentence. "I got a call from one of my mother's oldest friends back home in Glendale."

Margaret leaned forward, intrigued. Her mouth stretched into a capital "O."

"So far, we've only tiptoed around family issues, despite my best efforts," she said. "I really know very little about them, aside from Aunt Jackie and Mammi. I'd be interested to hear more about your mom."

I rolled my eyes at the request. Not necessarily at Margaret's desire to learn more about the woman who "raised" me, but rather the whole idea of speaking about her, out loud with actual words. A heavy breath escaped me, and long-buried resentment hung like lead weights. "Turns out she's being recognized and awarded for 'Outstanding Lifetime Achievement in Glendale Community Service.' I know it sounds hokey, but in a town like Glendale, Texas…" My words trailed off, and I wished I could take back the last twenty seconds.

"Well, do you know much about the area?" My cheeks grew hot as I twirled a strand of hair around my index finger, gently tugging. The muffled ringing of Margaret's office phone played as a backdropped distraction while I thought about my next move and waited for her response.

"I'm afraid not."

I chuckled. "You're not missing much. It's a four and a half-hour drive from here. Out in West Texas. Glendale's about forty-five minutes outside of Midland. A whole lotta nothin' out there besides flat land, lots of old, big-haired women wearing too much makeup and drinking too much wine at hoity-toity parties, and more 'blessed hearts' than you can shake a stick at." My jaw tightened in an unconscious attempt to prevent the rest of the words from exiting my mouth. "In other words, we're all somehow related."

"I'm not sure I'm following, Kacee," Margaret said, her brow furrowed together like a pair of long-lost Schnauzers.

I had to know this was coming sooner or later. Most kids "of wealth" embrace the family name. They toss it around like garnish on one of those heads of lettuce drizzled with dressing nobody really cares for, given a name mispronounced by most at an overpriced restaurant they alone can afford. I've secured the opposite end of the pole, a heroic attempt to keep my heritage hidden. As much as it can be anyway, with a name like mine.

"Have you ever heard of Havemeier Oil?" The household name reached much farther than the little town of Glendale.

Margaret's mouth fell open, but she recovered quickly. The muscles in her jaw worked overtime as the puzzle pieces clicked into place, the invisible headlines connecting: Kacee Marie Havemeier Robinson---granddaughter to the third wealthiest family in Texas, according to last June's issue of *Texas Magazine*. My mother, Ruth, wanted to make sure the family name would always be a part of me, so I have two middle names. It's weird. Thankfully, the article didn't show my face. I twisted my hair and inconspicuously yanked out a second curl.

"So, anyway, the story goes like this—my mother is getting this award and it's a big deal to the people living in her little town. There are still a lot of good people out there. Really good people. My oldest and best friend, Breanna, still lives there. We were super close until… well, anyway…" My thoughts trailed off in my head before the rest could run away.

"What is it, Kacee?"

"It's just… the bad has outweighed the good for so long. I guess I never…"

"This is good. Keep going," she encouraged–leaning forward. "You never what?"

Unshed tears pooled in the corners of my eyes. "I mean, I knew at some point I'd have to go back. Or I feared I'd have to go back, I should say. And I know I don't *have* to go back, but… I can't explain it. Either way, giving a definite to an indefinite time feels like a game changer." My grip tightened on the arm of the chair as I stared out the window, the air thick with nervous tension.

"Who's forcing you to go back?"

"Huh?"

"Who's pressuring you to go back?" she repeated, her tone revealing the irritation her face didn't show.

"Oh. My mom's friend, Edna. She called out of the blue. I did tell you about that, didn't I?" Margaret nodded. "Edna requested —No, demanded—that I be the one to present Mom with the award.

"She had the nerve to compare me to my mother. I stewed on this for a few days. Really thought about it. My life's work at TrueU is committed to helping families in need and victims of abuse, right?" Margaret confirmed with her silent bobbing head; the rhetorical question was not lost on her. "There are times I really want to tell some of them to run away. Run as far away as they can and never look back. I'm supposed to be offering sound advice and resources. I'm supposed to be a healer, and yet I can't heal myself. Hell, I don't even know if I want this part of me healed. Do you know what that makes me? A joke! A farce! Just. Like. My. Mom."

"You have a great deal of anger toward her, Kacee. Do you want to tell me what that's all about?"

"She was a terrible mom who couldn't even keep herself sane. She broke up our family, abandoned me, and now. Now. Now look at me!" I yelled, gulping in big lungfuls of air.

"What *about* you, Kacee? I see a very capable young woman sitting before me. A successful young woman. A caring young woman. Who do you see?"

"Who do I see? Have you not been listening?" Hot embers seared inside my chest as I stood up, paced the room, and tried to breathe. Had she not even been listening for the last *year*?

My hands took on a life of their own, waving at my sides as I spoke, fluttering and tapping at the chair. "I see a thirty-something-year-old woman who can't even go on a date. Who has never had a real boyfriend. Whose longest, most secure male relationship has been with her dad for goodness sakes---and I screwed that up---and the second longest is with her dog. I see a woman who is haunted by nightmares that she can't explain. I see a woman who substitutes perpetual work for a social life, because she knows work is the one thing she's good at. I know I can help other people. I just can't help my own damn self. And now? Now I see someone who may be going crazy exactly like her mother. That's who I see. And it scares the hell out of me. I'm missing something in my story. I have to find answers before I end up killing myself, or someone else."

Margaret sucked in a deep breath and turned to her mini fridge to offer me a tiny bottle of water. "Drink this, Kacee. That was a huge breakthrough, honey. Now we have something to work with."

"We do?" I wiped sweat I wasn't even aware of until it trickled down my brow.

"That was a very long time coming. You've been bottling this up for years. When you first walked through those doors, you listed your symptoms as 'stress' and 'not able to sleep.' I knew there was more under the hood. Now that we've started to get a peek at it, we will work layer by layer. It's hard work, but you can do this. You are a strong woman. We will do this together."

Margaret extended a gentle smile, and I exhaled loudly as I melted into the cushion.

"So… what did you tell your mom's friend?" Margaret asked, hands folded in her lap.

"That's the thing. I tried telling her no. I told her I was not at all the best person for the job, but she didn't listen. She laid it on thick, like molasses on toast. She rationalized it, telling me I was Mom's 'pride and joy,'" I explained, making air quotes with the last remark. Obviously, Edna never really understood our relationship.

"If I have to wade through all this childhood bullshit, I may never find the answers I'm searching for! I went back into therapy to reinvent myself. To work on *me*. Not to be dragged down by my past. I keep trying to shelve it, but it keeps rearing its monstrous head." I smirked to myself, noting the new brownish stain dotting Margaret's ivory shag rug and wondering its origin. "Did I tell you Dottie tried setting up one of those dating profiles for me?" I snickered. "I told her any sane man would be too scared of the monsters in my closet to ask me out."

"Our past does not define us," she said gently, her voice an even stream, "but there's no doubt that it does shape us. And when we are unsettled by our past, it's often best to resolve what's bothering us. Even if it's just internally. This type of healing is necessary before you can expect to find a truly happy future." Margaret's voice spoke over the calming buzz of a light bulb on its last days. "Kacee, you are not a fake or a farce, or any of the other words you used to describe yourself today. You do a great deal of good at TrueU Agency. Think about your driving force behind that."

I nodded my head slowly and took a sip from the cool water. "I know I'll have to face it all at some point. I'll have to face her, them, the whole damn ugly lot of a mess I left. But when I do, it should be on *my* terms. On *my* time for once…not because she's getting some two-bit award for doling out pancakes to the hungry! I bet those people didn't even know all the time she spent away from her own family. The terrible decisions she made, especially the one to break up the family smack in the midst of her only daughter- her only child's- preteen angst. When she needed her the most!" I shifted my weight on the sofa. It let out a tinny of a squeal as I did, and I stared down at my own spreading thighs. "At least Daddy helped people through his career as a surgeon. He helped those people *and* brought money into our household. Mom just wanted the recognition and didn't care that she abandoned me. She still doesn't."

I shivered from the inside out and wrapped my arms tightly across my chest in an effort to soothe the throbbing in my head.

Ding. The timer sounded, signaling the end of our session. I reached my arms down to gather the thin straps of my brown leather tote bag, still dabbing at my brow with the overused tissue, then tucking it in the front pocket of the zippered pouch.

Margaret placed her hand on my shoulder with a soft touch. "So, are you going to Glendale? When do you need to give them a decision? I'm happy to move up sessions if you'd like my help," her husky voice barely raised above a whisper.

My mind raced at the question, answering faster than my mouth could form the words. No. A hard no. When I left all those years ago, I'd put this drama behind me. My parents' ugly, nearly twenty-year-old divorce. My sordid childhood. My… my *mother*. Being the grand heiress to the Havemeier estate, Glendale expected "great things" from me. As long as my zip code reflected Cranston County, I'd lived under a complete hand of thumbs. Leaving to start my own life became my only chance of escape.

I paused for a moment to prime my thoughts, a technique I'd been working on for a while. *Think carefully before you speak, Kacee.* Daddy used to tell me that when I was younger, and I've found it to be some of the most valuable advice I'd ever received.

"I really don't know. I can't even think straight. I would like to meet again sooner rather than later if that's okay. Is Friday too soon?"

"Friday it is. I have an opening at 3."

"I'll take it. Thanks, Margaret."

I waved goodbye and trudged out the office door, my eyes looking down as I tied the belt on my coat. If there's one thing I'd learned from my childhood, it was to hold on to emotions only as a last resort. Feel when you must, then let them go as soon as you can.

I scooted past Margaret's next client in the waiting area, an older gentleman with frayed trousers and two-day-old scruff. I nodded and tried to eek out a friendly smile. Is that what will happen to me if I don't get closure now? I'll be seventy years old and parked in Margaret's office, still searching for resolution.

The old man's head remained down while his dark sad eyes followed me to the door. I couldn't help but wonder what answers he may be seeking as I walked out into the gray, blustery afternoon. I wondered if he judged me in his silence, his mind inventing stories about the reasons for my session at the therapist's office. I possessed a wholly irrational fear of being "found out." For what, I don't know.

My feet moved toward my pitiful little white car, the bumper boasting a small dent from last month's run-in with an elderly lady and her overzealous lead foot at the red light near the agency. The stoplight had turned yellow, so I slowed to a stop. Apparently, she accepted the change in color as a challenge, in a hurry to make her Wednesday night prayer meeting at the church and plowed full steam ahead into the back of me. She came out apologizing all over herself, leaning gently on her cane. I couldn't bring myself to accept her insurance. Poor thing was so shaken up, and the teensy little dent only accented my "I brake for cute puppies" bumper sticker anyhow.

The smell hit me, sucking me back like a straw full of soda. A man's scent. A familiar man's scent. The strong distinct woodsy aroma interspersed with sweetened sweat and a smoky overture. My head swiveled back and forth, and I was sure anyone staring at me surely thought I looked like one of those bobble head dolls. Yet the parking lot appeared empty, save two vacant vehicles—one gray truck and one black sedan. Of course, I couldn't identify the makes and models even if I tried. Daddy was the car connoisseur. I guess that was *his* religion. He'd acquired a new one nearly every time I saw him. One month it'd be a bright red two-door convertible. Barely three months later, he'd sport one of those jacked-up trucks with wheels so tall you had to pole-vault to hoist yourself into it. My favorite was the olive Jeep Wrangler, soft top of course. I kept driving the same old sedan I had, rattly and all, until the wheels fell off. It seemed such an unnecessary expense when the old one worked just fine. I suppose it boiled down to a difference in priorities.

I unlocked my car with trembling hands, the feeling of being watched returning and chilling my blood. Plopping safely in the driver's seat, I cranked the ignition and locked all the doors, manually of course. I turned the radio up loud, blaring country-era Taylor Swift and singing along about a redneck who was excellent at heartbreak yet terrible at lying. I pushed the thoughts as far down as they'd reach, at least until I hit the parking lot of the grocery store. The familiar stab to my temple as my vision went fuzzy made me sit for a moment longer before scurrying in to pick up my lettuce and chicken to prepare the night's dinner. With a touch of chocolate ice cream of course. I deserved it after a day like today.

CHAPTER 5

The next morning, I patted Barry's head as I plunged out the fiberglass apartment door and into the sunny yet frigid day, eyes bleary and looking over my shoulder from another night of unsettled sleep.

"Morning, Jeb," I said, as we passed opposite each other on the stairs. It felt odd to see him two days in the same week. He kept his head down; a familiar grunt followed. Surely Jeb wouldn't have broken into my apartment, right? What would he have to gain? My southern friendliness felt called into question, and Daddy's chastising words echoed in my ears.

A chill blasted onto my skin as I emerged from the tiny concrete stairwell. Raised goosebumps stood erect and spanned every square inch of my arms, and I shook them like embarking on the newest dance craze in an attempt to restore equilibrium to my exterior skin temperature. Cutting the corner a tad too close, I grazed my shoulder on the brick of the building and noticed the resulting pull in my new striped sweater, cursing under my breath. The temperature had plummeted overnight by at least fifteen degrees, and whispers of ice covered my windshield. I felt the cold straight through to the bone. I have never been able to put on enough clothes to keep my innards from shivering, even long after everything on the outside had stopped. I'd try to explain the feeling to Daddy, but he'd always shake his head and tell me I sounded just like my mother.

On a day like today, I'd catch him outside in nothing more than a worn-out t-shirt looking like a relic from the days of James Dean. He'd have it tucked proudly into his nicotine-stained jeans, the ones with the permanent outline from stowing a pack of Marlboro Reds in the front pocket. He liked to wake up early in the morning and stand on the back porch with his hip resting against a cedar post, smoking a cigarette and sipping his bitter black coffee from an oversized tin mug. No coat—especially not a white coat—no thermal socks, just a cigarette dangling haphazardly between his fingers, filling the space with thick smelly clouds. Me—forever afraid he might forget to dash the ashes before the embers burned down far enough to kiss his fingertips. His timing was impeccable, at least regarding his substance abuse. The tissue-thin material covering his chest barely concealed the long curly hairs that tried escaping from all angles—a simple man's attempt at protecting his heart. I thought of him often, yet my pride from our recent screaming match stemmed from the basic fact that he "forbade" me to even speak to Breanna because of some rumors she purported "threatened his career" and wreaked havoc on his life. I was, as always, in his corner, but I was no longer a child willing to be controlled. I was simply not going to be the bigger person this time. I'd been an adult my entire life, and it was his turn to come to me to apologize for his childish behavior. I sure did miss him, though.

As I drove toward TrueU in my basic white 2017 Ford Focus, passenger door rattling and in desperate need of a tire rotation, I contemplated my choices. Again. Each entry on my carefully curated pros and cons list for returning to Glendale swirled in my head. I also silently reminded myself to get gas on the way home. I hate getting gas and have a terrible habit of pulling into the gas station with the car all the way on empty, a tradition Daddy chided me for time and time again.

Option one: Stay here in Plantation and continue to go about my business. After all, my life and TrueU were here. People depended on me. Barry needed me. Life was relatively stable and predictable, purposefully distanced from the rest of the family. The agency had never run in my absence. We were growing and could not even keep up with the rapid rate and volume of the applications coming in. It disturbed me to consider how many women in such a small radius needed assistance to escape abusive situations. So many were looking for counseling, resources, safe houses, relocation. So many women entered our doors, down to the last dollar of their meager paychecks, with children to feed and nowhere to turn. Government assistance let them down. The state resources let them down. Law enforcement and the court system weren't acting fast enough to protect them. I wondered how many others were out there like Mary Hernandez, afraid to reach out, afraid to speak up, more afraid of the unknown than the devil they already knew. They needed help—and they needed it now. The number of women who *did* put their faith in TrueU was baffling, and I couldn't help but wonder who would be there for them if I left for several days on a fool's errand. People's lives were at stake, so it would be selfish for me to neglect potentially dangerous situations. I was already taking grants and applications home with me at night to review. Those were all very convincing reasons to stay.

Option two: Drop my entire life for a woman who made a feeble attempt to raise me—amidst bouts of personal chaos and psychoses—then abandoned me. Press the pause button on my own accomplishments and personal goings-on to stoke the vanity of an individual responsible for the gossip, town chatter, and embarrassment that haunted my family. Sacrifice my mental well-being for a woman who tried her best to ruin any relation-ship between my father and me, no matter the expense. *She* was the genesis of my high school nickname "Krazy Kacee" which my classmates bestowed upon me and likely hasn't changed to this day in dear old Glendale. This option would, however, allow me to get out from under the unsettled feeling I'd been carrying around, and perhaps enable me to uncover some unsolved mysteries in my life.

I took a moment to collect myself, pulled out my compact to apply a touch of red lipstick—not too dark—and dotted concealer at the dark circles under my eyes to mask the lack of sleep. Planting my feet firmly and confidently on the ground, I opened the frosted glass doors of the agency, the familiar swish followed by a soft squeak welcoming me home.

A loud pop sounded as I reached the threshold, and I hit the ground, bags splayed. I brought my hands to my head, shielding my face and my ears, knees curling up under me, trembling. *Why is someone shooting up the place?* I know emotions can get high here, but please don't let me die today, I pleaded with no one in particular. My eyes darted back and forth between the multicolored folders sliding out of my satchel and tubes of lipstick and mascara rolling about along with my unopened bottle of Diet Coke. As my breathing slowed and I realized no one had joined me on the floor, my logical brain took over. The assumed gunshot was likely the backfire of a truck in the parking lot. A familiar event, yet one that shook me to the core in light of recent happenings. I laid there a few moments, bordering on hyperventilation, before Angie from the back office waltzed up toward the front doors, extending a gentle hand, and asked if I was okay. I nodded slowly from the ground, my cheek suctioned to the cold tile and avoiding all possible eye contact. I thanked Angie, embarrassed at my reaction, smoothed the front of my red blouse, and stood up. I put on my best imitation of a confident boss as I gathered my belongings, scooping the contents back into my purse and realizing my anxiety had overtaken my morning. Maybe even consumed my life here in Plantation.

The warmth from the office rested in sharp contrast to the cold November wind, and it hugged my skin like a warm blanket, despite the shiver I felt quake my core. As I stuffed items back into my satchel, I deposited my wallet, makeup, and pens, depositing most of the items but not before plunking a little blue pill on my tongue and swallowing it down with a fresh Diet Coke still cool from the bag.

Once settled at my desk, I watched Dottie stride through the same front doors seven minutes late, just like normal. She'd stopped making excuses months ago. I tolerated a certain level of tardiness from her, which went against every part of my nature. I felt I owed her for sticking by me through some pretty lean and ugly times. Besides, I knew most of the responsibility of caring for her aging parents, her dad with advanced Alzheimer's and her mother requiring help with basic care, fell squarely and unapologetically into this young woman's lap. Her two siblings lived 1200 miles away yet rarely called to so much as check on their parents. Forget inconveniencing themselves with a visit or a helping hand.

The eyes of the black and white clock with the waggling cat's tail followed my every move as it hung proudly above the office door emboldened with my name. *Tick, tick, tick.* The kitty said eight-thirty-seven.

I didn't even allow her to sit down before summoning her into my office. She usually ignored me for the first couple hours, or until I'd had enough coffee to be civil, so this must have taken her by surprise.

Dottie gazed at me across the desk with a weighty expression, her jade eyes narrowed in curiosity as the pad of her thumb caught and released the long fuschia nail of her pinky finger.

"I looked at the names on the schedule this morning and there are no notes for my first appointment. Sue Schuster? You know I rely on your notes and she's due to arrive in a few minutes. What's her story?"

Dottie paused a couple beats before answering, "You don't *know* her?"

I quickly flipped through my mental Rolodex but came up short. "I don't think so. Am I supposed to?"

In a voice thinned with panic, she raced through an explanation, words tumbling out of her mouth. Dottie's sharp cheekbones pointed out her fire engine hair, giving her a razor edge instead of a soft curve. She had a way of hardening the edges all her own, though clients loved her, which was a trait difficult to come by—being both reliable and relatable. "She said she was an old friend and wanted to speak to you about agency services. I'm sorry I didn't question her further. It didn't seem appropriate at the time." The lines on her forehead were steeped in remorse, the corners of her mouth downturned.

My irritation threatened to bubble over despite the calming hum of the Xanax swirling in my bloodstream. I reminded myself it was an honest mistake and rearranged my face, forcing a smile. "Don't worry about it. Let's try to get a little more information from people when they call without being too intrusive. Maybe we can come up with a list of questions. What do you think?"

"Definitely!" she shouted, then covered her barbie-painted mouth with her fist. The breath she exhaled into it was audible. She lowered her hand to the armrest, stood, and flipped her long hair over her shoulder. "I'll see what I can find out about her in the next few minutes, then I'll start working on that list." With that, she turned and strode out of my office on mile-long legs held up by three-inch high stilettos, swiping her sheer ivory duster trailing behind her. Straight and tall like my favorite of Mammi's fancy perfume bottles standing at attention in a precise line across her vanity, barely used though containing so much value. Dottie prided herself on thrift-shop fashion, and she amazed me at her ability to pull together the most unusual of pieces to create tasteful and professional outfits. I often questioned if she missed her fashionista calling in life.

Alone, I typed 'Sue Schuster' into Google but came up empty. Facebook rendered one account, but the profile picture was a random bunny sporting a purple lei, and the account was set to private. I settled on that explanation and returned to the never-ending task of answering emails.

At 8:55, a buzz from my office phone severed my last nerve and broke my attention from the only article I could find. "Yes, Dottie?"

"Ms. Schuster is here for her appointment. Should I show her in?" she asked over the intercom.

"Pick up the phone, please."

I heard the phone clatter from its base. "Yes?" I could picture her huddled over her desk in the minuscule waiting room.

"Does she look familiar at all, now that you've seen her? Could she be a client's relative?"

"Not off the top of my head." I could tell she was cupping her hand over the receiver as she whispered. "She's older. Like someone's mother for sure."

"Do me a favor and ask her to fill out an information form like we do when new families come in and want to meet with me about services." The acrid river swirling through my stomach signaled something was wrong.

I pulled my sweater snug around my shoulders as a chill spread over me. The space heater buzzed below my desk, yet this was a biting cold from the inside out.

"I'm ready when you are, once the paperwork is complete." I paused in a moment of clarity. "But bring me her forms first so I can look over them before you send her back."

"Of course," she replied.

In a few moments, Dottie appeared at my desk, clipboard in hand, bangles jangling as she offered them. "Here are the forms." As she started to turn, she looked back. "I'm not sure they're going to be all that helpful to you."

Glancing down at the brightly colored intake page, I noted much of the information had been left blank. "Thank you, Dottie. I'm going to review this, and I'll let you know once I'm ready for you to escort Ms. Schuster back." Closing the door with a soft click, I buried my face in my hands and my eyes in the neon pages, searching for any clues.

Name: Sue M. Schuster
Age: --
Address: Hickory, TX
Phone: --
Emergency Contact: --
What Brings You to TrueU: Kacee Marie Havemeier Robinson
Are You in Immediate Danger? No
Do You Believe Someone Else is in Immediate Danger? Quite possibly
Have You Spoken to Law Enforcement/Therapist About This Problem Before: In a sense
What Services at TrueU Do You Believe Can Assist You Most? Kacee Robinson
Tell us a little about your current situation bringing you here today. ---

Then the thought hit me. *Could this be related to Mary Hernandez?* I don't recall seeing anything in her files about family residing in Hickory, but it's possible. Perhaps an older aunt or grandmother. Such a relative could provide additional key information in assisting Mary with the case against her wretched husband.

Schuster... I rolled her last name over my tongue. *Isn't that...? Shoot. Could Sue be my mother's childhood friend Susan?* She had used Havemeier in my name, and not many people in Plantation even knew I was a Havemeier. I closed my eyes with dizziness at the sudden realization of the connection. I turned down the heater under my desk, listening to the gentle hum fade to an uncomfortable silence, slipped on my purple flats nestled under my desk, and dotted my badly chapped lips with cherry-flavored lip balm.

Pressing Dottie's intercom button, I instructed her to escort Mrs. Schuster back. A soft, familiar knock came, followed by

Dottie's outstretched arm directing Mrs. Schuster toward my desk. Trailing behind, tall and rawboned like a darkened streetlamp, Susan Schuster extended a bony hand that delivered a limp handshake. Her face came into full view: jutting chin, short bob haircut, and those piercing blue eyes nestled just below the scar across the left side of her forehead.

A car horn honked outside my window, and time stood still. My safe space boxed in; my options suddenly narrowed.

CHAPTER 6

"What a pleasant surprise, Mrs. Schuster," I feigned, hoping my expression followed verbal cues.

"No, it isn't," she quipped, her face sullen. "And it's MIZZZZ Schuster now, if you don't mind. Going through James's death was hard enough. But to have people thinking I'm still married to that old kook. Well…" Her raspy voice, no doubt from years of smoking, trailed off as loose skin waggled behind flailing arms.

I worried she might snap an ankle standing in those two-inch pumps, dressed in preparation for court or perhaps an important interview. Her oatmeal-colored suit screamed businesswoman, yet the plain Old Navy style tee underneath suggested an afternoon lounging at a picnic or a woman desperately seeking notoriety. The gray shown through the temples and roots of her otherwise blonde hair, coiffed in a short bob, and her support-top pantyhose compressed her waist in a lumpy, too-obvious way.

"How can I help? Please sit down at least," I offered, gesturing toward the small love seat angled near the bookcase marked "Relationships." The intimacy of the sofa seemed more appropriate than the formality of desk chairs.

"I'm here about your momma," she blurted, taking a seat with hesitation in her actions. The deep creases around her mouth disappeared and reappeared like a silk folding fan.

Susan Schuster had popped in and out of our lives for as long as I could remember, but never stayed longer than a minute. I don't recall ever hearing her last name more than once or twice growing up—a passing mention here and an offhanded anecdote there now raced to the forefront of my memory. Mom said the pair of them were like sisters and would sometimes detail a fond high school memory in comparison to Breanna and me. The two of us had even made a similar blood sisters club like Mom and Susan. We each signed a written agreement, cutting and smashing our bloody prints beside our childish signatures. I still have my copy somewhere, but obviously Breanna broke that when she decided to start spreading those awful fake rumors about Daddy and tried reeling me into her baseless accusations.

"If you're coming to inform me of the ceremony, I am already aware. I've spoken with Edna McIntyre." I picked at a snag in the beige twill sofa, wondering how far it would unravel if I kept pulling.

"So you will be in attendance, then?" She crossed one bony ankle over the other and looked at me with unblinking expectation, a coffee cup tattooed pink where her lips had touched.

I winced. Feeling my own poorly manicured nails dig into my thigh, I squeaked, "I'm still deciding," surprised by the sound of my own voice cracking. All these authoritative maternal figures popping up at once had made me feel like a child in need of approval for my every action, my every decision.

Her eyes landed like steel on mine—squinty and focused. Her mouth puckered in preparation for a lecture, wrinkles gathering together, despite her undoubtedly expensive skincare and makeup routine. I could hear her breathing, heavy but quick, and smelled the perfume meant to mask any nicotine remnants.

We sat quiet for several moments before she pronounced, "I wish you could see Ruth like I see her."

She opened her mouth to continue. Then, thinking better of it, picked up her purse and stood to leave. Her head snapped like a rubber band popping back into place, and her body followed.

"I want to just leave this with you to read. I know you and your mom have been at odds for a long time."

"I haven't talked to her in—"

"I know you shut her out," she snapped, words cutting. Certain she'd not heard the truth in its entirety yet unwilling to argue with her, I allowed her to continue. Saliva mixed with stomach acid, and all this talk of Mom had me fighting the urge to vomit. "That's why I'm bringing you this. Read it or don't. But know this, Kacee. Ruth has been a warrior her whole life. She gave me one of her diaries years back, for safekeeping. We shared everything, so I'm not breaking any promises to her." She shifted her weight onto the opposite hip, bracing herself with her hand. "This is simply one entry to give you a glimpse of a day in the life of her childhood. She did the best she could. She loves you so much. The last thing she'd ever want to do is to hurt you."

Susan placed the folded paper on the table.

"Did you just come here to give me that?"

"I came to tell you some things about your momma. Edna told me you were giving the speech, and I thought I could help." The space heater kicked on, restarting the familiar white noise.

"As I said, your mom and I grew up together right there in Glendale. Practically sisters. It'd be impossible for me to tell you everything there is to know about her all in one sitting. What I can tell you is that she's a good person, Kacee. She's a good person who got the short end of life's stick, if you ask me." Susan shook her head, eyes downcast in reflection. "It all started with her momma."

"Mammi?"

"Yes. Her momma was tough on her. Not your normal set strict boundaries kinda tough, either. Much harder than she was on your Aunt Jackie. She held Ruth to a *whole* different set of standards. And Ruth already put so much dagum pressure on herself. Pressure to be perfect. She stayed so stressed out she was literally starvin' herself to meet your grandma's expectations by the age of twelve or thirteen."

"What kind of expectations did she have of her at *that* age?"

"Ruth's always been thin as a rail but thought she was Two-Ton Tubby. Couldn't get it outta her head. She tried and never could. And her momma sure didn't help none. Not one iota. If you ask me, your Mammi planted the idea like summer squash and kept on fertilizing it. Always had her on this diet or that. Your aunt was just born big boned, so to speak. I think she gave up on Jackie being her perfect Southern-belle specimen, so she did damn near everything but cram her own fingers down your momma's throat to make sure she stayed thin. Your grandma whisked her away to one treatment place after another, telling the town she was on a mental health retreat and leaving the masses to fill in the blanks with their own imaginations. The poor girl never had a chance of not developing a bit of unfounded 'craziness,' so to speak." Susan made air quote gestures with her fingers. "The court of Glendale public opinion had spoken, ruling her the unstable daughter. Your grandma sure as hell wasn't going to assume any responsibility or correct the inaccurate narrative. That might tarnish the hallowed Havemeier name. Ruth was Scarlet Lettered, and your grandma let it all happen on her watch." Susan laughed to herself. "When you think about it, I guess crazy was more acceptable than fat, according to Havemeier standards."

My mind boomeranged back to a Fourth of July family picnic with Aunt Jackie when I was a preteen. Aunt Jackie had packed her plate with barbeque, potato salad, and of course several brownies. Mom watched her with such disdain in her eyes it made me want to reach over and slap the food off Aunt Jackie's plate myself to avoid the ensuing scene.

"What?" Aunt Jackie questioned, noticing Mom's stare.

"It's like you haven't eaten in weeks!" Mom said, as she filled her own plate with exactly two spoonfuls of green salad, no dressing, and a tiny sprig of grapes.

"Not everyone can survive on air and water."

Aunt Jackie turned to me and winked. "I guess not everyone enjoys food as much as me."

The afternoon remained as uncomfortable as Mom remained bitter. Or perhaps she was just hungry and paralyzed by that demon.

The contents of the diary entry remained a mystery to me, as it lay unopened on the table, contemplating whether or not to read the words contained on the page. Susan stood to leave, and I shook her hand, not knowing if I was glad she'd stopped by or not. I found myself at a loss for words.

CHAPTER 7

March 2, 1973

Another of Mother's charity socials. If she hosted these events because she loved helping people or wanted to make the world a better place, that'd be one thing. Admirable even. But she doesn't. She's singly in love with the attention, the fanfare, the lights. Putting Sissy and I on display like show ponies, waiting her turn to grab hold of the bridle and parade us around the rink then make a deposit to our resting stable. Some sick statement to this pissant town that she's a good mother. Mixing and mingling, she just really REALLY likes guests whispering about the overblown price tag of her gown and the fact you could eat off the floor. Do they realize all this requires zero effort on her part to upkeep? Clinking ice cubes in her scotch with a gentle shake, I can see wheels turning as she thinks of her next victim. Her next pawn.

Mother assumes everyone is like her. God, please don't let me be like Mother when I grow up. I just want to hide behind the curtain, sitting with Sissy in the corner and drinking a fancy pineapple punch. How much smaller do I need to be to qualify as invisible? I tried to boycott today's event, locking myself in my room. As she yanked me from the closet by my hair, my only thought was, "I don't ask for much." Just a kid who wants to stay upstairs and read. My books are my only friends.

My only escape from this life she's crafted for me. But that would never be enough. I'll never be enough for her. Forced to plaster on a fake smile and listen to her adoring fake fan club sing, "Look how much you girls have grown! My how you've filled out; do you have a boyfriend yet?" Constant insipid chit-chat of decaying housewives with nothing better to do with their husbands' money than to throw it at the charity-of-the-month, some of which I question if Mother makes up in her runaway imagination the night of the events. The itchiness of Alencon lace around my collared neck feels unbearable.

CHAPTER 8

Stumbling up the creaky steps and into the counseling office with my tall vanilla latte in hand—extra shot of espresso, non-fat milk, no whip, of course—and a chai tea for Margaret, I flopped onto her couch and released a burdened sigh. "I've weighed all my options, Margaret. I've examined the situation up and down and beat this damn horse till it's black and blue. The only thing keeping me from going back is fear. I'm not sure that's decent enough reasoning. I don't want to be afraid." I dotted the moisture from the corners of my eyes with my index fingers, two of the nails bitten all the way to the quick, dried blood coloring my cuticles.

Not immediately returning an answer, but rather allowing time for reflection, Margaret opened then closed her mouth. She searched the pimply white ceiling for the correct answer. *There's always a right answer.*

"It's probably way more information than you need or care to know, but I've had chronic diarrhea since Edna called. I was visited by another of her friends since our last visit—Susan—and it sure as hell didn't help the situation. She came to the agency armed with a diary entry, supposedly written by Mom, and I can't get it out of my head."

"And why is that? If you're comfortable sharing."

"It was all about Mammi mistreating her. It painted my grandmother in a completely different light," I told her. "An *evil queen* sort of light."

"I see." Margaret shifted in her chair, taking a deep sip of her chai tea, and I wondered if she'd always been on the heavy side or if she was a stress eater like Aunt Jackie and my friend Harriet. It also made me think I should call Harriet soon and mentally began whipping myself for my poor friendship skills. The longest friendship I'd ever cultivated was with Breanna, which I had stupidly terminated just because Daddy said so. Even if she did say those hurtful things about him, I should have at least had the decency to accept her calls or return an email, if just to see what she had to say for herself. She made accusations that could have ruined his career. Everyone who knew Daddy knew they were false, and she had to be after money. Maybe she needed the money for something important. After all, I know firsthand, money makes people do things they'd never do otherwise. My mind raced as I sat in the chair, leg jumping up and down as fast as the ping-pong in my mind bounced between thoughts. Perhaps someone else put her up to it or there was an ulterior motive. Daddy was so hurt by the situation, though, and once legal got involved, I had to choose sides or be perceived as a threat. After almost fifteen years of friendship, you'd think I'd have reached out somewhere along the way. At least in an attempt to get her side of the story. It was all so out of the ordinary. I guess I screwed that up, too.

Lassoing ideas and turning back to Margaret, "What I'm telling you is that I can't eat, sleep, or even function properly until I make this damn decision about Glendale. On the one hand, if I return, I might somehow unearth my own path. Hell, I might even know why I can't sleep or even keep a friend. I might not get another chance to even see Mom. Aunt Jackie said she's been up and down with her health over the last year. But the last time I was in that town, I practically suffered a damn nervous breakdown!" I shouted.

Margaret's eyes widened as she straightened her snugly fitting skirt. "This is quite the decision you have. It wouldn't be easy for anyone in your position." She rose and crossed the room with her distinct left-lilting gait, hands shoved deep in the pockets of the skirt. "Now I know you don't like it when I psychoanalyze you," she said, "but I also know you are a well-read and intelligent woman. You know a great deal about psychology and the role our brain plays on our human behavior."

I nodded my head in agreement and caressed my fingers over the gold anchor hanging around my neck.

"Research shows that children of alienation or abandonment most often want nothing more than to be granted permission to give and receive love by those who left them in the first place. Whether that be a physical or emotional desertion, it seems to be—"

"We are only talking about my mother here," I interrupted. "My father didn't leave me. He wasn't perfect by any means. But he stuck by me. At least until last year," I revised my statement. "And, no offense, but spare me the psychobabble. I only need to figure out what to do."

"Fine, then. We will only speak of your mother. For now." Her eyebrows raised in a warning—warding off any opportunity to challenge her statement.

"I moved to Plantation to leave Mom and her antics behind. I'm certainly not looking for her love now. Not as an adult. I've moved past that and stopped wishing for miracles." Case closed. "Barry and my work provide all the love and support I need." We both knew I was lying about not needing anyone else, yet Margaret chose to push most of the issue aside and only focus on my maternal fixation that continued to circle.

Margaret skeptically harrumphed in her chair, not receiving the desired response. "Are you sure about that?"

"What's that supposed to mean?" I asked, somewhat indignant.

"I'm only making the observation that, if you were not seeking your mom's approval on some level, Edna nor Susan's opinions wouldn't make a hill of beans difference to you," she continued. "It's natural and normal to seek the approval of our parents well into adulthood—no matter the experience we've had with them as children. In fact, I'm sure you've seen some of this through your work with TrueU. Battered children who still feel guilty for speaking out against an abusive parent or an adult who tends to suffer from depression or chronic insomnia because she has never felt approval from her mother who abandoned her when she was seven. It's likely rooted in guilt. Does that make sense?"

I nodded, having never before made any sort of conscious correlation between myself and the children we serve. *I* wasn't that kid.

"What is your motivation for going, then—should you choose to attend? Are you going to make up with your dad, who you said still lives there? Are you going to relive old times with classmates like Breanna? Or are you going for your mother?" Margaret stared at me with her large open eyes, and I knew she'd remain silent until I provided an answer. But I didn't have one for her, and not for lack of trying; I'd spent more sleepless nights than I could count over the years in failed attempts at figuring it all out. Trying to understand why I attended Mom's damn church when she'd asked me, or ate her horrible food when she'd cooked it, or lived *my* life adhering to *her* dang lists, or even stayed with her, when all I wanted to do was to move to Daddy's. Guilt. Pure, unadulterated, southern-fried guilt.

I couldn't help but think of attending church with Mom one Easter Sunday. She dragged me there nearly every Sunday since the divorce. I watched with fury in my soul, the looks of pity from people whose backsides were nestled in the uncomfortable seats for the sole purpose of making themselves feel better and ensuring they had a front-row seat to judge the transgressions of the good people of Glendale. The whole congregation of the First Baptist Church felt sorry for us. Women dressed in their finest white dresses and shiny matching shoes, squishing up against one another on the long, blue-cushioned pews, knowing full well nobody wanted to be wearing those hot pantyhose. But no one dared challenge the chastity rule of revealing bare legs or fore-going made up faces in the Baptist church. Aunt Jackie, Mom, and I sat at the end of a row by ourselves. One can only extend so large a helping of Christianity before guilt by association sets in. Some of those folks believed divorce was contagious, like a good case of chickenpox. Mammi and Pappi were present and accounted for, seated front and center of the sanctuary where everyone could make sure to note their presence and Mammi could socialize and show off her new Easter hat. The white hat hung floppy on her head and featured white and baby pink magnolia flowers made from a gauzy material and draping from the hat down the side of her head, one of them nearly catching her dangling gold earring. Knowing my grandparents blamed Mom didn't help one bit. The whole situation approximated a pan of Jiffy Pop, and I was kernel number seventy-eight, biding my time until the appropriate moment of explosion when reaching the correct temperature.

Even though I didn't know how Mom could still believe in a sovereign God, she'd insisted we attend. She sat faithfully, head bowed and eyes scrunched tight as she begged for something. I couldn't know what she was praying for, but I liked to think she pleaded for forgiveness for breaking up our family. For making me the only kid in school who was being raised by a single parent. From time to time, I'd give her an askance look as she kneeled down, all penitent like that. In that look, I'd pour all my anger, frustration, disgust. *I hope He never forgives you,* I'd think. But then I'd scrunch up my eyes too and beg forgiveness for my impure thoughts—just in case He did exist. Karma and such. As I would beg, a part of me would become keenly aware that with my face scrunched in prayer and fingers tented, I must look a lot like her.

Placing two hands on her knees and pushing herself to a standing position while gathering her skirt together in one hand with some sort of magic trick, Margaret rose. "Well, it's settled then. Time to take back control. Guilt is no way to live. Wouldn't you agree?"

Surprised at her assessment, I looked up at her from my seat on the deep couch, my feet failing to touch the ground if I sat all the way back. "I, uh, yeah. I suppose you're right."

"Great. Then if your only reason is guilt, you will refuse the invitation, correct?"

"I, um, it's not the *only* reason," I said, unsure of myself and convinced the decision couldn't be quite so easy.

"Then tell me more." Margaret leaned in, her red manicured fingers folded neatly together in her lap.

"I do want to go. I mean, there are a lot of reasons for me to return. I think I could help solve some of my own issues. Talk with Breanna again. Visit Aunt Jackie. See Mom before it's too late. I'm not reaching out to Daddy. He will call me when he's ready." I felt one weight lift to immediately be replaced by another.

CHAPTER 9

The phone began ringing on the opposite end of the line, and what seemed like a great idea to call my aunt instantly dissolved into a clear absence of judgment. Listening to the first ring, I contemplated hanging up. By the second ring, I began praying to a God I'd abandoned years ago that I'd have the option to leave a simple message. I popped a little blue Xanax with a swallow of Diet Coke for good luck. Before ring three, that same God failed me yet again and Aunt Jackie's voice met mine; she was elated to hear from me.

Brash backwoods amplitude mixed with a bit of sugar-sweet care described my aunt to a tee. She'd do anything for you, so long as she liked you. But if she didn't, Katy bar the door!

"Hi, Aunt Jackie. How's it going? I've been meaning to call you for a couple days now, but I've been getting home late from work. And I know you aren't exactly a night owl. I—"

"Oh honey, you can call me anytime," she interrupted with her familiar southern lilt. "As long as it's before 8:30 and you ain't calling me late for supper," she cackled that infectious brand of laugh unique to Aunt Jackie. "I'm just pleased as punch to hear from you, Sweet Thang! Was plannin' to call you this weekend anyhow. I wanted to give you a talkin' to 'fore Ms.

Edna McIntyre sunk her clammy little claws into you. D'you remember that 'ol heifer? Full of piss and vinegar is what she is."

I tapped my pen against the golden Formica countertops, now chipping at the corners and contemplated at what point I'd spend long enough at home to map out all those redecorating projects I promised myself I'd launch into as soon as I took over ownership of this quaint little apartment. I wondered if it was possible puke green colored kitchens could come back in style as I focused on the moss wall color. After all, who ever thought crop tops and obnoxious blue eye shadow would make a reappearance in those fancy fashion magazines?

Chuckling to myself, I interrupted her rant. "She called me a couple days ago. Guess she beat you to the punch this time." I knew the revelation would send cartoon steam out of her ears, envisioning her grip tightening around one of her many stained coffee cups in the collection, perched at her avocado kitchen table and wrapping the phone cord nervously around her finger, her plump figure propped against the yellow-flowered flocked wallpaper. "Edna told me I *had* to come back to Glendale and give a speech for Mom. I wondered why you weren't the one to tell me."

"Actually, I—"

Not allowing her space to answer, I interjected. "I flat out refused Edna. Now I'm second guessing myself. I mean, the woman *did* raise me, I guess. Even if she stunk at it. I've lost sleep over this damn situation, and I don't know what to do. I'm hoping you can shed some light on the predicament. You're always my voice of reason."

I heard coffee slurping from the opposite end of the line, envisioning cats circling underfoot, whinnying an impatient banter my aunt seemed to understand like a second language. Shaky hands ran up and down Barry's overstuffed belly as my ears tuned to the sonorous voice blistering through the dark-corded receiver, his thick fur softening to a therapeutic touch as the problem at hand grew ever more imminent. His dark, droopy eyes inquired about my state of okayness.

"I'm alright, buddy," I assured him, bending down to pet his head as he leaned his face into my hand while I held my other over the receiver of the phone. "Let Momma get you a cookie." I stood to rummage through the top cabinet to produce a Milk Bone and kissed him atop his nose, to which all concern for me was suddenly forgotten.

I turned my attention back to Aunt Jackie. "What do *you* want to do, Sweet Pea? I think you've gotta answer this one for yourself. You're the one that chose to pick up and haul your cookies all the way out to Plantation. I'm not sayin' you didn't have your reasons. I'm just sayin' you gotta answer if you still got them same reasons or not."

I hadn't thought about it with so little guile.

"I've been thinking a lot about that," I told her. Headache creeping in, I put two fingers to my temples and began a circular massaging motion. The pounding from the inside told of a little toy soldier attempting to drum his way out through my left eyeball, drumstick first. I mentioned to Dottie about a month ago I might need to seek medical advice about my headaches, though doctors had always been a last resort. Since childhood, I had heard horror stories and town gossip about my mother and her medical trysts. I can't help but think little good comes from men in fancy white coats—my daddy being the exception, of course.

The latest swallowed pill kicked in and my head wavered somewhere between euphoria and "I have no idea what we were talking about." I zoned back into the action as she ranted on— defending her superior status to Edna McIntyre. "I'll tell you this much. I know your momma better than anybody, I s'pose. Edna's right about one thing. I'll give her that. Ruth sure would like to see you there. Whether you give that speech or not, she'd love to see your face. But that's up to you, darlin'. You gotta take care of *you*."

The mention of my mother's name jolted me. "Maybe you should call your momma *yourself* and talk to her," she advised, but my mouth, dry as parchment, rendered me unable to form a response to the mere idea of speaking to that woman again.

Picking up on my sudden silence, Aunt Jackie redirected the conversation. "How is everything else? How's that Barry? One of these days I'm gonna get to meet that cute little fella. I love seein' all those pictures you send through the electronic mail."

"Barry's doing great. I know he'd fall in love with his Aunt Jackie the minute he laid eyes on you. How are the girls? I hear them chatting up the place."

"Trouble," she sighed and slurped all at once, causing a coughing fit to ensue. "Them cats are just pure trouble. But I wouldn't trade any of 'em for the world. And don't you go on judgin' me for this, but I bought 'em a giant playhouse for all three to share. You gotta see it when you come." She paused. "*If you come*," she clarified, knowing that pushing me into anything would be the easiest way to get me to revolt. Some things never change. "That thing's bigger'n the neighbor down the way's whole front porch! They love it!"

"Oh, I bet they do. And I have no room to talk, if you were to ever see Barry's toybox," I chuckled as I eyed Barry, digging through his third pile of tennis balls and assorted stuffed and squeaky farm animals before landing on a final selection of a crinkly hedgehog.

The phone line between us inflated with uncomfortable silence like a balloon, soon to release its air and shoot off course. Shattering the quiet, she asked, "Will you promise to let me know your plans?"

"I pinky swear. I need more time to sort this all out in my head. Truth is, there've been a couple of weird things happening here, too. I think coming there for a few days, even to take a break from Plantation, might not be so bad. I mean, I guess it doesn't matter if my first intention is to speak at Mom's ceremony as long as I see her, right?"

"I s'pose you're right. What kind of weird things, Sugar? Do I need to be worried?"

I rubbed my hands over my forearms for comfort. The scars left behind yielded little, only serving as more evidence of pain from an internal battle I'll never win. "It's hard to explain. I found my door unlocked and things in my apartment moved around. But the only thing I can find missing is one single book. Well, and some letters. And, heck, I mighta even have loaned the book out. I don't know. I'm second guessing myself on every-thing these days. I also thought I saw or at least smelled…" Remembering the familiar, musty peat smell wafting by me yesterday as I strode out of Margaret's and later recalling the familiar shadow, I decided against bringing it up to Aunt Jackie after all. First of all, it'd send Aunt Jackie into a panic. Second, I'm sure my nerves had clinched my reasoning and tainted the situation. It didn't even make sense.

"Saw what? Smelled what?"

"I'm just seeing things is all."

With a sigh, she said, "You're working too dang hard up there, is what you are. I used to be like you, ya know? Child, I warned you about this when you took the job over there. You need to take a break from that place. Go get a pedicure or—heaven forbid—go on a date. You know any guy would love to take out my beautiful niece."

"Ugh."

"Just think about it. Promise you'll think about it. Don't learn the hard way by burning yourself out like I did. You've got a lot of good to give, Punkin' Pie."

"I promise. I already feel better talking to you." The death grip I'd placed on my glass now relaxed. Shredded pieces of paper napkin lay in an adjacent pile.

Aunt Jackie always remembered and appreciated the little things in life. She retired early to spend time in her house out in the country with Katy, Trixie, and Macy. Those cats became her entire life.

"Do you know I haven't had an overnight visitor since your mom stayed here last? Our sisters' experiment, as she called it. Oh lordy, that woman hates my cooking. She wasn't here two weeks before she took over the grocery shopping. Especially since mine typically consists of chocolate and coffee." She chuckled to herself. "I gotta ask 'fore you come down here to stay… Do you make lists like your momma, Kacee?"

"Oh my goodness," I laughed at the notion. "Mom and her lists." It was a comedic and painful childhood memory wrapped all in one. She had lists for her lists.

"Why did Mom come to live with you the last time, anyhow?" I watched the ice swirl in my glass and slowly melt with the low freezing point of its contents.

"Oh Sugar, she was in no shape to keep up independent living following her last stint in the psych ward. Wait." She exclaimed, as if suddenly remembering. "I think I'm supposed to call it a mental health unit. Yes. Anyway." I could tell she was pleased with herself at the correction as she continued. "I'm thankful you didn't see her in that condition. I thought I'd prepared myself for the worst, but she came outta there more broken than she went in. I know you remember one of her first in-patient stays with a nun's conscience. The one when you were about ten." The mention of the incident knocked the breath out of me. I'd never forget. "Take that and throw about three dollops of stress on top. That's what this one looked like.

"The facility called me at initial admittance this time, because I was listed as her next of kin. I raced to St. Joseph's Behavioral Hospital to be by her side. Nurse Ratchet stopped me at the door, and your momma didn't even look like herself. Eyes wide, flitting around. Her body couldn't sit still. Hair plastered all to her face from tears, snot, and not showering. And she prob'ly weighed eighty pounds soaking wet. Didn't look like your momma at all." Aunt Jackie paused. "She didn't even recognize me. That one hurt the worst. But she got better. She just needs some help every now and then."

"Fine. I'm coming," I blurted.

"What?!" Aunt Jackie exclaimed.

"I was leaning that way, but talking to you, well, it's the right thing to do." I paused, "I mean if it's okay with you for me to stay there."

"Of course!" she trumpeted. "I'm so thrilled!"

I heard shuffling in the background, then she began again. "Now I gotta get you off the phone so I can clean up or you're gonna think your aunt—" her voice trailed into a lost thought.

"I don't care what—"

She cut me off, snipping out final instructions.

"Make sure you bring a nice dress. Edna says this is going to be *some* shindig. You know Edna'll invite that highfalutin' crowd she likes to call her own. Though most of 'em talk about her 'fore she gets her back good and turned 'round. I think Edna's like your Mammi was, in that sense. All about the status."

"Fancy dress to impress Edna. Got it. Anything else I should know or remember to bring?"

"Not that I know of. Just yourself. And that little cutie-patootie, Barry."

"I think you might be just as excited to see Barry in person as you are me," I teased. "And you know he isn't little." I laughed.

"Not quite as excited. But he's darn sure a close second. And size is relative and sometimes how you feel in your heart. So there."

Barry certainly did *feel* small, as evidenced by his lap sitting. A long pause followed as if she was considering saying something then decided against it.

"Well, I'd best be tidying up this place, or you'll think your aunt's an old maid." Her burst of laughter filled my ears and my heart.

"I'll call when we are close, Aunt Jackie. I love you."

"I love you more, darlin'."

We hung up, and for the first time in a long time, I felt at peace.

A text message gave rise to a collaborative vibrating of my hand and kitchen table. I snatched up the phone, wondering what Aunt Jackie had forgotten to tell me and impressed she'd typed out a text so quickly. The phone fumbled in my hand as I saw the name listed was my code name for Mary Hernandez.

MARIANNE: He made contact with #2 at school.

I deciphered the carefully worded message. Robert had found a way to contact her daughter. #2 was a cipher for the middle child, who was also a bit of a Daddy's girl. This meant he wasn't far behind on her trail. My search for a safehouse switched into overdrive, and I banged out emails to confidential contacts and searched for leases in small, remote towns. Pulling out all the stops, I fired off a quick message to Terry J, my most trusted private investigator, to wrangle in his services. I considered looking at other locations besides the original permanent plan of Arkansas. Mary was relying on me, so I knew there'd be no sleep until I found some potential options.

CHAPTER 10

kept turning Susan's intake form comment about danger over in my mind.

What did she mean by someone being in danger? Was it Mom? Me? Why didn't I ask her when I had the chance?

I considered Aunt Jackie's suggestion to give Mom a call and let her know the good news. I wouldn't even know how to start the conversation. I grabbed my quilt off the back of the sofa and rubbed at the yellow tufts. Barry nuzzled close by; his head rested heavy in my lap. Sitting in the small brown accent chair positioned in the cozy living room, I tapped a pencil at the edge of the walnut coffee table—its click, click, click seemed to whittle away at my rapid succession of pros and cons list. The reasons not to call Mom winning by a long shot. Maybe there was something to the hereditary list-making after all.

Staring at the phone, the receiver sat in its cradle. I began to quiver. I reached for the phone and dialed the number all in one quick movement before my brain could stop my muscles.

"Hello." Came a somewhat unfamiliar — yet never forgettable — voice on the other end of the line.

"Ummmm, may I speak with Ruth Robinson, please?"

"This is she." A weak voice came back, then a pause followed by audible tears. "Kacee, is that you?"

I gulped in uneven mouthfuls of oxygen. The feeling as if I'd been strangled under the weight of her voice suddenly overwhelming. A burst of pain shot through my ears, and they began to ring—stifling my hearing. I wondered how long it had been– Four years? Five years? It felt like an eternity. "Yes, um, hi Mom. It's me."

I heard loud sobbing on the other end. I envisioned her sitting in a tiny white box of a room, tears flowing down her hollowed-out face, splashing to the ground. She wouldn't bother to get a tissue. The cries were surely a mixture of joy and sadness —from both of us. Her enfeebled body probably perched on a chair or propped up on the bed, all 5'2" of her. I knew her exact height, because I'd aspired to be taller than her when I was a kid. She was petite, and I thought I'd outdo her, in at least one area. I recall the sting of disappointment when the pediatrician announced he was certain I had reached my maximum height at a whopping 5'1"—I'd literally fallen short again.

"I, uh, heard you were getting an award," I blurted. "Congratulations." *I hoped it wasn't supposed to be a surprise and I'd just blown it.* After all these years, I was still at a loss for words and terrible with surprises. I'd prepared so long for this very moment, yet suddenly couldn't remember any of the things I planned to say.

I should have made a list.

"Edna called and asked me if I was coming." Three deep breaths and count to ten. "I know we haven't had the best relationship over the years, so, um, what do you think about the idea?"

"Oh honey! You were thinking of coming *here*? To *Glendale*?" A schoolgirl squeal trapped beneath the surface of her words.

"Truth is I have some unanswered questions of my own about my childhood, Mom. I'd like to be able to support you and also maybe talk to you about some stuff that happened, stuff that's been bothering me for twenty years. Would you be willing?"

"Oh, of course, sweetheart! Anything you want to know. You're old enough now to know anything and everything you have questions about. I realize I wasn't the best mother. One thing I want you to remember… no matter what, I always tried to do right by you." She was nearly impossible to understand through heavy gasps of sobs. "I really tried. I'm just so happy to think I'll see you again. I'd honestly resigned myself to thinking I'd lost you. It was the toughest belief in the whole world to come to terms with."

"Then how could you just up and leave me, Mom? How could you break up the family like you did? And then support Breanna trying to ruin Dad and his reputation when she was accusing him of…of…of what she did? He had to go before the surgeon's board for it all." I couldn't even bring myself to voice all the horrible accusations out loud to her. "I'm angry. I'm hurt. It's gone on too long."

I waited, tapping my foot against the teal base of the table storing more books and more papers. Hearing her breathe heavy on the other end of the line, I began to worry if I'd pushed too hard, considering her living situation.

My words had flown out in a flurry. "Kacee, sweetheart, I did so much wrong. *So* much. I won't deny any of my part in the undoing of the family. However, I didn't break up the family by myself and neither did Richard. It takes two people. I will tell you there's a side to your father I hope I shielded from you, even if it meant you grew to hate me. I decided long ago I could go to my grave with you hating me as long as it meant you stayed safe." I chewed at my lip as she spoke, tasting blood from biting down too hard, a twinge of disbelief at how she could still be placing blame on the one parent who was there for me. "And the situation with Breanna is not what it seems. It's also not a conversation for the phone. If you decide to come visit, I promise to hold your hand and tell you in person. The whole truth." She paused before stating, fire in her words, "and I *never* left you."

Swallowing a small piece of my pride and pushing down the monstrous lump formed at the base of my throat, I whispered, "Okay, Mom. I'll be staying with Aunt Jackie, so I'll have her set up the visit with your facility." My voice softened. "She said it's a nice place."

"That's great, honey. And it *is* a nice place. They monitor all my medication. I'm even able to work a little one day a week. They help me manage the severe manic episodes and other breaks. They also make sure I eat when I can't bring myself to do it. You know how anxiety affects my appetite. I wouldn't say my living situation is ideal, but it beats having to go in and out of the hospital. I've been sick for the last few days but hearing your voice sure is making me feel better," Mom sounded weak but happy.

"I'm glad I'm coming, Mom. See you soon."

I hung up the phone and collapsed across the sofa, listening to the cushions release a familiar and comforting sigh under my weight. I replayed the words, as they sent a bitter taste in my throat. My contacts were cloudy, and my eyes burned. I hadn't talked to her in so many years, but she had almost made it feel like it was yesterday. I wondered if there could be more to the story I'd ignored all these years. For those few minutes, the anger and the hatred I felt toward her had faded—just a little. And she'd agreed to answer my questions, which gave me some hope.

Walking into the bathroom and washing my face, I stared in the mirror at my reflection. Having removed my contacts and what felt like tiny pieces of sandpaper rubbing underneath each one, I placed my glasses squarely on my eyes and looked at my reflection. I blinked hard. Staring back at me was a remarkable resemblance to Ruth Havemeier Robinson. I didn't want to see it, but I couldn't help it. The hard jawline, yet soft features. The oval eyes, blessed with long lashes yet premature smile lines.

Just another of the many contradictions that made up my mother- and now me. I shook my head.

Flushed and sweating, all I wanted to do was escape. I phoned Margaret, who surprisingly answered. I blurted, "I'm going back to Glendale. I need to sort this all out."

She sounded pleased as she said, "I'm glad you've made the healthiest decision for you, Kacee."

That's what parental approval looks like in my daydreams.

CHAPTER 11

Checking the time, it was only nine p.m. Not too late to call Dottie. She was likely getting ready to go out for some social activity, dinner or drinks with friends.

She answered with a cheerful, "Hey, Kacee! What's going on?"

"I'm sorry to bother you during the evening, but I wanted to let you know I'm going to be leaving town on short notice. I'll leave tomorrow and be gone for several days." Thinking, I added, "In fact, don't plan on me being back before next week. I have some family business to attend to, and, well, it's just a little sticky. I'm going back to Glendale."

"Is everything okay?" she questioned, concern filling her voice. "Does this have to do with that Sue lady coming to visit and telling you to go home?" She paused, and I swear I could hear her puzzling out how to phrase her next move. I beat her to the punch.

"Oh sure. I am fine. And it does. I just wanted you to know since I won't be at the agency. There's a folder on my computer labeled Plan B, just in case anything was to ever come up and I had to be out. All emergency contacts are in there. I will still be working as much as possible and checking my emails and voice-mails. Feel free to call me if you need to."

"Heavens to Betsy! I knew you'd do the right thing after that meeting," she blurted.

Shoving folded shirts into an already overstuffed suitcase, I paused---brown and white flannel shirt held in one hand---and gingerly lowered it to the bed at her comment.

"Why do you say that? And if you had a strong opinion, why didn't you tell me when I asked you?"

Dottie sighed before speaking. "I didn't think it was my place to voice my opinion. I know you asked me, Kacee. I'd be lying if I said I didn't punch the air just now." She laughed in her infectious chuckle and said, "You've only got one momma, Kacee. You gotta make this right, or at least find a way to move on and keep this part of your past from steering your ship."

I shifted, looking at the phone. "You're pretty and smart," I teased. Most clients who walked through the doors of TrueU grossly underestimated Dottie's brains because of her Barbie doll figure. It was a running joke between the two of us.

When I hired Dottie, she was at a point in her life where she was trying to turn herself around and reform her life from a not-so-positive upbringing. Drugs and crime had littered her child-hood, and she was determined to do better for herself.

"We are planning to take off first thing in the morning. I hope to not leave you for more than a few days." I paused for a moment. Remembering Mary's odd text message. "And if you happen to hear anything, anything at all in reference to Mary that came in the other day, please let me know right away, okay? And I'll do my best to hurry back."

"Um, sure. I mean, you're the boss," she teased.

I laughed. "I guess in theory. Thanks, Dottie."

CHAPTER 12

Letter from Mom:

February 2, 2019

Dear Kacee:

I know you probably won't open this letter, but I have to try. I simply must. It's embarrassing to even write to you, knowing you don't want to speak to me, but it is my only outlet, and my therapist says it's healthy. I am getting stronger again. I want to make you proud. I know I have let you down so many times, honey, and for that I am sorry. I also know you are being told some misinformation. It is said I am plotting against you and trying to ruin your new career through false rumors about your dad. That is simply not true. I want to talk with you more than anything. Now that you are an adult, my therapist says I should try and help you understand the mental illness I am personally struggling with and also that it has nothing to do with those rumors. She suggested, if I was comfortable, sending you some of my writings. You know how I feel about my writings. You know how personal they are to me. To show how much I trust you, I've plucked some pages of my private journals to share. These are my innermost thoughts, and some are going to be painful to read. I hope you can use them for personal growth, for relationship growth, and just to know your mom as I truly am, since talking to me is not an option right now, if ever. I will keep sending them, Kacee, and hope you read them. Now or one day. Maybe it will help you understand me. And that I have always only loved you and done my best.

Love, Mom

Mom's Journal Entry:

March 20, 1987

It doesn't seem like Richard and I have been married for over a year already. We're figuring out a lot about each other. Marriage is a lot different and a lot harder than I imagined. He wants dinner at 6 p.m. every night and would like for me to plan out menus. I'm fine with the planning, of course, but my cooking skills are limited. According to him, there must be red meat of some sort with every evening meal. I stopped by the library today and checked out some new cookbooks to help. Driving half an hour into town each day after work to gather up ingredients is tiring. I need a master list to cover a couple of days. I'm just no good at cooking and end up burning meals about every other night which frustrates Richard then frustrates me. At least I'm trying. I regret not having one of the cooks teach me more when we were growing up. One of the many things I took for granted. I thought everyone had a cook when they got married. It's also hard, because I've had to adjust my shifts at the hospital to try and get home on time. I suppose I never expected this would all be so time-consuming and draining. Tomorrow we are going out with Susan and her new boyfriend James. Anxious to meet him. He's a firefighter, and Susan says she thinks he might be "the one!"

March 29, 1987

Last night started out fantastic and ended as a complete disaster. We went on our double date with Susan and James. Susan and I got our hair done together earlier in the day at the new little boutique in town, Cut and Curl. Mary Beth had hers fixed there last week and came out with the most fabulous curled flip ever! The lady curled mine to perfection and feathered my part just right. Susan's short bob always looks stylish and chic. We treated ourselves to a little shopping spree at Boutique on the Square and picked up brand new outfits. I bought the cutest royal blue crop top shaped like a giant bow to wear with my jeans and white blazer. I was excited for Richard to see me in it. That's where the demise of the evening began, as he quickly pointed out how my stomach poked out when I sat down. He told me it was probably made for thinner girls and laughed. I didn't find the humor in it and rushed to change into a more conservative tank.

He insisted on driving, and we picked them up from Susan's house around seven. Susan looked darling, and I caught myself eyeing her posh yellow mini dress. The wide red belt and flats accentuated her perfect figure. Of course, she could get away with that because she didn't live with stomach rolls like me. Fat. Fat. Fat. I hate being fat.

If James was a Disney character, he'd be Goofy. Clumsy, perhaps not the brightest bulb on the tree, funny, and impossible not to adore. You could tell he was smitten with Susan, which makes me happy. We all ordered a first round of drinks. Richard was on his third; everyone seemed to be chatting it up, while his words sloshed in his mouth, barely audible. His thick sandy brown eyebrows furrowed in distress. I leaned over, patted his leg with my hand, and whispered in his ear asking if he was okay. He glared at me, fire in his eyes, and barked, "No I am not okay! I'm not okay taking you out to a nice restaurant and watching you flirt around like a hooker trying to get tips to take back to her John!" I sat in disbelief. Stunned. Tears pricked my eyes. Tears of hurt, anger, embarrassment. Not knowing what to do or how to respond. He'd never spoken to me quite like that before. I lifted myself from the table, head hung, and walked to the edge of the restaurant. He ruined my night, humiliated me in front of Susan and her new beau, and threatened to wreck a friendship. Susan came outside after a few minutes and put her arm around me. She asked what that was all about, but I couldn't even tell her. I didn't know why he was speaking to me that way. She hugged me, and I hugged her back and apologized for the night. At least she still seems to be my friend. I didn't speak to Richard after we arrived at our house. I slept on the couch, and I feel like I'll be sleeping there for a while.

CHAPTER 13

The rain let up, and I knew we must be getting close when sulfur plugged my nostrils---nothing like the scent of rotten eggs in the morning. We passed a successive slurry of oil derricks, kissing the ground and rising back up for breath, only to repeat the familiar pattern. Single-story houses with large porches hugging their breadth spread wide apart amidst sprawling acres of flattened land. Old cars, many of which probably hadn't run in decades, parked cattywampus in the dirt, rusting in annoyance of no one in particular. Cows grazed the sparse greenery, in no hurry and late for no meetings. I'd forgotten the lazy pace of West Texas. Time spared for manners. For observation. For breathing in honeysuckle-flavored life. Amidst all its faults, lots of good remained here. The closer I inched toward Glendale, the more it felt like home. I reached over to the passenger seat, fumbling for my phone to call Aunt Jackie.

After two rings, she picked up. "Aunt Jackie? We crossed through Hitown about thirty minutes ago and we just drove by the old freight train graveyard. So I suspect we'll be out to you in another half hour or so. Do you need anything on our way in?"

"Oh no, Sugar. Y'all just bring your little selves on into me. I've already got some biscuits and grits cookin' on the stove, so I hope you're hungry." Before I could answer, she asked, "What's that noise?"

"The bottom fell out of the clouds. What you're hearing is Barry showing his, um, bravery." I giggled, realizing she must be hearing his soft whimpers coming over the phone. Although Barry was not the pluckiest, he was a great listener. Sometimes I wondered if he ever grew tired of hearing about my troubles at work, my frustrations with my childhood, my lamenting over never having a date. Then I realized it was hard to have a fundamental argument with a dog, and perhaps that's why he'd stayed my best friend for so long. Plus the unconditional love aspect could never be underestimated.

"Aww, you get that sweet boy over to Aunt Jackie and let me fix him right up. Ain't nothing a good 'ol bacon biscuit can't cure. I'm gonna fry him up some crispy bacon right now."

Shaking my head as I said goodbye, I pressed "end" on the phone. Food had been Aunt Jackie's love language as far back as I can remember. Mom used to chastise her for it, saying it led to her not "having a man." Well, the eating of the food, anyway.

Mom would say Aunt Jackie didn't have one sweet tooth; she had a whole mouth full of them. She'd work subtle comments about Jackie's weight into regular dialogue, with or without her present to defend herself—not that she would bother. I'd always considered my aunt fluffy, but I'd never consider her fat. Mom's comments seemed hurtful to me, lobbing bits of conversation like grenades and shoving them into the "adult bucket."

A perfect example: my tenth birthday party. Aunt Jackie was present and accounted for. My friends were there, and Mom served as the cruise director. Daddy hadn't made it home yet. *He was coming.* Mom's stress level had crept up to the high mark like the meter at the state fair. The one where you get close to ringing the bell and the siren sounds. I understood early on that once Mom hit a hard point with her anxiety, she was effectively punch-drunk. You either had to accommodate or evacuate.

The backyard crawled with ten-year-old girls whose collective squealing had soared past rockstar-worthy decibels. Mom was carrying bowls of pretzels and grapes, and I scanned her face for her tell-tale red flags—forehead wrinkles and red splotches growing larger right between her eyes. I swear sometimes I could see the skin stretched taut over her skull begin to melt because of her brain overheating. She was a master at keeping it together in front of most people, but there were times she'd dissolve into a puddle before my eyes. Sometimes in front of Daddy, but I was less threatening and safer. I had caught a glimpse before the upheaval, during mid-race of the Slip and Slide. Inside the house, pouring lemonade, I heard five girls scream in unison. The type of screeching only ten-year-old girls know how to perfect.

Mom snapped, "That's enough, Kacee! Either you quiet those girls, or I will. Everyone stays outside for fifteen minutes. I need some Mom time, or I'm going to lose it. And where the hell is your dad?"

It was my birthday party, but I knew for our own good we needed to respect that request. We stood under the overgrown oak out back, counting to ten and taking turns jumping as high as we could in attempts to reach the orange tied on a low hanging branch, a makeshift piñata game with no fun shapes and no candy reward. After seventeen and a half minutes, Sally Zuman jumped high enough to grab the orange, pulling it down and squeezing slightly too hard so as to produce a sticky, squirting mess of juice. I nonetheless breathed a triumphant sigh at accomplishing the task handed to me. I prayed I had bought enough time.

Marie and Kesha barreled into the living room, smelling of fresh citrus, while I trailed along behind, all of us carrying our sweaty, oxidized stench from playing a little too hard. Marie asked Mom if she'd heard from her mother regarding her forgotten sleeping bag. I held my breath for Mom's response, hoping her nerves had restored to their unfrayed state.

"She hasn't called yet, Sweetheart, but don't you worry one iota. We'll take care of it." My mother, the perpetual peacemaker, had made a reappearance. The "real" Mom speaking. Not "crazy Mom." She'd retreated to her back bedroom, popped some of her medication, and now she was okay. *Thank God for those little blue magic pills.* To the casual observer or to those closest to her, she would make everything all right. Even if it wasn't, she remained as convincing as a prosecuting attorney with a murder confession in hand.

"Mrs. Robinson, I have an emergency," came a quivery voice behind her as I looked up from across the room. I spied Breanna, donned in her neatly braided pigtails with purple flower clips to match her purple cuffed shorts and purple socks, not wanting to make eye contact with anyone other than my mother. Mom turned to face my friend. Pulling Breanna close toward her and guiding her toward the guest bathroom, Mom put a hand around her shoulder. I remember a shroud of puzzlement hung over me for a long time, and I never asked Mom about the secret she and my best friend shared. The mystery was solved when I turned thirteen and was initiated into the same unlucky club. One I wished every month I could opt out of.

As the afternoon of that birthday party drew to a close, Dad's continued absence weighed heavily on Mom. At first, she'd excused his truancy at social events by saying he was delayed in surgery, touting the importance of his career of saving lives. Eventually, the bitterness kicked in and she began resenting him for not being present with parenting. She was all about control. She crinkled up her forehead in a peculiar way, her right eyebrow higher than her left, the spot right between her eyes growing redder the longer the anger festered, her hand touching her head in distressed repetition, as if that would somehow help stave off the brewing headache. The details are still a mystery to me, but the breaking point had been hit. In that instant, I remember hearing Aunt Jackie make a comment about cutting the cake.

"If we cut it now, we can all have our second piece later," roistering the words with laughter and good-hearted fun.

Mom hissed, "If you wouldn't *have* seconds, perhaps you wouldn't carry those extra pounds, and you'd have a *husband* to go home to."

Time stopped. All of us girls turned in unison, staring a hole through both of them. I cowered toward the back of the group, afraid to breathe. In true Aunt Jackie fashion, she made a joke of the whole situation. "Girls, who wants two pieces of cake until my Prince Charming comes with the chariot?" I remember wondering how Mom could be so cruel. A bully? I felt angry with myself for not standing up for Aunt Jackie as she had for me so many times before.

Mom apologized to Aunt Jackie by the end of the night, the only time I ever recall the vitriol toward each other quite so unpretentious.

Over two decades later, I still found myself trying to decipher my mother's precise love language and feeling guilty for not coming to Aunt Jackie's defense that day.

I thought about Breanna often—probably more often than I'd like to admit—and wondered how she'd been doing following our last row. I heard she'd had a baby and landed a teaching job in town. I'd picked up the phone a hundred times, but couldn't bear to betray Dad like that after her last visit and the rumor mill she tried stirring up to take him down. The town of Glendale didn't have many doctors as it was and even fewer with well-known positive reputations. She and I had been through so much together and I never thought she'd betray me or my family. Yet another misjudgment of character to add to my collection.

The roads were nearly desolate save one dark-colored truck in my rearview, following a little too close for comfort if you ask me. I slowed and eased to the edge of the pavement so he could pass, but he slowed his speed as well. Odd, but to each his own. A long row of ranch-style wooden fence marked off a subsection of houses, sprawled wide on two or three acre lots. Houses flew giant Texas flags with pride, many stationed immediately subordinate to the American flags, in proud patriotism for both country and state. Homes spread far enough from each other to allow for plenty of privacy, yet close enough to call themselves a neighborhood. I flicked the blinker out of habit, knowing the nosy truck would be forced into a decision. It slowed, as if considering, then sped around me, leaving a gray fog in its place. What was wrong with these people? Miscreants. I licked my tongue over my cracked lips, vowing to pull out my trusty lip balm once we arrived at Aunt Jackie's and returned my focus to the stretch of road ahead, visibility clearing.

Winding along thoroughfares where trees made way for homes, yet streets stood named after them: Live Oak, Red Oak, Ash. Aunt Jackie lived on Whispering Willow, which only seemed fitting with her love of gossip. Once I spotted her log cabin in sight, I rolled down the window and pointed it out to an exuberant Barry. His head poked out the open window, ears flapping in the wind, and made his own call out with a "Ruff!" It rang through the calming quiet. I couldn't bring myself to pull down the gravel driveway, so I put the car in park just down the road and sat for a moment. Trees turning the colors of deep ruby and golden sunset. The remnants of cut grass, bales of hay and wild grasses tossed about as if random pieces of colored confetti had been thrown from an omniscient hand. Plantation was technically in the country, but it was more of a town. More concrete and industry. Glendale held old money, farms, and a gaggle of judgment. I took an extra moment to breathe in the familiar surroundings and guided the car up Aunt Jackie's driveway.

CHAPTER 14

'm heeere!" I announced, stepping onto the wooden porch ladened with clanging wind chimes that looked like little red birds and bright yellow butterflies, their wings threatening to show bare glass at the edges. The space lay cluttered with overflowing baskets of hanging begonias, ivy, and petunias in an array of colors, the scent nearly knocking me over with one strong whiff. With a heavy-breathing Barry in tow, I swung open the barn-style wooden door to Aunt Jackie's house. The high-pitched squeak bemoaned its lack of visitors.

Her cumbersome, sock-cushioned footsteps rushed toward me in a queer rhythmic pattern; her booming voice paired with Southern twang. "Well butter my butt and call me a biscuit! If it ain't my favorite niece," she exclaimed, sweeping me off my feet with one of her famous bearhugs, her blue and white housecoat swooshing in the breeze. It took exactly one second before Barry decided he'd like some Aunt Jackie attention as well; he couldn't hold his licker any longer. He showered her with warm, slobbery kisses, to which she responded with a vociferous laugh born straight from her soul.

She turned to give him her full attention, and ruffled his ears as she cooed, "Well, hello there. You must be Barry, you sweet 'lil thang. I'm your Aunt Jackie, and it's so nice to meet'cha." His tail wagged like a mottled blur of black and white fur.

"Where's your luggage, honey?" I didn't have the heart to tell her she'd regret asking that question when she saw the number of bags stuffed in my trunk.

It'd been a long time since my last visit to Aunt Jackie's, at least a few years. Mom used to say, "The older you get, the faster time goes." I rolled my eyes every time I heard her say it when I was a child, and even though I had come to think of her as foolish in other ways, many of her mantras ring true in my adult life.

I spotted Henry ambling over from next door. His broad shoulders and sturdy stature donned the same everyday denim overalls.

"Is that Kacee?" he boomed.

"Yes sir, it sure is! Hi, Mr. Henry. How are you? How's Miss Ethel?" The question left my lips as I watched his face drop, eyes turned downward behind his black horn-rimmed glasses. Immediately I knew I'd said something wrong.

"Ethel died seventeen months ago, honey."

"I'm sorry. So, so sorry. I had no idea." Shame burned the tips of my ears and slithered down the back of my neck.

Did Aunt Jackie tell me that? Surely, I hadn't forgotten… had I?

I gave him a big hug and felt Mr. Henry soften in the grip, my transgression forgiven. He rubbed my back, the rough texture of his hard-working hands creating the sound of sandpaper against my fleeced shirt.

"Let me help you with those bags, little lady. Good to have you back. I know your Aunt Jackie will be glad to have you here for a while. How long ya' stayin'?"

"Just a few days." We trotted out to the car, both of them happy to help assist with my belongings.

"Good Lord, child! I didn't know you were moving in. Say,

aren't you burning up in that sweatshirt?" Aunt Jackie tugged at my sleeve, and I yanked my hand away, a rush of blood filling my face. I knew if I took the shirt off, she'd see the scars on my arms.

"I'm always cold," I justified.

"That's what the boys say, anyhow—cold blooded," Henry scoffed, belting out his familiar belly laugh and slapping his leg with a th*whap*. He feigned a backache, pressing his hand to his lower back as he lifted the three suitcases from the trunk of the car.

I couldn't hide my smile, mostly at Henry's heart-warming giggle. "Hey, Barry has some luggage thrown in that pile, too," I said in defense, shrugging my shoulders before turning to lock the car door. I held up a rather large bag of Milk Bones and shook them, adding substance to my claim.

Aunt Jackie thanked Henry for his help, and I introduced him to Barry. Technically, Barry introduced himself, jumping and licking his newfound friend, neither of the pair ever having met a stranger. I overheard Jackie inviting Henry for dinner the next evening. She pinky promised to make her famous chocolate chip brownie pie for dessert.

"I'll be there… but only if you're gonna slap some ice cream on top of that," he bargained, and I caught the twinkle of humor in his voice.

Aunt Jackie rolled her eyes in mock annoyance, but it was clear she enjoyed his company. "You got it!" she said, matching his twinkle with hers. I heard the front door close, and it was just the two of us girls again. An old familiar feeling cast over me.

I followed her round figure to the back bedroom, admiring her thick curly hair as it swooshed from side to side, falling over the side of the wide neck of her housecoat.

She stepped aside at the threshold, and I stopped abruptly as I saw inside the room that had always been mine when I came to visit. She'd tidied up and put fresh linens on the bed, and sitting square in the middle was Bob the Unicorn, my prized possession and childhood confidante. The scene before me took me right back to my teenage years on a weekend getaway to her house. Time spent at Aunt Jackie's meant following *none* of Mom's rules and all of Jackie's (which involved a lot of late, giggly nights and equal amounts of ice cream). Our days together stretched in sticky taffy ropes of brownies for breakfast and entire fall afternoons spent painting and napping, junk shopping and then creating the most fantastic art pieces out of that junk---just because.

"Where's Katy, Trixie, and Macy?" I hollered across the house to Aunt Jackie. On a typical visit, they'd be greeting me at the door, knowing I'd waste no time grabbing the treat box and distributing tuna-flavored goodness.

"Prob'ly hiding. I betcha my friend Barry here is a tiddly bit much for them. They'll find their way out sooner or later. Lord knows they won't skip a meal," she chortled. "Speaking of, come sit down and eat some breakfast. Are you hungry?"

Aunt Jackie and her cooking. I suppose neither sister was blessed in the kitchen.

We sat at the familiar green table, eating canned biscuits and talking about the drive with little bits of Aunt Jackie's latest book club meeting thrown in for good measure. When she told me they had read *Little Women* last month, I suggested something a bit more contemporary. She scoffed, telling me the majority of the club members were "old biddies" who only wanted to read the classics and examine "the good old days" when women and men had predefined roles. Hearing my sigh and watching me shift in my chair, she quickly changed course. "That's why I keep my dirty romance novels hidden in the quilt trunk, Kacee," she confided.

Aunt Jackie's house still smelled the same, a mixture of lavender and sage incense, and looked as if nothing had ever been touched, save for a swipe or two of a broom and a feeble attempt at dusting. An oversized curio cabinet was packed to overflowing with more Precious Moments than one could count, and the same brown sectional stuffed inside the tiny living room. Laying my eyes on its multicolored throw pillows tattered and threadbare from years of wear caused a warm feeling to spread through me. The constancy brought comfort at a time when a lack of both prevailed. Evidence of the cats' playtime was strewn about in the form of frayed rugs, scratch marks on the baseboards, and random snags on Aunt Jackie's favorite red recliner. A six-foot sisal climbing tree stood in the corner, Trixie perched atop its highest platform, rendering a one-eyed half interest in me.

I rolled the largest of my suitcases into the compact room, and Barry made himself at home on the bed, the exact same bed that had been in that room for at *least* fifteen years. Soft and cushy, yet creaky as a hundred-year-old lady's knee. I considered how many talks Aunt Jackie and I had had sitting on that bed and the buckets of tears shed over boys or Mom and Dad or silly teenage problems right there on that very same quilted duvet. I breathed in the familiar mixture of dust, baked goods, and Chanel No 5 and recalled running away to Aunt Jackie's the first time the Krazy Kacee nickname bubbled out from the cracks of the playground. There were times I wondered if Barry realized how fortunate he was for his primary concern—the source of his next belly rub.

The little bathroom that would be mine for the duration of my stay displayed pink tile flooring—the tiny square variety. The coordinating pink vanity boasted a half-used can of Aqua Net and two tubes of lipstick likely close to my same age, along with an impressive line-up of perfume bottles standing at attention, some short and squatty, some tall and trim. It reminded me of Mammi's bathroom and playing there when I was a child. Tidying up didn't equate to purging.

As I began sorting clothes into drawers and settling in, I pulled out an old Foo Fighters t-shirt hidden in the back of one of the drawers. Lifting it to my nose and inhaling, I swear I could smell faint whiffs of marijuana and wishful sweat beads of Dave

Grohl. Breanna and I had wanted to attend that concert so badly, but of course Mom forbade it. Daddy would have allowed it, but Aunt Jackie stepped in and saved the day again, offering to drive and supervise us. The t-shirt, now riddled with frayed edges from too many washes, stayed at her house, as it was coupled with the oh-so-short cut off jean shorts, and I reminisced of the days when my legs could espouse the tiny pieces of denim with the confidence of vinegar tasting sour. Breanna and I had smoked our first cigarettes that night at the concert, and thought we were so cool, though neither of us admitted to the other they made us sick. It wouldn't be until years later I'd learn Aunt Jackie watched over us with binoculars from ten rows back the entire night, letting us be fourteen and knowing sometimes learning lessons firsthand is the only way to make them stick. I folded the clothes back and shoved them where I found them, unable to hide the huge grin on my face and suppress the storm of emotions from missing my friend Breanna.

I stacked the rest of my clothes neatly in the remaining drawers and stood to push back the worn, limp, rose-colored drapes in hopes to brighten up the room filled with shadows of my past. The space came into focus as light illuminated pictures on the dresser, family, friends, a couple of me and Aunt Jackie when I was a child, all caked with thick layers of soot.

Good thing I tucked my inhaler in that bag.

Aunt Jackie is the photographer of the family, the one to capture and record every important moment. A prominent photo of Aunt Jackie and Mom as adults sat displayed on the dresser. They were quite the dynamic duo of posterity: Mom wrote, and Aunt Jackie snapped photos. I had noticed a photo of Aunt Jackie and some friends, including Henry, when I walked in. I wondered if there was more developing than just neighbors and friends, especially since he'd lost his wife. I picked up one photo framed in chipped redwood. The clip boasted Mom and Aunt Jackie snapped at a high school pep rally when they were teens. With Aunt Jackie's quintessential wide smile and feverish energy, it was clear she had soaked in every moment of her high school experience with her sister fastened tight to her side like an extra appendage. Mom, stiff-armed and sporting a pinched grin, the obvious effort exerted for her to enjoy herself written all over her face—their polarized personalities captured in a single photo.

CHAPTER 15

Ring. Ring. Buzz. Buzz. Diiiiiinnnng. What the heck is that? I checked the circa 1978 LCD alarm clock on the nightstand. The bright red numbers said it was 5:57 a.m., and my cell phone sounded frantic to wake me. Attempting to untangle myself from the web of sheets I'd spun in my sleep, I rolled toward the edge of the bed and kicked my right leg free before I stood. I lurched toward the other side of the room where my phone lay charging on the chest of drawers, its flashing lights growing more insistent by the second. I rubbed my right hand in a feeble attempt to dispel the pins and needles that poked and surged in protest of having my arm raised above my head all night. Careful not to disturb Barry during his log-sawing duties, I stepped over him and fumbled the phone into my left hand, swiping across to make the racket stop.

I brought it to my ear. "Hello?"

The warble of Dottie's panicked voice woke me in an instant. Her jumbled words poured through the phone at five hundred miles a minute, in her sorority-girl-meets-horror-movie-villain tone, and none of them made a lick of sense.

"Slow down, for heaven's sake!" I yelled in a brief pause as she took a breath. "I can't understand a damn word you're saying, and you woke me out of a dead sleep. This better be good."

"I'm sorry to call you so early, but I received a message from Detective Amanda Bower. She is canceling! What should I do?"

"No one knows better than you, Dottie," trying to infuse calm I didn't feel into my voice. "This event is our second largest fundraiser, drawing hundreds of people, and we've already sold over two hundred tickets this year. Amanda Bower is the draw for many of these folks. She's the most revered veteran in the field of child abuse. Did she say why she's canceling with only one week until the event?" My anger began to subside. After all, this was hardly Dottie's fault. I could feel her panic pulsing through the phone as she stumbled over her words.

"Why would she do that to us?" I demanded, knowing full well Dottie knew as much as I did about the good detective's decision. I wanted to believe she had a good reason. "Is she deathly ill?"

Detective Bower had been our constant and, for lack of a better term, the most successful money-maker for the agency. Folks flocked like gnats to a light every year to absorb her knowledge. She had so many nearly unbelievable stories of the abuse she saw in the field. Her gentle-but-authoritative tone provided a unique way to convey the dangers of child predators to each audience member, emphasizing how the responsibility for reporting resides with us all. The first time I heard her speak elicited daggers of emotions within me to the point of excusing myself from the venue. I'd never before heard terms such as "grooming" and the sick concept that one pedophile may abuse as many as seventy victims before he is caught. Hands sweaty, stomach churning, I had no choice but to escape through the back door on weakened knees. I learned right then and there I was not cut out to be the initial intake point for severe child abuse cases. Detective Bower has provided the agency with an invaluable community resource since that day years ago. I couldn't fathom what was keeping her away. The people needed the information, and the agency needed the funds. It was a true win-win, or at least it was up until this year, it seemed. The pulsating knot in the back of my neck held the festering frustration, yet none of the solutions.

"She wouldn't give me a reason and said that due to 'circumstantial changes and departmental constraints', she would no longer be able to fulfill this year's obligation to TrueU Agency." I envisioned Dottie's skinny fingers dotted with hot pink nails making air quotes to punctuate each statement. "She also said to wish you the best of luck and safe travels on your journey back home. Which I thought was an odd thing to say, personally."

So did I, I thought to myself. I sat in silence, twisting my now matted thick locks of gold round my forefinger and unwinding them again, while wiping the fuzziness out of my eyes with the balls of my hands.

I needed time to think of a solution. Praying seemed somehow inappropriate, since I'd abandoned the idea of religion years ago. Mom's God had never been of much use to me, anyway. He'd failed her time and time again, refusing to provide her with the help she needed — the help *we* needed— after Dad left. Correction, after she *made* him leave. Or that's how it seemed in my mind. She prayed. She gathered others to pray. She asked her God to intervene with Daddy. With me. She asked for us all to be a family again. Nothing happened. If he was such a powerful God, he could have fixed it, but he chose not to. "Almighty" should be just that… omniscient and supreme. Lazy and apathetic had seemed more appropriate descriptors at that point.

Even though she was just a headless voice on the phone, I could picture the sweat beads forming near Dottie's flaming red hairline, sympathy extended as I realized she'd never been entrusted with this amount of responsibility. I softened and suggested she call Detective Bower and inquire about a reschedule date. *We needed to give those who had purchased tickets something; we couldn't afford refunds.* This would at least provide a talking point and, perhaps she would volunteer a reason for her abrupt cancellation. Worst case, we'd schedule a backup speaker on the same topic and send out an email correction to this effect. Dottie deserved to hear from me that she was not going to be canned on the spot, as if she had something to do with Bower's mysterious change in plans mere days before the occasion. The fact that my life resembled a poorly balanced upside-down cake had nothing to do with her.

A dull pain in my jaw told me I was gritting my teeth. "Look. It's going to be alright, okay? I'm sorry I snapped at you. I'm under a lot of pressure down here dealing with my family. It's stressful for me to be away from TrueU as well. This event is important to me for… well, a lot of reasons. If you would please make the call to Detective Bower and see if she can reschedule for some time soon, that would be great. If she can't, call me back right away and I'll take it from there. I appreciate you letting me know and everything you are doing." It was tough to handle the agency all by myself, but it may have been even tougher to let go of something so personal. I'm slowly learning the value of positive affirmation—Margaret says it's good for me, but I'm not ready to admit she might be right.

Dottie needed a different type of motivation than me. We're only eleven years apart in age, but we were raised in alternate universes. She fell victim to a subset of the "everyone's a winner" era, through no fault of her own. She was part of an entire generation of people who were awarded trophies for effort and not achievement. I believe we did this slew of folks a psychological disservice. It made them weaker. I chuckled to myself a bit in thinking of how my father would have reacted to such an attitude—no weakness. Though I can't say he was wrong about that at least. In my day, if you failed, you were told you'd failed. No rewards provided for showing up; participation ribbons would have been laughed out of existence. Some of us won, some of us lost, defeat was used as motivation.

Mom was the dreamer of dreams, believing in fairytales and

happy endings. She refused to allow the almighty dollar to rule her life, likely because that's how she grew up. She didn't talk poorly of Mammi and Pappi; the mindset was blatant in everything my grandparents did. Their worlds revolved around money, money, money. Cash conflated self-worth. In contrast, my happiness remained my mom's utmost priority (at least that's what she said). Telling me I was "enough" seemed to be her method of validation, though I never quite met her measure in my mind's eye. The stories of my parents made a perfect segue into a completely messed up childhood, extending into adulthood and manifesting itself into a now thirty-four-year-old overachiever with massive trust issues and the self-esteem of an average fire ant. Never knowing whom to believe at any given time, I eventually landed on Dad. His stories made the most sense and fell in line with the town chatter.

Daddy was the parent who truly raised me—taught me how to ride a bike, how to stand up for myself, how to make decisions. He tucked me in every night, planting a kiss squarely on my forehead. Mom spent her time gallivanting around town saving the good people of Glendale with her volunteer efforts, changing out of her scrubs and into her superhero cape to benefit everyone but her own daughter while Dad and I spent hours at home alone. Watching movies, eating popcorn, learning math, making pacts, and figuring out the world's problems.

Once I left for college, I'd check in with Dad every semester to make sure he was aware I'd made the Dean's list. I wanted to tell him about my successes in school, despite him not believing I had a real major or intended to pursue a viable career. Once, during my sophomore year, he came out to visit and took me to lunch. I ordered a steak and loaded baked potato, something I couldn't afford on my regular student allowance. He ordered a double Jack Daniels and Coke.

"Dad!" I exclaimed, "why didn't you order food?"

"I grabbed a burger on the way over," he explained.

The way his eyes were already swimming told me his pit

stop wasn't for just a burger if it entailed food at all, but I tried to wipe the thought away. I hadn't seen him in several months, and the last thing I wanted to do was aggravate him. Mom used to call him out on his drinking. It always ended with a verbal explosion, a shouting match that escalated to unforeseeable heights. Why couldn't she just leave him be and let him sleep it off? He was never aggressive toward her that I knew of, well, unless she provoked him. I finished every bite of my lunch, and the waitress dressed in a blue and white apron brought an extra diet Coke for me and another Jack Daniels and Coke for Dad.

I swirled the ice in the sweating glass with my straw, watching the cubes slowly melt into the brown liquid. "Guess what?"

"What?" he said, his voice taking on the thick, raspy slur that indicated he was on his way from buzzed to sloppy.

"I changed my major to social work with a minor in math."

He sputtered, liquid escaping his mouth in a spurt across the table, as his hand gripped the edge of the wooden top, white knuckles showing. "What on earth will you do with that combination? Nothing that's worth a shit, I'll tell you that right now!" His voice was too loud.

I hadn't expected him to be overjoyed, but I had anticipated a *little* support. I hung my head, brushing off the comment and pretended it didn't hurt me.

I recalled the many conversations from when I was small in which he'd told me the only good options were attorneys or physicians. "The rest are for losers," he'd said. The anchor necklace burned against my skin, the white button-down shirt feeling scratchy against my arms, suddenly aware of the fresh scars that lay below. Did he still really expect me to major in medicine like him? What major would I need to make sure I turned into a drunk? I quietly seethed inside, immediately chiding myself for my thoughts.

He wasted no time reminding me how hard he worked, why he was rewarded with being the parent who could pick and choose his hours while Mom---as a lowly nurse---was sidled with picking up random shifts. I didn't want to work like that, did I? He sacrificed so I could have what I needed and what I wanted. The least I could do was to make my education worthwhile, he'd said.

After he paid the bill, I insisted on driving him home, and he rebelled, lashing out. "You are NOT the parent here, young lady." By the time lunch had concluded, my exhaustion had reached its limit, and I felt like telling him he wasn't either (or at least he hadn't been acting like one). I'd clung to our unspoken agreement that I'd never do that. I never corrected him about his drinking after that one incident in my teenage years. Always a Daddy's girl.

It'd be a long time before I'd ever admit it to anyone else, but I had always been a little afraid of him. Perhaps it was a healthy fear. We had a special bond that Mom and I would never form, no matter how hard she tried. No matter how frustrating that may be to her. Dad and I shared secrets and inside jokes. Ever since the divorce, they had each struggled to be the favorite. Neither waved a flag around nor counted their stars in public, at least not at first. If you waded below the waters, lifted the lid a teensy bit to peek into the pot of treasures, their neediness glared like shiny gold coins. Most days it was blinding. They both wanted me to choose them. Nobody asks your opinion when you're a kid. Sure, the pompous, highly compensated, never-had-anything-go-wrong-in-their-lives idealists and counselors would tell me, Mom, and Mammi that the "best" thing for me was to pick up and move on. To participate in activities and refocus my mind from the divorce. Didn't these losers realize my entire world as I knew it had vanished with one swipe of the judge's pen, and they wanted to know if taking up tennis would be good for me this summer?

Mom tried to find a happy medium, and I wanted to believe her more than anything. "We are going to be just fine, Peanut," she'd tell me. "God has a plan for us. We might not be able to see it now, but we've gotta keep moving forward. I know none of this is easy, Sweetie. We've got each other, and we are gonna make it." She spent most of her days working extra shifts at the hospital and throwing herself into volunteer opportunities, thereby avoiding the need to perseverate on the fact that our lives had splintered into thousands of tiny pieces that had been scattered to the four winds.

For years, we subsisted solely on Hamburger Helper and girl power, the concept of "stronger" not being on my own radar. Truth be told, Mom looked obstinately feeble and defenseless six out of seven days of every week. Dad remained the same: formidable, powerful, and drunk. Mom was ever changing, ever working, and unpredictable.

Drunk became a way of life for Dad. His resting state, his regular frame of being after a while. Most of the time, he was a functional drunk. He had to be—he was a surgeon after all, and he had to look and act sober. His job depended on it, so he hid his habit, only allowing the truth to seep out under the periphery of his safe circle, which included me. The entire town of Glendale depended on me keeping his secret. But Daddy and I'd been sharing secrets for years, so I never let him down. We had a pact.

I recall sitting knee to knee, shoulder to shoulder, rivaling one another at games as a kid. Me with my bottle of Dr. Pepper. Dad with his short glass, two cubes of ice, half Jack Daniels, half Coca Cola. His breath, syrupy sweet, drifted through my nose and into my core memories as he'd lean toward me to say, "I win!" I'd rub his bald head and laugh, as he chased me around the game room, losing his eyeglasses somewhere along the way. We'd giggle as he hovered over me on all fours, pinning me to the floor with his leg and tickling me relentlessly. He'd leave me lying on the floor in a puddle of laughter, unable to breathe.

Maybe this was a version of how everyone's parents behaved. I never thought it to be the kind of thing you ask your other friends. Well, except Breanna. We were secret constituents of a club we hoped no one else ever found out about. We both wanted more than anything to revoke our memberships.

Breanna had once confided in me that her parents yelled a lot too, and her dad threw things—when he was home. She'd often come to school, in the middle of Texas September, wearing sweatshirts. Other kids made fun of her, but I knew why. Some scars are impossible to hide, although I'd tried myself. Hers were mostly from bruising and getting cut by bottle glass. Mine, in contrast, were self-inflicted. We were both searching for ways to make the pain stop. Perhaps that was one of the reasons I flocked to social work. But you can only get blood on so many towels before explaining it away no longer works, at least with Mom.

Daddy told me he left because no one could live with Mom. Killing his soul, his passions, his creativity, and his love of life. Who would want to live with someone like that? I tended to agree with him, being the one who had no choice. She continually implemented rules for everything, even things that never needed rules. No going out with friends, even on weekends, until every shred of homework and every project was completed. She didn't care that wearing those stupid sweaters (that left exactly zero skin showing) she'd gleaned from the sale rack of the local department store obliterated my reputation and abolished any tiny glimmer of hope that I might ever enjoy a modicum of popularity as I embarked upon my freshman year. Once I got older, she refused to allow me to accept a dating invitation until she met the boy and his entire family. I was the poster child for overprotective parenting. Her helicopter blades blew away any hope of a serious relationship.

Barry climbed atop my chest, bringing my thoughts back to the present. He hefted his body weight over mine as if he believed himself to be a twenty-pound toy poodle. He'd always been completely oblivious to his size, and I've always considered this to be part of his charm. Scooching Barry off me, I pulled out my laptop and hooked up to the hotspot on my iPhone. Elated to find Terry J's response affirming the townhome was still available. I'd located a townhome within Mary's budget—a three-bedroom, two-bathroom place nestled in a small Arkansas town. I was pleased to know the two boys could share a room, and both Mary and her daughter could have their own rooms. I needed these kids to feel safe. Being raised in the midst of a personal battleground carried with it lifelong effects.

I replied back immediately. "Book it."

My inbox blinked with another waiting email, entitled "MH." I knew this stood for Mary Hernandez but did not recognize the sender. Hesitant to open it, I took my chances. The body of the text read, "Stop digging now. While you still can."

I leaned back on my body pillow and clutched my quilt, rubbing the yellow nubs the same way I did when I'd escaped underneath it as a young girl. My face felt hot, yet I began to shiver. Who knew of my involvement and was threatening me? Staring without blinking at the screen, every name I could conjure began running through my head. I came up empty for motives. I started to think I was in over my head.

Perhaps I should turn this over to the police. Nopety. Nope. Nope. Nope. I will help Mary. She tried it their way. I'm going to help see this through for her. It's personal now.

Not responding to the mystery author, I emailed Mary the information I had, omitting the details I'd nailed down confirming Robert and his ties to the suspected drug ring as well as the odd email. No sense in adding to her already frazzled and overloaded bin of stress. She had her own family mess to deal with, and I knew she'd be excited to learn of me finding a location for her. I carefully omitted the precise details and arranged for Terry to meet her at a separate location to take the family to their new home. I sighed, smiling as I typed it. A strange sense of vindication floated from my heart to my fingers.

I sent the email off, then refreshed my inbox. No follow-up email from Dottie yet.

CHAPTER 16

"Morning," I crooned, startling Aunt Jackie out of her trance as I shuffled into the kitchen.

She bit her lip, lost far away in her mind and parked firmly at her green kitchen table.

"Oh, good morning, Sugar Pie. How'd you sleep?"

"Eh… alright I suppose. You?"

"Just a rough 'ol night, kiddo," she said, her smile doing very little to hide her worry.

"Have you heard any updates on Mom?" She shook her head as I poured the coffee into my cup, shaking three sugar packets into the black abyss.

I sat across from her at the table, neither of us feeling much like talking, yet both tugging at the familiar urge to interrupt the silence. Attempting to change the subject of Mom, I spoke first. "Dottie called this morning to let me know our speaker for Stop the Abuse canceled. So that's definitely not great news."

"Isn't that your big conference? Why did she cancel?"

"Yes. I mean it's only the second biggest fundraiser we have all year and just a few days away. And she didn't give a reason. Not anything feasible, anyway," I sighed.

Aunt Jackie pushed herself from her elbows to extended

hands and tended to the whistling tea kettle. Pulling the flask from the pocket of my pajama pants while Jackie's back was turned, I dumped a hefty amount of vodka into the cup. As I replaced the flask, I reached in my other pocket and felt around for my little blue savior. In one deft motion, I tossed the pill into my mouth and swallowed it, wincing at the bitter taste. I just needed to take the edge off. "We raised over $17,000 for the agency at our last one. Did I tell you we had a single donor who gave $5,000 alone? I was hoping to do just as well at this year's conference. But without our big-name speaker, that seems doubtful. "

"Wow, kid, that's super-duper impressive! You musta had a fantastic turnout. You are doing some amazing things over there. I'm crazy proud of you. You know your momma would be, too, if you'd share stuff like this with her." She paused. "And I betcha it'll work out." A smile spread across my face, but lingering worry dulled its shine.

Emotion lodged in her throat, so I continued speaking.

"I really have no idea what's going on." I sipped my vodka laden coffee and felt my face heat up. "Dottie said she didn't even leave so much as an explanation. This detective's been with us since the agency opened. She's the best in her field of abuse prevention and reporting. Kind of a legend, to be honest. Detective Bower is an icon across the state."

Coughing and sputtering as my words reached her, she swallowed the tepid drink, spraying a healthy dose of the liquid across the rickety table, then wiped her mouth with the back of her hand. "Did you say Detective Bower? As in Amanda Bower?"

"Yes, why?"

I detected a strange pause in her voice. "Oh, uh...I just know her. That's all."

"How do *you* know Detective Bower?"

Aunt Jackie fidgeted with the edge of the tablecloth, twisting it up with one hand while spinning her coffee cup around and around with the other. "We've, uh, crossed paths before. It was, um, on a case. You know I worked with lots of detectives and stuff when I was doing social work." Her voice didn't seem entirely convincing, and it was clear she wanted to avoid the topic, but I wasn't ready to let this go so easily, especially considering her odd behavior. Aunt Jackie shifted in her chair and dropped eye contact with me. Something was off. I decided to drop the subject for now but made a mental note to circle back to the topic of Detective Bower.

"Did you decide to help me sort through this mess with Mom? I could use some good news this morning, but if not, I'd rather pile on all the bad right now," I pleaded.

"Kacee, you know you're my favorite niece, and—"

"I'm your *only* niece," I interjected, sarcasm spilling from my lips as a halfhearted chuckle surfaced. I fidgeted with the loose arm of my glasses, not having worn my contacts in days.

Aunt Jackie swiveled to face me. "Minor details. You're still my favorite. There is nothing I wouldn't do for you or your momma. But I've gotta be honest. The more I think about it, the more I'm sure it'd be unfair for me to tell my version of your parents' relationship. You see, one thing all those years of social work taught me is that ten people can watch the same dang things happen and give eleven different accounts as to what *actually* happened. It's the telephone game. You ever play that with your friends when you were younger?"

I nodded. I remembered playing at Breanna's birthday party with Kesha, Moses, and Sarah Spears when we were in middle school. We started with something like, "Sarah went to school and got a kiss from Matt," but ended with, "Susan ate a purple egg with a bat."

"Well, it's kinda like that. If I tried telling you about your momma and your parents' relationship from my point of view, somethin' might get lost. Tainted with my bias. It's all about perception. And perception is reality. Wait, somebody famous said that, but I can't remember who it was." She paused for a moment, staring up at the white ceiling as though the answer would fall into her lap. "Phooey. Memory ain't what it used to be." She threw her hands up. "Anyhow, the only true reality that mattered was that of your mom, dad, and you. Since your mom ain't in any shape for questioning at this moment, it's me and you here now. Best I can do is pull out her journals and let you go through 'em. She brought 'em all here when she came to stay during the sisters' experiment. We piled the boxes in the junk room, and I've never bothered 'em. Figured it to be her personal business." She paused, aimlessly spinning a saucer with her middle finger. "But I don't think she'd mind if you want to read through 'em to help you piece things together. I'll do my best to help you fill in the blanks if something don't make sense."

Tapping a topaz-emblazoned gold ring on her coffee cup and sliding her hand back and forth through the handle in expectant warning, she added, "You need to know, child, it's certain you're going to find some things in there that'll push your limits and shore make you question what you thought you knew. Your momma hasn't had it easy as you might think. So, there it is. Whaddya think?"

Aunt Jackie let out a breath that could extinguish eighty candles. The tension in the room softened then crumpled to the floor in a useless pile as Trixie leapt from the kitchen counter and into her lap. Barry perked up, gave a one-eyed head tilt, considering his cat-chasing option, and resumed his nap on the cool kitchen floor. Aunt Jackie sat back in her chair, stroking Trixie's thick mottled fur, and awaited my reply.

I sat motionless. My face froze in shock. *Mom's journals?* I didn't think I could enter that sacred haven. I'd only ever read the one from Sue and then the snippets she sent me contained in the letters I'd dared to open before they'd vanished. Mom wrote relentlessly. She recorded everything. Lists, goals, recipes, ideas, random thoughts, and more lists. I swear there were more pencils and Post-it notes in our house growing up than food.

They were her tried-and-failed method of keeping her world level.

In high school, I was the only student still getting notes in my lunch from my mom. As much as I wanted to pretend to hate it, I never did. The random "Have a great day, kid!" came in handy on occasion.

Aunt Jackie's suggestion of breaking that seal was too much to bear. I'd heard Dad's side. Mom hadn't communicated hers with me in years, and even then, it was mostly through explosive fights that ended in slammed doors. But the chance to learn her side through her journals had been presented to me. *I thought I was ready to go visit her, but I wasn't ready yet.*

The facility had called last night to tell Aunt Jackie my mom had taken a turn for the worse. Her psychotic outbursts were becoming more and more frequent and increasingly self-injurious. The plan was to increase her medication, though this would necessitate sedating her for nearly eighteen consecutive hours. Given the fact that her celebration was only a few short days away, Aunt Jackie worried for her ability to taper off her meds long enough to enjoy the day and remain coherent enough to understand the honor being bestowed upon her. I knew the worst thing would be for her to attempt to make a public appearance or a speech of some sort while she was doped up on medication. Worse even yet, I imagined her falling down the stairs of the stage in a ball of pity, unable to maintain a level of socially acceptable behavior. Just like the time in school when Mom took too many anti-anxiety pills, but still insisted on bringing cupcakes for my classroom birthday celebration. She'd started singing in a boisterous tone, "Happy Birfday, dear Kaceeee…," allowing each word to hang on a little too long and swaying so much that I stood behind her to make sure she didn't tip over. Her skirt wormed its way around her left sandal, threading through the buckle and catching as she passed a pink-frosted mini-cake to Breanna across the table. Mom tripped, splaying face down on the desk and emerging with a fully iced pink nose, underwear partly exposed. My friends thought it hilarious as she haphazardly wiped her wild golden locks away from her face, apologizing profusely for the embarrassment, and took mine in hands, squeezing my cheeks like a five-year-old.

I couldn't bear the chance that I'd come all this way to visit her and watch her receive an award she was too sick to accept! She would never refuse an opportunity for the spotlight or to be surrounded by people.

Why couldn't she just get it together?

With regards to the journals, I thought perhaps she may have used them as a roadmap or narrative for me to understand her better—with that very situation in mind. Mom always thought ten steps ahead of everyone else. After careful consideration, I addressed Aunt Jackie. "I might need a bit of hand holding, but let's give it a shot."

Aunt Jackie slapped her knee, startling cats and Barry alike. "Sure as shootin', you got it honey." She paused, thinking. "Now, before we get started… you wanna run next door and see if Mr. Henry'd like to come share some of these eggs I'm about to whip up?"

Grinning, I lightly socked her in the arm and reformatted my question. "So is there something going on between you two I oughta know about? I mean y'all have always been good friends, and he is single now, so technically—"

She cut me off. "Oh good Lord, child. I'm too dang old for the mushy stuff. Henry's alone out here. I'm alone. So we look after each other. How many times are you gonna ask before you believe me?" Waving her hand as if shooing away a gnat, she ordered, "now scoot!"

I scampered out the front door and down the creaky steps, wishing I could make my plants at home bloom in such perfect profusion as those adorning Aunt Jackie's porch. Hanging baskets ranged from ivies to bright red wisterias to vibrant pink begonias. She had honeysuckle vines climbing up the cedar poles of the house, the aroma yanking me back to Mammi's house when I was a little girl. Out at the base of the porch grew tall rose bushes in sunshine yellows, cotton whites, and flamingo pinks, and I thought about all the poor plants I'd gathered over the years. Only one remained alive, and my pitiful red rhododendron had suffered enough of Barry's wrath to call it quits. Approaching Henry's darkened stoop, the contrast was startling. No plants, no color, just weather-worn wood below foot. A green vine crawled down the side of the house, almost as if by accident, its leaves browning on the edges from neglect. A porch swing hung from above by rusty metal chains that let loose the most awful sound with each whisper of the breeze. Peeling yellow paint had once matched the faded, weather-beaten siding on the house. Mr. Henry must have heard me on the creaky porch steps. He swung open the door as soon as I'd reached the top, greeting me with his signature toothy grin and denim overalls.

"We were wondering if you'd like to come join us for some breakfast. Don't tell Aunt Jackie I said this, but I'm sure the company will be better than the food." I giggled, but I thought Henry was going to crack a rib from laughing so hard, his overall clasps jangling as he bent over and held his sides.

"Now don't you go on bein' so critical of your auntie," he reprimanded amidst his laughter. "She's a might fine woman."

"So is that a yes?" I asked. A smile played on my lips.

"I shore would like to come on over. Let me grab a jug of my special sweet tea to bring, Sugar."

"Mmmm… I love sweet tea!"

We crossed through the wide yards, avoiding uneven terrain caused by the persistent homemaking of local vermin. While we walked, I listened to Henry carry on about my Aunt Jackie and how thankful he was for her, especially since Ethel had passed. When he said his wife's name, I heard a catch in his voice and looked over to see his downturned eyes rimmed with moisture and the skin around his mouth taught with grief. It occurred to me that relationships work all kinds of different ways.

CHAPTER 17

My laptop sat perched slightly ajar on the kitchen counter as a loud *ding* from it startled me. I hopped up from my seat on the cushy recliner, hopeful the alert might be a message either from Dottie about the conference or from Terry about Mary. Neither proved to be the case.

One new message popped bold and unread in my inbox. The sender heralded "MatchMe.com." My head began spinning at the rate of a football being lobbed across the end zone at a college bowl game.

Three deep breaths and count to ten.

Steadying my breathing, I focused on the screen.

MatchMe.com: You have four new likes, and one new wink.

I gathered the heavy device into my arms, balancing my Diet Coke on top, and made my way to the family room. I planted my butt on the floor and slid my legs under the coffee table.

Aunt Jackie sat in her familiar chair, feet kicked up, dressed in her favorite floral housecoat and reading one of her trashy romance novels. She looked as relaxed as she ever had, sipping her black coffee (with a half teaspoon of sugar, of course). Her gaze drifted toward me as I entered the room.

"Want to have a little fun this afternoon?" I asked. I needed a little lift before delving into the depths of my mother's journals. Just an hour or two of mindless enjoyment with my dear Aunt Jackie—truly the most fun woman I knew.

Her eyes widened and brightened at the mention of fun. "Sure. I'm always game for shakin' things up." She sat her "I Don't Give A Sip" coffee cup aside as if ready to shove the known off in lieu of something new and exciting. "Let's hear what you've got in mind, darlin'!"

"So, my friend Dottie and *her* friend Janice started this online dating craziness for me. I've never really checked any of these guys out, but wanna take a gander? We could even set one up for *you*." Thinking back to my earlier suspicions, I followed my statement with, "unless you and Henry have a thing, that is." I lobbed an exaggerated wink in her direction, bidding her to divulge juicy information on their relationship and waited for her response.

She balled up her fist and shook it at me. "You stop that right now. I done *told* you. This ol' gal's just about ready to be put out to the pasture when it comes to datin'. But you *know* match-makin' is my area of expertise." She leaned back in her chair, smiling her approval as if a secret memory occurred and she'd just picked the lock. I flipped open my laptop and logged onto the MatchMe website. We began pulling up possible companions and laughing until our sides hurt.

"Here's one," I said. "Screen name 'Fredfromtexas.' He likes long walks, camping trips, fried fish, and shoot-em-up movies." Next, I read from the laundry list of qualifications for his ideal female partner, including a minimum breast size of double D.

Aunt Jackie audibly gasped when I read it. I tee-heed at the audacity of someone in this century making such a requirement, not to mention one so bold as to write it down. Another of our favorites included "Doglover2682." I thought this one might offer promise, since canines were a big part of my own life. After scrolling through his photos of nothing but dogs: dogs with hats, dogs with sunglasses, dogs in tutus, dogs on boats, and dogs in bathrobes, it soon became borderline obsessive and creepy.

"This one's interesting," I told her. "Yet he loses points for screen name creativity. It's 'Jpeg.' His profile picture has shoes! And nice ones. This could be right up my alley. He's an attorney and likes dogs." I scrolled down the page. "No real photos. That's curious. Or maybe suspicious."

"Give him a thumbs up. What the heck," Aunt Jackie encouraged.

Giggling, "A wink, you mean?"

"Thumbs up, wink, pat on the back, whatever you kids call it these days."

We heaved from laughter, finally catching our breaths. When the room grew uncomfortably quiet, I thought for a moment, weighing the scales as to whether or not my next question should travel from my brain through my mouth. Pushing the envelope a bit, I asked. "Did you have anything to do with my mom and dad getting together? Was it *your* doing?"

"I most definitely did not," she said, the look of insult infusing her face. "I said I was a *good* match maker." As soon as she said it, she realized her mistake and shot me a look of apology. Words wouldn't come, and I waved my hands in dismissal to keep her from trying. I knew she meant no harm.

"We haven't talked about Mom too much today. How is she doing? I mean, when I spoke with her before, she was glad I was coming down, but how is her health today and what exactly did the facility say?"

"Honey, she's on a lot of meds. She's getting the award for the things she did when she was in her prime. I realize you cut ties with her, and I'm sure you had your reasons. All that aside, I know she's glad you're here." She took a deep breath. "Your momma's struggled more the last several months with balancing her meds. This last month or so, she's been doing pretty well, but she still has her ups and downs. I believe you being here and her finally getting some well-deserved credit in this town and drawing out some of those haters may just be the boost she needs."

I wanted to feel happy she was doing better, but I still harbored such long-standing resentment. Mostly, I wanted to bury it all. I almost regretted bringing her up while we were having such fun.

Sighing loudly and standing up to toss a toy across the room for Barry, I said, "Let's see what this profile looks like."

"And just to be safe… I'll make some hot cocoa," she added in an attempt at recovery. I watched her pull a fresh bag of marshmallows from the pantry. Knowing the giant puffy ones remained my favorite, she dropped two into the warm goodness and watched them melt.

We spent hours on the site, laughing and viewing more pictures of hairy men with paunch bellies, men with mullets that were more "blast from the past" than "reclaimed retro" who hadn't even bothered to groom before begging their buddy to snap the profile picture. Most of these were topped off with their favorite can of beer or their fresh kill from hunting. Some sported terrible mullets and others Oscar-worthy comb overs. Aunt Jackie had a story about each imagined date, complete with a charade-like skit so funny I came close to peeing myself at one point and had to literally run to the bathroom.

Barry cocked his head to the side, as I'm certain he'd never heard me howl at such volumes. It turned into the cackle of a witch mixed with a wild hyena, which set Aunt Jackie off and her living room aglow with pure glee. It felt so good to get lost in laughter; I couldn't remember the last time I let all my worries go and allowed joy to spread throughout every inch of my mind and body. Only Aunt Jackie could do that for me, and perhaps I for her.

Amongst the banging of skillets being extracted from under the stove as we began to prepare dinner, the phone rang. It was Mom's facility. Jackie turned from me, speaking in hushed tones. After a few moments, she hung up the phone and turned to me, placing hands on my shoulders. Before uttering a word, I could read the sentiment in her eyes. Scoops of grease heaved into the Teflon-coated pan with a metallic crack of the spoon, and I watched it dissolve into liquid as noises and voices receded into the distance. "It's going to be okay, honey. She's had valleys before. They are going to keep me posted."

She turned back toward the refrigerator, pulling it open a little too hard as the contents rattled inside, and returning the bowl of raw chicken to the countertop.

"Why don't you help me fry up this chicken?"

I rolled the chicken in batter as she dipped it over in the grease, the sizzle matching that of the nerves I felt certain each of us felt. We cooked in silence, as cats and Barry circled underfoot. Thoughts a million miles away.

CHAPTER 18

After dinner, we sat side-by-side on the threadbare sofa, full well knowing I'd stand up with an entire cat's worth of fur on my backside but caring little, Aunt Jackie's hand on my knee. "Ready?" she asked.

"As ready as I'll ever be." I needed to learn these truths. I needed to be prepared to see Mom and to give her a proper speech we could both be proud of.

Though I agreed to rummage through Mom's journals for answers, my stomach fluttered like a flag caught in the wind, twisting and flipping over itself. This could provide the answers to questions that should have been asked long ago, some tougher than others.

Aunt Jackie nodded and without a word, stood and walked toward the back of the house. I had no choice but to trudge behind her into the office, *or her junk room* as she affectionately referred to it. The whole collection was a commingling of past and present, but my gaze landed on two brimming plastic containers and one dingy cardboard box. I took a deep breath before freeing the corner of the lid from the box. The familiar smell of Madison Avenue rushed into my sinuses.

Taking in the look and smell of all the boxes packed with notebooks and journals, I asked, "How far back do these go?"

"Oh golly. Your mom kept some type of diary or journal as far back as I can remember. I reckon there'll be stuff from back when we were kids. I've got her latest one she was writing in before she left to go back to the residential facility."

She walked over to her sweet-tea-ring-stained desk and lifted a faded pink notebook with tiny white flowers embedded on the cover. Peeling gold letters spelling out "Di--y" and the flimsy, broken side lock indicated years of use. I wondered if the condition of the latch foreshadowed the contents I would find inside. Broken.

February 4, 1978

Susan is my new best friend. You wouldn't believe it, but she came over and we hung out all day. It's double good for me, because she's a popular kid. My nerd factor seems to be climbing at a lightning-fast speed. I talk myself into failing a test or at least trying to get a B, so I won't always look like the straight-A nerd. But at the last minute, my emotions override me, and I just can't do it. Mother would be so disappointed. Lots of days I wish I could be more like Jackie. She just lives her life. She isn't expected to be perfect. I expect it of myself, but Mother expects it of me, too. I wish I could tell her I'm not perfect. To stop it. But it would break her spirit. So, I must be perfect. My new best friend can help me at least be more popular while keeping perfect.

Why would Mammi put this level of expectation on her and not on Aunt Jackie? I don't know much about her childhood at all, yet I'd adjudicated a life sentence based on rumors and opinions of others. Rumors that she was crazy because of her struggle with mental issues. I suppose I bought into it, because Dad had said to trust the masses. I never offered her the chance to explain what might have driven her to that point. I took Dad at face value for most everything. Once my relationship with him began unraveling, I saw holes in his stories. Stories about Breanna. Stories about Mom. Stories about town gossip. I began to question myself and everything I knew to be true. I sat unsure of how to trust myself once given permission, even by her, yet the pact with Daddy and the idea that he was my trusted parent lodged in my consciousness.

I kept digging. The question of "exactly for what" remained nebulous in my mind, almost like "I will know it when I see it." I knew instinctively it was the right time in my life. I couldn't hold down a relationship of any sort. I hardly had any friends, let alone a romantic relationship. What I had to show for myself was a deep-seated inability to trust another human and pick apart every flaw of everyone and everything, starting with myself. I still didn't understand why Mom wanted to break up the family. I had so many questions, and I felt as if I was at a point in my life where I couldn't move forward without truly understanding the clandestine nature of my past.

I expected the same level of perfection from Mom as I now saw Mammi doled out. I'm not sure why, but I still felt justified. Pulling my quilt over chilled legs, I was compelled to keep opening and reading, determined to solve my own equation this time.

May 5, 1978

I got my first B today. Pretty traumatic. Mother got all fired up and started sloshing her adult drink this way and that. She exploded, telling me I might never get into a good college now if I kept going with grades like this. I mean, I'm upset enough. I've made it all the way to the eighth grade without one B on a report card and all she can do is look at the bad. No wonder Father works all the time. He probably can't stand to be around her. She isn't flawless herself, but no one dares tell her.

I've seen the way she treats the nannies, as if they are little more than the dirt on her shoes. Truth is, they are raising us kids. Josephina answered all my questions about sex the other day. I'd heard stuff at school but was too scared to ask Mother. (Jackie would have made fun of me). Josephina carefully explained to me how you can use your mouth and have sex at the same time like the kids at school say; that it's different and still something I shouldn't do until I'm much older. I don't think she'll tell Mother or Jackie. But Mother... my mother looks at her like she's a slave. Like garbage.

I wanted her to hug me and tell me it was all right. That I'd still get into a good college. It was my best chance of getting out of here... Just one random display of affection by the ice queen herself is all I needed. Of course, it is NOT all right, because she's correct. Colleges are going to go through my transcripts and that B will glare at them like a flashing neon sign. Failure. Failure. Failure.

Hands shaking, I brushed the hair from my eyes, and my stomach knotted. Not the neat knots like those ornate bows Mom secured to the end of my perfectly matching pigtails. Ugly, messy, bird nest knots.

August 25, 1978

I started making lists to help me get things done and stay organized. To remember tasks Mother wants me to complete or when I am supposed to weigh in or practice my piano. Looking at my thighs the other night when I sat down for dinner, they spread out like half-melted sticks of butter, all squishy and gross. I could hardly look away. I've begun losing some weight. I overheard Mom telling Judy she wished I could get rid of my baby fat. I've been sneaking into Mother's room and using her scales. I started at 101, and I'm down to 94. I also made some written rules. I tucked those away behind my dresser mirror. Just in case I forget those butter stick thighs and want to reach for a second biscuit at dinner, yet not visible enough where I would be questioned about them.

Mother says we must "look and act like perfect ladies" if we want to find a man. It's not my focus right now, but Mother says this is the goal of a happy life. Sure, we must go to college, but that's sort of a backup plan. She didn't even finish college when she met Father and look how things turned out. She's one hundred percent taken care of, she has a great house and doesn't have to work (especially on herself).

She's having Jackie and I start cotillion classes next week. Supposedly, we will learn how to properly dance with boys (gross!), eat with the right silverware (but not too much), and use the correct words when around adults. I think we do a decent job of all those things, but she says it'll make us more marketable to boys. Whatever that means. I guess it's a toss-up. I want to have kids someday, so getting married is important to me. Nobody wants to marry a fat girl. Svelte = quality life. Mother has made that VERY clear.

But no matter; I have a foolproof plan for attracting the right boy. For keeping Mother happy.

1. Weigh three times a day.

2. Eat no more than seven hundred calories per day.

3. Measure upper arm by ability to circle it with thumb and forefinger. If thumb and forefinger cannot touch, reduce calories by 100 per day.

4. Avoid social events where food is served.

Number four is going to be tough with all of Mother's parties she makes me and Jackie attend. And I don't want to make her mad. Though she's typically too ensconced in her own drama to worry if Jackie and I are eating food or not. I can avoid social events for things my age, like birthday parties and hanging out at the ice cream shop downtown. A sacrifice, but worth it. My skirts are a little looser, but I can still see that disgusting roll on my stomach when I sit down. Bigger clothes are more comfortable. That way, people can't see the fat. Mother tells me I look frumpy, but I'd rather be frumpy than fat. I'm super nervous about school starting. I don't have as much control there.

Weak and fuzzy-headed, I began to see patterns in shapes I didn't want to recognize. I am not my mother. I'd never be my mother. And why did Mom portray Mammi in such a negative light throughout her journals? Was she mistreated by her for the entirety of her life? Mammi was a hugger. An overhugger to be specific. Every time I saw her, she squeezed me with the pressure of a push pop, squishing until I was certain my orange insides might gush forward, streaming down the side in a puddle. Sure, she had advice for me on my hair or makeup, but never anything cruel. And she was my confidante. Oh, how she loved Daddy, too. Sometimes I thought she loved him more than her own daughter. Come to think of it, she frequently criticized Mom on most visits, but in a Southern coated way only she could. She'd say things like, "Ruth, I don't think olive is your color, honey" or, "How is working at the hospital these days? It doesn't seem like you are juggling very well. Richard looks thin." The memories rushed into my brain like water flooding in from a broken dam.

Emerging from the room, I shouted, "Aunt Jackie, I'm running up to Harold's General for a few things. Do you need anything?"

"Oh, Sugar, I think I bought most of your favorites. Whatcha need?"

"I need some country-flavored oxygen. I've barely started reading. This is a lot tougher than I thought," I admitted. "Is it okay if Barry hangs out with you until I get back?"

"Of course. Take all the time you need." Her hand waved above her head, mimicking a bird's wing. "And if you happen to pass by Cookie's, pick us up some of that famous chocolate ice cream," she added with a devilish grin.

"I'll sure do that. I won't be gone long. I just need to breathe and orient myself first." I laughed to myself, "Boy, I never thought I'd be saying that again about Glendale!"

Turning my attention to Barry, I kissed his head, gave him my stern eye, and uttered a word of warning. "Be good, please." He perked one ear toward my direction, his rough tongue grazing my hand.

CHAPTER 19

'd barely stepped foot out the door when my phone rang. "Hello? Yes, Hi, Dottie."

"I'm sorry to bother you, but you said to call if Detective Bower couldn't reschedule. And, well, she returned my call... with not-so-great news. She said it wouldn't be possible for about a month."

"A month?" I hollered, then remembered who was on the phone with me. Took a beat. "I'm not upset with you, Dottie," I clarified. "This is just getting ridiculous. I'll make a few calls to some of my last-option alternatives. This event cannot fail, and I'm livid she'd put us in this position, especially on such short notice. Thanks for following up and letting me know." We said goodbye and ended the call.

Pulling up the trusty address book on my phone, I searched for Detective Lee's information. Half as good a presenter as Bower, but—fingers crossed —she'd be available. I dialed the number as I got into the car. "You have reached the voicemail of Detective Rebecca Lee. If this is an emergency, please hang up and dial 9-1-1. If this is a matter that can be handled by one of our other detectives, feel free to press zero and be redirected to the first available Plantation Detective. If you need to speak with me directly, leave me a message, and I will get back to you at my earliest possible convenience. Please understand I am not in the office every day, as much of my time is spent out in the field."

That was the longest dang message I've ever heard, I thought to myself. After the beep, I began speaking while attempting to siphon all pitiful begging tones out of my voice. "Detective Lee, this is Kacee Robinson. We have a bit of a situation down at TrueU. I was hoping you could help us out. Stop the Abuse is creeping up on us, and we've just gotten word that our keynote speaker is, um, unavailable. You were the first person I thought of," trying to boost credibility and a massaged ego into my message with my words in hopes it might persuade her to say yes. "Would you consider coming to speak for us? There's a small stipend allotted for the event that could help make up for your time. Please give me a call back at your earliest convenience so we can talk. Thank you so much. You'd be a great addition to the event. Really… anyway, so… thank you for thinking about speaking." Realizing I was beginning to ramble and rubbing an old scar on my arm red and raw, I hit "end" on the phone before I realized I hadn't said goodbye or left my phone number. Not that she didn't have it, but that was dumb.

Breathing a sigh of hope and relief all rolled into one, I pulled away from the house, waving at Henry outside on his front porch. A warmth ignited in my stomach as I realized what he was doing, painting that old porch swing. A new sign of life.

CHAPTER 20

Bumping along backroads that felt as if I were driving on the surface of the moon, I seethed about Detective Bower's sudden cancellation as I wound my way to Main Street. It was amazing how little the town had changed. I believe the ratio of smooth road to bumpy road has altered a bit, even in the last few years since I'd last visited---and not for the betterment of the vehicles driving on these gravel-encrusted dirt streets.

The same overgrown grass displayed on the shoulder of every road with the occasional and unexpected wildflower patch popping up. It even felt like I'd seen some of those same broken-down trucks in front of the same weather-beaten, tired houses years ago. A few more store fronts had grown deserted than on my last visit, which saddened me. No used bookstore with fanciful holiday window displays. And no lights glimmered inside Winifred's Boutique. I wondered if Winifred had died, sold the business, or maybe it was just closed today. Afterall, Winifred Mayhew was old when I was a kid.

As I drove, I wondered what Mary Hernandez must have been like as a kid and especially what it must have been like for her marrying Robert so young. She'd told me they married when she was only fifteen, her parents basically betrothing her to him, a twenty-one-year-old man at the time. She grew up dirt poor, she'd confided, and only wanted to be loved. I suppose that's all any of us really wants in the end, and it's why she'd stayed so long. She convinced herself, despite all the bruises and the name-calling and the broken glass, that he truly loved her. She'd said it was only when he'd become violent with the kids that she'd had the courage to begin seeking out options. Even that proved to be harder than she'd planned. It seemed Robert wielded a layer of invisible protection around himself, rendering him untouchable, for reasons yet to be fully unveiled. I wondered if Mary ever performed in the school choir or had a sleepover.

Mom might have been overbearing and she wrestled with the gods of the mind, but maybe she tried in her own way. At least she didn't marry me off as a teen.

Harold's General Store stood as a staple for as long as I can remember. We'd come here after school for a soda or to buy last minute groceries. Dad frequented the place to purchase beer, and he'd let me choose candy from the barrels. My thoughts turned dark.

From about the age of thirteen, I'd go to Daddy's for the weekend, per Mom's strict adherence to the court-prescribed schedule. I liked spending time with him, but it meant I missed out on plans with my friends--- mostly Breanna. "A rule is a rule," Mom would say, and that was the end of the conversation. Mom and her rules.

At Dad's house, I'd find an oversized fridge stocked with wine coolers for me and plenty of Coors Light for him. I loved the fuzzy navel ones and could guzzle at least three before I passed out. Sometimes he'd make it a game.

One Friday evening of my sophomore year, I'd arrived at Dad's to find a brief note scraggled on a scrap piece of paper and strewn across the counter: "be back in ten." I was sixteen and old enough to look after myself. I shimmied down into the soft, cool comfort of his slick cocoa leather sofa, curled my body around a cozy maroon blanket he kept there just for me, and flicked on the 60" television to HBO. Mom didn't splurge for such luxuries at our house, as she encouraged reading over television. Just as I got comfortable, he bolted through the door, loud and boisterous.

"Hey baby girl!"

"Hi, Daddy. Where have you been?"

"I went to buy more beer and picked up some hamburgers on the way. Wanna eat?" he asked, unloading brown paper sacks of groceries from the counter to the refrigerator, along with grease-soaked bags containing fries and cheeseburgers. I stood to make myself useful.

"Absolutely. I'm starved!"

As we sat on his Italian leather sofa and ate our burgers from TV trays, he made quick work of two more bottles. His volume rose as he spoke, inquiring about school and friends. He asked after Breanna, just the background noise of the *Mean Girls* movie accompanied our dinner. Daddy glanced up at the screen a few times, rolling his eyes ever so slightly at my choice of show, yet said nothing. His drinking had increased since the divorce. I wanted to ask, but I'd seen how he reacted to Mom if she broached the topic, even if she wasn't trying to be unkind or if she left off her holier-than-thou voice. Sometimes she genuinely seemed to care about him. Either way, under no conditions did I want to endure *that* wrath. I was beginning to feel like I was walking on eggshells over here, too — and I didn't like it. My TV tray creaked beneath me as I scooted it on the auburn-stained concrete below. Dad's almond-shaped eyes glanced up but said nothing. He gave me a crooked smile, mischievous in nature, though for what I wasn't sure.

"Can we make Coke floats?" I asked in an effort to stimulate the conversation and somehow work my burning question into our evening.

"You can make a Coke float, and I'll make a beer float," Dad answered. His intoxicated laugh rang in my ears. He wasn't falling for my diversion.

The little voice inside of me begged to keep quiet and remember my place, yet I foolishly ignored it. "Dad, I think you've had seven beers since I've been here, and you were drinking before I came." I paused to push my heart out of my throat. "I'm concerned." I caught the familiar flicker of irritation in his eyes. The stiffening in his body as he clenched his fists then released them.

I shouldn't have gone for it.

"Oh, hell, she's turned into her fucking mother. You've been counting? You think you know when I've had enough? You think you're the goddamned beer police? Well guess what, little girl. You're not. Do you want me to turn you in for drinking those fuzzy navel girly drinks I let you have, do ya? Just to remind you, young lady, that's illegal."

I stared at him, fire in his eyes, watching him look at me like he used to look at Mom. Half of me felt guilty and the other half sat plain old terrified.

"I've had a rough day, and I deserve these beers. Shit, girl, I've had a rough ass LIFE because of your worthless, good-for-nothing mother! She married me, lied to me, used me, and it now turns out she never even loved me. I thought at least *you* believed in me. I thought we had a pact. Did you forget about that? I guess it's not important to you. *I'm* not important to *you* either." He began to gently sob and stood to cross the room to the kitchen, tossing the empty bottle into the oversized trash can. It rendered a high-pitched clink as it landed on top of its partners in crime.

This was my fault. Even though I longed to run from the house, slamming the back door in anger and splintering its wooden frame into tiny particles, I instead reacted in true Kacee fashion — by apologizing.

I'd learned long ago he needed me to be on his side, no matter what. It was my job now to keep Daddy happy. Only I could see both sides to him—he could be so good or so horrible. I had to focus on the good and make everyone understand the good. I had to. His reputation depended on it. He depended on me. The pact depended on my loyalty. I could not fail him.

"I'm sorry, Daddy. I'm so sorry," I pleaded, reaching for his hand. "I didn't mean to get on you. It's just...just...I guess I just worry about you because I love you. You *are* important to me. The *most* important."

With those words, his bloodshot eyes lost their fire, and he hugged me with such intensity I thought he might never let me go. He grasped my ribs, and his fingertips dug into my skin in a way that told me not to move. When he finally released me and took a step back, holding both hands, a desperate fear had spread across his face.

Frozen in time, I was broken out of the memory as I heard someone calling my name. I was still standing a few feet from the door leading into Harold's, palm on the handle.

"Kacee? Kacee Robinson, is that you?"

Out of instinct, I jumped and swung the plastic sack behind my bag, crinkling the brown paper bag inside as it rubbed against my leg. I'd stopped at the nearby liquor store before heading into Harold's, certain I was alone. I should have known better. In Glendale, I'd never be alone.

The deep female voice calling to me is familiar, slightly nasal yet cheery. Its owner laid just out of my memory's reach. I turned around and my whole body felt it may collapse under the weight of my shock.

Breanna.

CHAPTER 21

Sucking in a sharp breath, I stood my ground. There was no avoiding her now. Sun glistened off her short dark hair, reflecting her maze of waves and sparkly lip gloss. Her bubblegum pink nail polish glinted as she reached with one hand to remove her leopard sunglasses. Her retro Nirvana tee-shirt was relaxed, and her frayed jeans held together only by the grace of a higher power. The light bounced off her phone screen held in her left hand and onto her face, giving her an ethereal glow. I couldn't help but notice she looked spirited. She accelerated quickly down the sidewalk toward me, and I looked at what she was pushing in front of her with her free hand as the last dot connected. Maya. The child in the stroller she was pushing must be Maya. The last I'd heard, Maya was just a baby, now here she was, a beautiful little toddler.

I raised an unsteady hand in acknowledgment.

"Oh my gosh! I can't believe it's really you," she gasped. "What are you doing back here?"

"I'm, uh, I came back for Mom's celebration. Some type of lifetime achievement award the town is giving her. For her community service..." I stumbled over my words and wondered why she was acting as if the last time we'd spoken, it hadn't been a complete fiasco. In fact, our harsh words had been thrown like daggers, intended to harm. That was almost four years ago, and much longer since we'd seen one another.

"That's amazing! I heard about it and have seen the flyers up around town. Can I give you a hug?" she asked. "I know our last conversation was, um, bad." She threw a glance in the direction of Maya, and I felt it was a secret signal begging me to please not elaborate for the sake of the child.

There it was. Breanna always stating the obvious. Would I look like more of a bitch if I said yes or no? And she has her kid right here. What kind of example would that set?

"Sure," I stated flatly, avoiding eye contact and shifting my weight from one Converse foot to another. A horn blared as a nearby motorist ran the stop sign at the corner of Main and First Street. I snapped my head in the direction just in time to watch the near collision and brace myself for the *crunch* of two cars colliding. Thankfully, none came. What I did see was a gray truck swerving to miss a little blue car of some sort. A gray truck.

Surely there are a million gray trucks on the road and it's just a coincidence that I've seen a gray truck in the parking lot at Margaret's, behind me on the road into town, and now here. Right? I'm being paranoid.

Even the loud disturbance failed to deter Breanna's train of thought, plowing forward toward her mission of a reunion, and I redirected my thoughts, resigning myself to be realistic.

Breanna reached out her arms for an embrace, and I fell into her. It was easier to hate her from far away. It was much tougher to erase all those years of friendship when you can feel each other's heartbeats.

I released her grasp, wiped my face, and directed my attention to the cobalt stroller streaked with cookie crumbs and smelling faintly of sugar, urine, and oxidized toddler. Two bright blue eyes stared back at me. "You must be Maya." She shook her head in affirmation, pigtailed curls bobbing.

"Maya, this is Kacee. She and I were best friends all through school," Breanna said.

"Is she still your friend?" The child's innocent question sucked the breath from my lungs and brought me back to my own days of innocence, as fleeting as they were.

Had I ever asked Breanna why she'd said all those horrible things?

"Yes, I suppose she is. If she wants to be, I mean. We've just grown apart a little," Breanna explained, as Maya's face screwed up in confusion. "It's hard to understand adult stuff, sweetie." Then she added, "even for adults sometimes."

Her statement was true, if nothing else. She'd extended the proverbial olive branch, waiting for me to latch on or drop it. I tugged. "I'm only here for a few days. Maybe we could meet for coffee tomorrow? I was just thinking about you."

"Yes! Yes, let's do that." Breanna turned her attention to Maya, hunched with both hands on her thighs in a catcher's stance as she squatted in front of the stroller. "Would you like to have a little playdate with Granna tomorrow?"

"Yea!" The youngster began clapping her hands together. "Granna lets me have ice cream for breakfast and lets me play with all the don't-touch-me things in her house," she proudly pronounced to me. "She has *a lot* of don't-touch-me things," she added, as if confiding in me a secret.

I smiled down at her. Pivoting toward Harold's in an attempt to gather my thoughts, "Most grandmas tend to be like that." I winked at Breanna, and we both laughed, remembering Mammi's stiffness when it came to her collectibles. "I'll plan to meet you tomorrow at Coffee Beans. Two o'clock work?"

"See you then. And I'm so glad we ran into you today. The Good Lord has a way of putting His hand in things." She held her hands up toward the sky.

I felt a slight eye roll at the last comment. People 'round here always wanted to credit everything bad happening as the "Devil's work" and all the good "happenstances" as divine intervention. It was always my belief that some things just happen for no reason at all.

"Bye, Miss Kacee," Maya called, waving feverishly with her tiny hand, mine on the door handle as the cold wind sucked the door in with a swoosh.

CHAPTER 22

strode into the store, its familiarity allowing my thoughts to dart like pinballs ricocheting off springs, toggling between newfound information of Mom and my reunion with Breanna. I was so distracted, the malodorous combination of horse grain mixed with fresh onions barely registered as my feet shuffled along the concrete floors, their perpetual layer of sawdust swirling around me with each step. Stacks of dry goods lined the shelves and large barrels of loose candy stood at attention at the end of each aisle like oversized toy soldiers.

As I headed to the register to pay for my Diet Cokes and peanut butter, with some twisty pretzels thrown in for good measure, a woman behind the counter squealed my name. "Kacee Robinson. Well, I'll be a monkey's uncle! As we live and breathe. I can't believe you're back here in Glendale." Annamae Armstrong stood before me, best known for her county fair prize-winning blackberry cobbler with butter crumb crust.

"Oh, good afternoon, Ms. Armstrong. Been a long time. How're you doing?"

"I'd be doing a lot better if Social Security didn't screw me out of all those years I worked. Now I gotta pick up shifts here at Harold's." She sighed and shook her head, propping her hand on the rough cedar countertop carved with initials, dug out from years of scratches, and splintered at almost every sharp edge. I noticed the purple veins protruding from her thin skin and age spots dotting her arm and hand as it rested on the surface. "Oh, it ain't too bad, I s'pose. Spending some days countin' out cash and keepin' a sheet full of tick marks to track how many bags of this and that we sell." Shielded hand to her mouth as though she was spilling top secret information, "God bless his soul for lettin' this old woman work a few hours."

Speechless for a moment, I scrambled to find a note of positivity to dash atop the conversation. "You look great!"

"Thank ya, sweet thang. You don't look a day outta high school. Comin' back to see your momma for her shindig?"

"Yes, ma'am. That's the plan." Leaning into the countertop, I breathed deeply the sweet smell of sugary treats set out near the register to entice kids as they waited for their mothers to finish gabbing. I felt the outer shell I'd grown so long ago begin to fissure. Flashes of Mom swatting away at my own hand for reaching in one of those barrels. Images of Daddy gathering up six packs of beer and cheerily encouraging me to dig for treasures of such sugary goodness. The disparity was overwhelming.

The front door jingled, and Ms. Armstrong glanced toward the front of the store as a look of distaste spread over her face. Her eyes narrowed, and her lips puckered into a frown, lines becoming visible like road maps to her thoughts. "I don't know why them kinda couples come in here, parading unnatural relations like that. But I s'pose as long as they buy stuff it's not my place to say nothing. Just gotta keep an extra eye out."

Not knowing what she was talking about, I turned to spy a short African American woman of about twenty. She wore a long mustard dress and short heeled chestnut booties I wished I could add to my own expansive shoe collection. When I made eye contact, she smiled, accenting her shiny pink lip gloss, and strode across the store alongside a Caucasian man who must have been close to six feet tall and donning pressed khaki slacks and a white button-up dress shirt. I knew better than to argue with the mentality. I grew up here and knew racism was still alive and well in these parts. As I turned back to face the counter, I noticed a smallish Confederate flag mounted in the far back corner of the store, disguised among exposed ceiling rafters.

This old world changes every day, yet some folks refuse to change with it. That's where life gets us into real trouble.

This thought forced me to reflect on my own situation. I need to acknowledge and fully understand my past before I can move forward and make a better life for myself.

Ms. Armstrong turned her attention back to me, and I caught snatches of conversation about my mother, already in progress. "I put a flyer announcement out in the winder so everybody could see it when they came in or passed by. Did you see it?"

"No, I'm afraid not, but I'll look on my way out. Thanks for doing that."

She pulled a serious face, her pupils narrowing. "Your momma is a good woman, Kacee. I seen it with my own eyes. She deserves to be celebrated like one of them people on TV. Now I know you may not want my opinion, and I know you went and got yourself some expensive education so's you can make better opinions yourself. But right now, I don't see you're in any position to listen to nobody else." One hand rested on her hip and the other gestured out as if to indicate no free-standing audience, a stained white apron tied around a dress that, at one point, was probably her Sunday Best.

"People 'round here talk. *Too much*, you ask me. Then and now. And they go poking their noses where they don't belong. Truth is, I was one of those people till my husband died a few years back. Some cockamamie rumor mill started up I's the one who killed him!" She threw her hands up in disgust, red-faced with gusts of gray hair falling between her glasses. "Can you believe that?" Not giving me time to answer her rhetorical question, she continued in a huff. "I saw firsthand how fast gossip can spread 'round here. Like a maggot on roadkill. Even if that theory's got no teeth in it, some people don't care---so long as it's juicy and a distraction from their own pitiful lives here in Glendale.

"I used to listen to everything your Mammi said about your momma and believed it to be true as the Gospel straight outta the Good Book. Lotta people round here did. Listened to her opinions on damn near everything and took it for the truth because of the Havemeier name and its status in this here community. Now I ain't gonna speak bad about the dead, but I'll just say your momma put up with a lot in that woman. God rest her soul." She raised her right hand toward the sky and gazed upward. "She put up with more from her and your dear daddy than most could stand."

I opened my mouth to protest the comments degrading two of my closest confidantes, but snapped it shut again, having enough manners to avoid an argument with an elder. Overwhelmed by the confusion building in the wake of Annamae's diatribe, my words were held hostage.

Unaware of the mental turmoil she was causing, she continued, "The town chatter and rumor mills, coupled with your momma's own demons she's 'a fightin'... well that's too much to 'spect anybody to stay outta them mind hospitals."

She leaned forward and cradled my face in her hands. "If you're back here anyway, give her a chance. We all watched her fall apart when..." Her voice trailed off, as she turned toward the tinkling bell atop the front wooden door, signaling the arrival of another customer. She dropped her hands and lowered her voice. "You're her lifeline, Kacee. And you ain't perfect, neither." The last sentence said was delivered with a wink to soften the lecture.

Hanging my head humbly, I had no choice but to tell her what she wanted to hear. "I know. I'm coming to believe there may be a lot I don't know." A sense of defeat spread over me. Confusion.

Did I know anything about my own childhood or were all the memories I'd spent a lifetime burying a complete farce?

"Young lady, if you wanna know somethin', you just walk your happy self right back down here. I've been around a long time and seen a whole lotta things. Life ain't always pretty, but my experience says true colors'll always show by the time the credits roll."

Not sure of a response, I took the bag of groceries from Ms. Armstrong. She squeezed my hand as she passed them off. Taking special note, as promised, of the flyer reading "Community Service Award and Celebration Honoring Ruth Havemeier Robinson" on the way out the door, I felt hot despite the cool, blustery afternoon. I turned to look back through the window, watching Ms. Armstrong keeping a close eye on the couple that had entered while we were chatting. I shook my head and headed back home to Aunt Jackie, via Cookie's, of course.

If what she said was true, it was possible Mom fell victim to the Glendale rumor mill just like Annamae. I believed that Mom was an unfit parent… because the town told me so. And because I didn't like her parenting. But, now that I'm an adult, I understand few teens like being parented. I believed Mom broke up our family and was impossible to live with… because the town told me so. I believed Mammi had my best interest at heart… because the town told me so. I believed Daddy was the loving and responsible parent, because, after all, he was a surgeon at the hospital and Mom was a lowly nurse… and the town told me so. Most of all, I teased apart every action of Mom's and criticized it, because Daddy had taught me to do this and report back to him. I had a special pact with him. She followed rules. She made up her own rules. She told me I was enough, yet I never measured up to her version of enough. The town of Glendale supported Daddy, not my "crazy" Mom. Everyone knew Mom was great at volunteering for things and had a good heart. Nobody could out-volunteer her. And, truth be told, I have a feeling Aunt Jackie pulled some strings for this award in the first place to boost Mom's mental health and well-being.

The town never felt she could fully be trusted, because she couldn't get her mental health stable. I began to wonder if the town rumors had ultimately led to her prompt firing from the hospital she loved so much. She loved working with the geriatric patients in the rehab unit, then she was suddenly let go without notice or much explanation at all. Ms. Annamae's story about the strength of the town rumor mill made me question everything I thought I knew to be true.

In the middle of my reverie, my nose caught a distinct peat smell of whiskey mixed with wooded soap. My head jerked to attention, and my eyes scanned the surroundings in a panic.

Could it be? Where is he? Or is my crazy getting stronger?

I saw the box marked on Susan Schuster's intake form scroll across my brain. *"Someone may be in danger."* Maybe that someone wasn't Mom after all. Maybe it was me.

CHAPTER 23

Aunt Jackie sat drumming her fingers and drinking her fourth cup of coffee at the kitchen table when I returned from the store.

"You had me and Barry 'bout to send out tha ding-dang search party!"

"I'm sorry. I ran into Breanna, and…"

"Oh how lovely," she said, standing and squeezing my arms in an embrace all in one quick motion. "Come tell me all about it."

I strode over to the kitchen, opening and closing cabinets as I stocked the snacks away. The tension in my shoulders melted ever so slightly with the familiar hiss as the top of the soda bottle spewed out carbon dioxide, but my headache crept back up my neck and into the tippy top of my head.

Something deeper than a sigh rose in my stomach, and I exhaled forcefully enough to alarm Barry. "We agreed to meet for coffee tomorrow," I blurted. "On my way back here, I kicked myself. After knowing she set Dad up a few years ago, it seems like such a betrayal. But Ms. Annamae Armstrong, oddly enough, brought up a good point about the Glendale rumor mill. I think I should hear Breanna out."

Aunt Jackie's voice remained steady and matter of fact as she rose toward the sink, filling a watering can to tend to her plants and avoiding eye contact.

"And I came here to unravel the truth about Mom. Maybe she has a perspective I hadn't considered before. Seems like everyone else in town does," I scoffed, unable to shove the excitement swirled with dread far enough down into my stomach to keep it from seeping out of my mouth. I'd waited years to talk to Breanna again, unsure if it'd ever happen. Unsure if I even *wanted* to speak to her. Now the groundwork was set, and my psyche tousled every emotion like a windstorm through my brain.

"What does that mean?" She stood at the door, leaning over the large ferns that spread like hands welcoming each visitor.

"Seems Ms. Armstrong has some awful robust opinions about Mom: the way Mammi treated her, the reasons she ended up in psychiatric care." I paused, unsure of whether to mention the rest, but realized it *was* Aunt Jackie. "Even about Daddy."

I reached down to rub Barry's ears, trying to distract myself from the awkward silence. A guttural moan escaped him, and I knew it was his version of a satisfied purr.

Stationing herself once more at the sink, she refilled her water can with her head still down, focusing on the task at hand. "Do you know who Winston Churchill is, Kacee?"

"Of course I do." I rolled my eyes though she hadn't bothered to make eye contact.

"He once said, 'Men occasionally stumble over the truth, but most of them pick themselves up and hurry off as if nothing had happened.'"

She turned the water off, lowered herself into an easy chair, hand placed under her red coffee cup, and said nothing more as her eyes wandered up to meet mine, almost as if by circumstance. My move, yet I had no idea what Chess piece to choose, so I sat in silence as Aunt Jackie stood back up and continued her plant duties, unfettered by my quiet.

My phone buzzed in my back pocket, and I reached for it. Glad for the disruption. Notifications of junk mail weaseling its way into my general inbox. *No, I do not need 20% off at a store I've never heard of, thank you very much.* Then came a nice surprise, a new inbox message from the dating website. Someone new gave me a "look" and sent a message, although no photo was attached to it. The profile picture space was filled with one red Converse, and a pink Louboutin pump, crossed at the toes. JPeg. The same guy Aunt Jackie and I winked the other night. A welcomed distraction to the uncomfortable moment. He'd returned the wink with a message.

Dear KHav:

I looked at your profile, and I'm intrigued. I live in a nearby town called Trenton, about an hour northwest of Plantation. Your non-profit work seems fantastic. I grew up in a single parent household, and much of my law practice focuses on contentious divorce cases, where I do quite a bit of pro bono work. Probably because of the way I grew up—dirt poor. Either way, what you're doing with your non-profit is admirable. If you're interested in learning more about me or extending me the privilege of learning more about you, please call or text me. My phone number is 314-1111. Hope to talk to you soon. ---JPeg (a.k.a. Jason)

Still unsure of venturing down the road of online dating, I smiled to myself and tucked away the private flattery without a response. I wanted to sit on it for a while (unless I decided to pull it out for a rainy day). Another lesson of my mother---life is always better with a plan and a list. But something struck me as different about his approach. He appealed to my work and not my looks. He used proper grammar—a definite notch in his cap. Self-supporting—another check. And he should have no idea I was a Havemeier, perhaps the crowning jewel of tick marks.

"I'm going to need to think on some things," I told her. "I feel like my world is turning upside down," to which she gave a simple nod.

CHAPTER 24

marched myself back into Aunt Jackie's office. Nestling up against the back of the old rocker and pulling a crocheted afghan over my legs, I settled in with a new diary and began reading. Time became melting wax with each turn of another page.

April 3, 1980

I'm happy about my weight loss, but this hair all over my body is getting annoying. I feel like a blonde Bigfoot. At least my hair is light. I think I'd die if I had dark hair up and down my arms and on my face. Long sleeves are best, which work out since the world is freezing nowadays. I'm gaining hair everywhere except on my head. Good thing I have a ton of it up there, since it's started falling out. I'm finding giant clumps in the shower. Annoying. I checked out a book from the library on weight loss. Supposedly if you master a super low level of body fat, your body tries to insulate itself by producing extra body hair. I mean, right there in writing it says I am achieving my goal! I'd rather be fuzzy, bald, and have these dang brittle fingernails than be fat. Fat is the ultimate enemy. The capping insult. God's supreme punishment. I'd sacrifice my own life to stay thin. Mother used to make crass jokes about my bubble butt and now she harps on how "no boy will take a coat hanger for a wife." It's the only part of my life I can control, and I'll be damned if she's going to win.

Fingering individual strands of hair and letting them fall back toward my tense shoulders, I wondered what would make me sacrifice my own well-being. Nothing seemed quite so important to me, yet many days I questioned the sum total of all my blended days, refracting one another toward a blinding light. Perhaps that's why I numbed the pain the best I knew how. Cutting gave that same satisfaction, I'd guess. Watching the blood trickle. The vodka helps too, although I'm not addicted. It just helps when I need to take the edge off. Maybe she did, too, on a different sliding scale. I bit the end of my glasses and rubbed at my stinging eyes. Her journals read like Rapunzel-meets-concentration-camp-survivor.

May 2, 1980

Mother decided I must be shipped off to some bogus treatment facility when I no longer fit into her picture-perfect party life. I'm now 67 pounds and a junior in high school. She doesn't ask my permission or even my thoughts. The only thing that matters to her is that women "of distinction" have begun asking questions. I'm not sick. I'm just better at calorie restriction than she is. I think she's jealous. I've learned to show more discipline than she. I can subsist on less than 100 calories a day, and she could never do that. She thought she was teaching me self-discipline, and the student became the master.

I think treatment facility's just a rich person's way of saying psych ward. She's feigning concern, when the only possible concern she may have lies in how my weight may impact potential male suitors. She couldn't care less about my health. But NOW she's playing the role of concerned mother, because it gains her some sympathetic attention. I think Jackie put a bug in her ear that she's worried. My sister almost always has my back, sometimes more than I wish she did. Mother's too aloof to notice any damn thing not directly related to her or her precious social functions. "We are telling the community you needed a hiatus for healing." She had the nerve to say it with a wink. Like we were keeping some sister-sworn pinky secret between just us girls. Unbelievable. Now the whole damn town thinks I'm crazy because she doesn't want to look like a less-than-perfect mother.

I almost felt sorry for Mom. Almost. She felt out of control and was trying to exert control over her life by managing what she could--- her weight. How could Mammi ship her off to a cold, sterile facility just to save her own reputation? And to think she actually encouraged Mom's eating disorder is unthinkable. I shut my eyes tight and imagined her face and what she must have looked like at that age. One of her monster horns suddenly grew smaller in my mind. I was starting to see her as a real person again and Mammi as a tiny monster under her bed.

I'm not sure how to handle the idea that my entire childhood may have been built on false foundations and incorrect assumptions. Each piece of these people identifies me, and pleasing them, respectively, has made me who I am. If I have so grossly misjudged so many, then who does that make me?

June 14, 1980

I returned home today from that godforsaken place. I sucked in southern air filled with fried potatoes and fresh cash. I've spent the last six weeks suffocating in sterile air. They can fatten me up a little, but it won't last long. It was comical to see how easily the staff of so-called professionals was fooled by a teenager. Didn't anyone ever notice the bars of soap or bottles of lotion missing from their desks at weigh in? Do I look like I've gained nine pounds since I left? Maybe three at most. Those items fit neatly in pockets and bras. Just scream and make a scene one time and they'll never check those areas again, I guarantee. Fools. I may be psychotic, but I'm not stupid.

Not everyone falls prostrate to Mother's demands. That Bitch doesn't care who touches her own daughter. It's not important if a boy rapes me like Tommy Taylor did last year, but my God let's make sure we create a positive and thin appearance for the neighbors to see. I wish I could let loose. I'm sick and tired of being so damn accommodating.

She pays people to be her servants, and I wonder if that's even legal anymore.

I'm forced to play nice for one more year and then I can be all on my own. Creating me to be such a fusspot then punishing me for her own method of raising. Nobody realizes how hard it is to keep up this facade of a perfect life. Mother doesn't ask anymore. She just <u>expects</u>. Her mothering isn't about me. Never about me. I've been the albatross around her neck in private and the showpiece for her curio cabinet in public.

On the outside, Mother is the one who gets credit for raising two great daughters, all while donating oodles to charity. She's the one whom everyone in Glendale looks up to as a pillar of the community. Yet she can't have an honest conversation with her own daughter. She can't bother to walk into my bedroom, sit down on my bed, put an arm around me, and ask if I am doing okay. Nope. I don't think I can ever bear to have a child. Putting another human being through a mere one hundredth of this much pain, knowing I caused it, is enough to make me want to take that knife out of the top drawer (under the second gray sweatshirt, nestled in the left sleeve) and cut. Again. Deep. I think she birthed me for pure social status.

Mom cut herself, just like me? She did always wear long sleeves under her scrubs when she went to the hospital. Even in the summer, you rarely found her without a jacket or a thin sweatshirt. She'd tell me she was just cold by nature, and I never questioned it. One time, when I was about seven, I'd gone to bed and then crawled out because of a nightmare. I found Mom on the couch reading. It was July and she was wearing just a t-shirt and jeans. As she was comforting me back to bed, I remember rubbing her arm. It felt bumpy in weird places. I'd asked her about it, and she told me they were old scars from when she'd clumsily taken some tumbles as a kid. At seven, that explanation made sense. I hadn't conjured the memory since that day. I stared at my own arms and realized how similar they must have looked to my own. Perhaps even more alarming was Mom's admission of being raped.

Why did we never discuss this? Come to think of it, we never had many discussions at all about the dangers of dating. I guess I'd shut her out by that time.

July 23, 1980
I think it would be easier on everyone if I just died. That is all.

I ran to the bathroom, hand pressed tight over my mouth. The release came, and I listened to the echo of my lonely howls reverberating off the tiled floors, beating my fists against the shower as I turned it on to hide the noise. I let the water rush over me, fully clothed, and let it rinse the sick off me. She must have felt so filthy at that moment. To be violated and have nobody believe you---not even your own mother---to the point of taking your life. Right now, I wanted to wash it all away—all of her injustice, all of my own sins, all of my failures.

How could the Mammi I knew and loved have had such animosity for her own daughter? And how did Mom shovel that down so deep it disappeared on the surface?

Issues I couldn't put a finger on as a child suddenly unblurred like learning to color inside the lines for the first time. It all made sense. She'd repeated to me like a trained parrot, "You are perfect just the way you are, Kacee; you are enough." She didn't want me to live a life constantly criticizing myself. Yet, I had become another person telling her she wasn't enough. As much as I thought I couldn't measure up to her standards, she felt she never measured up to Mammi's. Then, I'd intensified the feeling by rejecting her over and over. I came all this way to see her and had yet to do the thing I came for. I had been controlled by fear of yet another rejection. Fear of upsetting her and making her worse. Fear of hearing something I didn't want to hear. Fear I might need her. Fear she might not be the monster I made her out to be. I knew there was only one way to find out.

I jumped at the sound of a text notification from my phone. Shutting off the water and drying my hands, I tried pulling myself together. This is it. This is the text that will allow me to save Mary, I thought. Atonement for my past transgressions. I reached for the phone, hopeful.

Disappointment overtook me when my eyes slid to see Dottie's name, though it didn't linger there for long.

DOTTIE: I just wanted you to know things are going smoothly. I'm not sure what you are going through. I know I'm younger, but I've been through a lot in those years---for me, for my parents. I'm here if you need me. Thanks for trusting me.

An unexpected pride filled my heart.

I wonder if this is close to a maternal feeling, even though she's just over a decade my junior.

I'd watched her grow since arriving at TrueU as a recovering addict three and a half years ago, needing a job and wanting to make a difference in the lives of others who might be in a similar situation. She needed a chance, and I was willing to give her one.

Why couldn't I have done that for Mom? We could have waded through some of life's trials together.

I regularly found myself laughing at the difference in generational customs between Dottie and me, yet if I tasked her with a job, I knew it would get done. At the young age of twenty-three, she was teaching me to trust others.

ME: Thank you, darlin'. I am learning a lot about myself and am looking forward to coming back. I am lucky to have you to hold down the fort. Please call or text me if you need me. Thanks for reaching out.

DOTTIE: (a plethora of heart and smiley face emojis, spanning two lines of text—just one of the many generational gestures I didn't understand but knew meant well).

Thoughts clunked into place and memories whirred back to life. *For the first time in thirty-four years, I'm beginning to understand my mother.*

I watched an ant crawl up the baseboard, headed for the water of the bathtub. He was only trying to better himself. He was walking uphill, and instantly I related to that little ant.

Even through my rejections of her and her parenting, she'd shaped me. Because of or in spite of who she was, I had become strong and fiercely independent—and was finally reaching the point where I could admit it when I was wrong, particularly to those I loved and had hurt the most. I'd come to learn that sometimes those people were one and the same.

I couldn't go back and tell her, "I'm sorry" for what happened during her childhood or even apologize for my own actions in not believing in her all those years. Saying I'm sorry for not giving her a chance against Daddy or the town rumors wouldn't change anything. Two words wouldn't come close to being sufficient. I knew I needed to find something more substantial to explain my need to understand, and I was obligated to do so in person.

CHAPTER 25

lifted my phone off the bed, though it hadn't made another peep, sick with worry I'd missed an important call about Mary. Clutching the device in my fingers I turned it over, only to be filled with disappointment as I found it devoid of missed messages from Marianne or Terry J. To make matters worse, no further communication followed about the event from Dottie or Detective Lee. The event was almost here and not even my second-choice speaker seemed eager to respond. I heaved myself up onto my elbows while lying prone on my stomach.

Aunt Jackie knocked on the door, her gentle rap a portent of the shape the next few minutes would take. I gathered the pile of tissues surrounding me and stashed them under the pillow. My tears were flowing freely by that point, so I yanked four more Kleenex out of the box in front of me and did my best to mop up the deluge. It was pointless. I couldn't let her stand out there endlessly while I failed to get it together.

Four more tattered Kleenex found their way under my pillow. "Come in."

Aunt Jackie floated in as if traversing a gossamer thread and perched daintily (as daintily as Aunt Jackie did anything, anyway) on the edge of the bed. I felt the dip of the bed behind me, felt her hand on my back. She said nothing. Just waited.

"Did she seem like she was struggling back then, or has she always put on a good face?" I asked her once I was able.

"Your mother became Mammi's scapegoat. I'm not proud to say it, but I allowed it more often than I shoulda. Even on the worst of days, she couldn't let down her guard. The momma you came to know and convinced yourself you hated was a mask, a *defense*. She lost herself in that whole mess, trying to save you and the rest of the family."

I melted into a pillow, thinking how Mom pretended everything was always perfect when, clearly, it wasn't. She tried building this bubble around me, treating me like a glass figurine that would break if dropped. I could never even go anywhere without her, leave the house without her explicit knowledge, or join a club at school without her approval. My friends made fun of her—and me—for her overprotective, obsessive, mental-spiraling behavior. But I was starting to wonder: could all this have been an attempt to control her own life and protect me—in her own way—from Mammi and maybe even from some behaviors she saw in Daddy?

"I screwed it all up, Aunt Jackie. She will never forgive me. I may never forgive myself." My head fell under the weight of my guilt.

"Listen to me, young lady." She reached out and her rough-textured hand lifted my chin, so I was forced to look her in the face. "Your momma always pardons wrongs, Sugar. That goes double for you. You should give her a chance to prove it to you herself." She patted my leg twice, stood up, turned on her heels and crossed the creaky hardwood floor. I sensed she needed to escape before breaking down herself. She closed the door behind her, leaving Barry inside.

The tinkling of my phone tried to interrupt the silence left behind in Aunt Jackie's wake. Ignoring the sound, I turned my attention back to my recent revelations. The ringing began again. Someone needed me. Afterall, I had been dying for it to sound just moments ago. One glance at the caller ID told me I needed to pull myself together, and quick. I used my sleeve to mop my tears and forced out my most cheerfully professional tone. "Good afternoon, Detective."

Rebecca Lee inquired as to details for the Stop the Abuse event, approximate number of attendees, purpose of the event, precise date and time, and other similar questions. I tried my best to convey the importance of the occasion. If we could stop just one person from committing an act of abuse on another or teach one individual the signs of abuse to allow for early reporting, we would have done our job. I've never been much of a saleswoman, but I knew I had to sell this conference to Detective Lee. At the end of my mini-speech, I heard her speak through a smile as she said, "okay, where do I sign up?"

My heart leapt out of my chest, thrilled that I'd pulled it off and the day would be saved. I told her I'd call the agency and let Dottie know and to expect a phone call regarding her bio because I was currently out of town.

"I totally understand, Kacee. No explanation needed. You are allowed a little personal time, you know?"

"I cannot thank you enough, Detective."

"It is my honor. And call me Rebecca."

I bounded into the living room to share the good news with Aunt Jackie.

"Well, if you didn't turn your frown upside down!" She exclaimed, as she kicked back in her recliner, two cats perched atop her fuzzy blanket pilling at the edges from one too many washes and reading an Agatha Christie novel I'm certain she'd read several times before. She'd read every Agatha Christie novel several times before. When I detailed the phone call, she congratulated me and gave me one of her famous bear hugs.

"I'm going to go call Dottie."

"Okay, sugar. I'll be right here, stuffing my face with this Blue Bell cookies and cream. Sure, you don't want some?"

"Maybe after I make this call." I grinned then floated off to my room to spread the good news to my apprentice and continue my epistolary pursuits.

CHAPTER 26

saundered into the kitchen and flopped into a bistro chair, sending it reeling backwards as I tipped myself off balance. I'd have preferred to unsee some things I'd read, but that wasn't bound to happen.

My mind spiraled like a honey ham at Thanksgiving as I noticed a handwritten post-it stuck to the fridge. I never before realized that Mom and Aunt Jackie made the same little squiggle on the end of their T's. They both write in some form of barely legible chicken scratch, though Mom's is a teensy bit fancier. It's funny how you start noticing small nuances once your brain has picked up on such things. It makes me contemplate how much I've missed while focused on a singular issue.

Katy darted across the living room, yanking me from my thoughts, stopping only briefly to use her claws to snag the shag rug laying near the front sofa. Just on the verge of a hissy fit, Aunt Jackie's voice boomed through the house. "Katy! Mind your Ps and Qs and stop that, little lady!"

A streak of black and white taunted her new sable-colored roommate who selfishly dared to steal a fraction of attention. That sneaky cat was prepared to put on a show. Against my better judgment and before I could stop him, Barry fell hook-line-and-sinker into her trap and a full-on chase ensued. Aunt Jackie set down her coffee cup and took off after Katy while I attempted to corral Barry, the four of us forming a crazy dog, cat, and human conga line. Both listened equally well, which was to say, not at all. Round and round the living room they went, Barry's tail knocking over books and Katy mocking him as she wedged her way under armchairs, emitting a low growl. We finally managed to separate the two and sat back down, coated in sweat and doubled over in hysterical laughter.

"I declare. She's the dickens to fence in." Aunt Jackie cackled as she rose a few minutes later to rinse out her cup. "I gotta hand it to Barry. He held his own with her."

Not being able to drop the question that niggled at the edges of my mind, I blurted out, "Did Mom even want to marry Dad?"

Taken aback, Aunt Jackie pivoted from her place at the kitchen sink in slow motion. "Of course she did. I reckon your mom loved your dad as much as any wife's ever loved a husband."

"That's what I mean. Did she marry him because she *wanted* to, or because she was *supposed* to? Because it was the right thing to do?"

Aunt Jackie's face wrinkled right between her eyes, the way it does when she has something to say that won't be easily received. After mulling it over, she admitted, "Both. Like I said, she gave everything to your dad. She'd have crawled over broken glass for that man. I feel like marrying your father was also her perfect break from Mammi. Your grandmother dearly loved your dad. He was a doctor with lots of earning potential. He fit in with her form of society. And he seemed nice to your momma." Pausing, she added. "At first, at least. Her eyes darted toward me then looked away in a questionable glance. She set the plate down in the sink, turning to me and drying her hands on a towel as she made hard eye contact. "I don't recall ever seeing Ruth or Mammi any happier than when they wed, except of course when you were born."

A twenty-year juggernaut fell off my shoulders. Maybe she was in love with him and thought he loved her too, yet the whole time his behavior was a reflection of possessiveness and sick jealousy. It festered after her attention was split with me and grew right along with his alcohol tolerance. My head felt four sizes too big—and spinny. I hated feeling out of control.

I reached under the chair and scooped up Trixie, by far the most docile of the bunch, and stroked her velvet orange fur. "You know, I've been commissioned to write this speech for Mom. I've been digging through these journals feeling like I'm reading about a stranger. I may have bitten off more than I can chew."

I'd found myself writing and rewriting pieces of the speech. Scrawling paragraphs about how she'd make sure the bows on my pigtails matched and how she taught me to appreciate every book on that library shelf from an early age, only to scratch out half the sentences I'd written in hair-pulling frustration. The journals helped me order my thoughts, yet they each seemed to come at an expense. With each passing journal I delved deeper into her mind and not sure this was where I needed to be or even where she wanted me to be. Before this all started and before I cracked open the first journal, I was sure I knew the entire landscape of my mother's life. I knew how it went, because I'd traveled it with her. And the parts for which I wasn't present, I'd had reliable narrators detail them to me. Now, it feels like I wasn't even there. As if her life had blossomed and expanded while hidden under the earth like a potato plant and all I'd been allowed to view were the leaves lying listlessly on top of the soil. I fumbled for the bottle, hands trembling and shook out another blue pill. Maybe that will help me think straight or at least calm my nerves.

On the one hand, I felt as if I knew my mom better than I'd ever known her, as sad as that was. On the other hand, I felt a pang of betrayal, like peeking around the corner as a little girl overhearing my parents' private conversations. I didn't think it would be this difficult. Not to pen a simple speech about my own mom. But what do I say? She took care of me the best she could while going crazy and dealing with Dad always three sheets to the wind? I screwed it all up by blaming her and hanging on to Dad, because he was more fun and at least he tried telling me the truth. I had a conniption when most of the time she was just trying to protect me, adding to the pressures placed on her by her own mom and reinforcing her need to be perfect, an unattainable target for which I set her up for failure and berated her as she fell short.

"She hid so much of herself from me, her own daughter," I voiced in frustration to Aunt Jackie. "Why wouldn't she talk to me about who she was? Especially when I got on up to the teenage years and was struggling with relationships myself. Maybe it could have been a bonding opportunity for us. Heaven knows we needed some by then. Seems like I was relegated to the periphery of her life, and I'm not sure anyone got into the center circle, even my dad. Why wouldn't she sit down and tell me she had problems growing up? Maybe I could have related to some of these issues. I mean, it would have been nice to know she wasn't born perfect at least. It took these damn journals to even realize she was a cutter like me!" I cupped my hand over my mouth at the realization I admitted this out loud.

Aunt Jackie's face formed into a scowl, the kind of lopsided grimace I'd seen only once on my friend Harriet's dad after he'd had a stroke. Her brows ruffled and lips pursed. Both hands slammed open-palmed onto the counter. "Just hold your horses with the stone throwing, young lady," she warned, her volume rising. "Would you have even listened, Kacee? By the time you were old enough and mature enough to have those conversations, you'd already made your mind up that everything was her fault. She couldn't talk to you. Plus, it isn't a parent's job to confide in a child. Your mom was trying to glue it all together. She took a medicine cabinet full of drugs just to get through each day. Mammi used to always tell us to 'act ladylike,' which meant to show no emotion and do what we were told. I was horrible at it, and your mother had perfected the skill by age seven."

Then she added, "She sure as hell wasn't going to use her teen daughter as a sounding board to the shitshow created by your father and grandmother."

Jackie spoke with a passion I'd never witnessed, leaning into me and jabbing an index finger in my direction, spit flying as she spoke hard and fast. "Once the divorce happened, you began isolating her and making assumptions that would forever change the trajectory of your relationship. You had decided you only trusted one parent, and it wasn't her. All she wanted was your love, but everything she said or did was wrong. Not exactly a heart-to-heart environment. Before long, you and your dad had her wound so tight it was a wonder she didn't snap like a rubber band when you touched her. You tossed her out like last week's kitty litter."

By now, Aunt Jackie was red faced and little balls of spittle had collected in the corners of her mouth. Her eyes had narrowed into tiny slits, and her perfectly-drawn eyebrows danced a coordinated conga.

Her voice calmed but her passionate diatribe continued. "I know these words are harsh, but you asked me to be honest. You weren't at fault, merely a child given false information from a source that *should* have been trustworthy. She didn't care about winning a popularity contest or being your friend. She wanted to be a good mom. She wanted nothing more than to build a relationship with you, but you made a fateful decision early on that has yet to be undone. Much like your mom, once you set your sights on something, it's not easy to change them. You're here now, so take advantage of the gift you've been given, Kacee. Know her now."

She pushed back in her chair and breathed like she was in Lamaze class, forcing out air that seemed to have been trapped in her lungs for years. Maybe it had.

I knew she was right, but how could I reverse time? I'd

believed for so long the rumors of her craziness, both from the community and from Daddy. I'd believed she caused him to leave. I lived with her overprotective parenting style that bordered on imprisonment. I'd lived with a cabinet full of drugs, which Daddy said she used to get high and escape the responsibility of parenting me. I'd heard the fights and the broken glass and watched as she said nothing while Dad accused her of letting her anger get the best of her. I'd watched Mammi—her own mother—tell me Daddy was the superior parent. And if that wasn't enough, she had tried to sabotage him. Which is the reason I had to stop talking to her for good. Breanna tried to get him fired from the hospital and ruin his name by accusing him of sexual abuse, and Mom wouldn't discredit her. It was unthinkable at the time. Yet her journals told a different story. Something didn't add up. Of course, that was my sole rationale for requesting Aunt Jackie's assistance. She knew more than she'd told me. Maybe the remainder of the journals will tell other parts of the story or secrets nobody wanted to tell me—or perhaps nobody knows. My whole life I'd looked to Daddy for the truth, but now I didn't know what to think. But we'd made a pact. The pact.

"Do you have the number to her room handy?" I blurted. "I'm going to call her."

"Tonight?" Aunt Jackie sputtered, knuckles turning white as she physically gripped the edge of the chair.

"Do you think she can handle it?"

She rose without a word, shuffled into her bedroom and returned in silence, producing an orange post-it note. On it was scribbled a phone number and the words "Room 1125."

"You have to go through the operator at this hour," was all she said.

My insides trembled, panic-stricken. The emotion paralyzed my head, yet my body remained in motion as I dialed the number to Mom's facility.

CHAPTER 27

After four rings, a voice answered with too much enthusiasm for the job and time of day. Her bubbling demeanor and decibel level were deemed inappropriate by my standards. "Mainstay Rehab, how may I help you?" she chimed in between audible smacks of gum.

"Um, hello? Room, I mean, hello," I slipped on my words like wet tiles on a stairway. I took three deep breaths and counted to ten. Composing myself, I began again. "I'm calling to speak with Ruth Havemeier Robinson. Um, Room 1125. Please. If she's available, that is. Please."

"Let me check," the lady on the other end of the phone responded brightly and loudly. Another loud smack followed before placing me on hold, and I wondered if anyone else had found this as annoying as me.

A moment later, a hauntingly familiar voice came over the line. "Hello?" My trachea kinked, cutting off all air with that one word.

"Hi, Mom," I managed.

"Kacee!" she exclaimed in a breathy voice. "Two times in one week. Well, it's nice. I could get used to this," she said.

She sounded so happy I could almost feel her warmth. But

she also sounded weak. Frail. Weaker than a few days ago. Or maybe sadder.

"How are you feeling?"

"Pretty well, honey. I've just had a little setback. I'm sure I'll be back up and running before you know it. I can't go to work at the Senior Center right now. But don't you worry. I'll be good as new soon."

From what I'd been told, she'd been volunteering at the Senior Center for quite a few months now, helping check blood sugars, blood pressures, and conduct general well checks. It kept her active, both her mind and her spirit. Not to mention she provided a great service to the grossly understaffed center in the little town.

"Oh, that's good. I, uh, am glad you're on the road to recovery again." I paused with discomfort. "I wanted to talk to you." I paused. "If you feel like it, I mean. I got into town a couple days ago. Aunt Jackie gave me access to some of your old journals." Suddenly feeling guilty or as if I betrayed my beloved aunt, I quickly backpedaled. "Well, she thought you wouldn't mind and that it'd help me understand what I might have missed as a kid or just didn't know…"

Mom interrupted me. "Kacee, stop honey. It was my idea in the first place to open up those journals to you, if you chose to read them. I knew you weren't ready to talk to me, but I told Jackie you might be ready to *read* my point of view." Laughing, she said, "After all the time I made you spend reading, it's a little comical you'd learn things about your own mother's life by reading, when I'm right here. There's a level of irony in there, kid."

"We're still going to come see you before the ceremony. I mean you couldn't have visitors for a while and then…" My words trailed, and I felt myself spiraling. *Three deep breaths.* "I'm trying to get things ironed out in my head as I go along. It's just that these journals are turning everything I thought I knew about my childhood on its head. And I don't understand. I have so many questions, I'm not sure I could bundle them up and ask them all."

"Well, honey, as long as I'm around, I'll spend the rest of my life trying to make any amends to you. That includes answering your questions." She paused, and I could hear her fidgeting with something and swallowing. "I might be receiving an award for my volunteer work, but I know I'm not winning any parenting awards. I screwed up with you. Therapy has taught me to take accountability for my part in the situation and that continuing to perseverate on past negative relationships will not be productive." She sounded as if she'd regurgitated the information from her own therapist's mouth.

It struck me in the gut, as I could hear Margaret repeating similar words to me.

"I thought all this time you were the one forcing Dad to leave. I thought you didn't love either of us. And then Mammi—"

"Stop, Kacee," Mom interrupted, with a firm yet gentle tone. "Let me try to clear it up one at a time. Let's start with your grandmother, because I think that answer will be the easiest for you to digest. Your grandmother and I had a difficult relationship. Aunt Jackie probably didn't give you those journals because, well, they weren't necessary to your understanding." I cringed, wondering whether to come clean on this or not. I wasn't sure whether I should tell her I'd already read about how Mammi treated her like a second-class citizen, not even qualifying as a daughter. How she'd paraded her as a prized dessert at a county fair for her friends to see, shipped her off to skinny camp against her will, and given her a complex about her body her entire life. How she'd taught her she'd never be enough or measure up to some pre-fabricated and unattainable standards set by my prim and proper grandmother. I decided that was not a conversation for the phone, but I'd save it for an in-person visit. Who knows? Maybe I'd come back more frequently after the celebration. I snapped back to the conversation. "—so because of that, we just had a difference of opinion on a lot of things, is the best way to put it."

The forty-year-old red oak stood tall outside Aunt Jackie's window, the wind escorting some of its freshly-turned maroon leaves to the soft browning grass below, bidding others to join their change-of-seasons dance party. I thought of playing amidst Mammi's big oaks when I was small, catching lightning bugs and trapping them in Mason jars, only to bawl my eyes out the next morning when they lay motionless at the bottom of the glass, despite Daddy's heroic number of holes punched in the top with Mammi's ice pick.

"Wait. Because of what?"

"Kacee, were you not listening to me, honey?"

"I was, but I just didn't hear that part," I lied.

"Because your grandmother and I differed on how women should be viewed. She thought a woman's main job was to serve a man. I wanted to go to college and nursing school. That was the last straw, so to speak. It started way before that when I was young." Mom sighed. "She expected a lot from me, I suppose you could say. She left your aunt alone to be herself. Maybe because she was the oldest." She audibly snapped her fingers as if to switch gears. "But anyhow, that doesn't pertain to you. What I was going to tell you was just that very thing. I tried real hard to put mine and your grandmother's strained relationship behind me when you were born. Your father and her hit it off, so that helped. I wanted you to love and adore your grandmother, as any little girl should. I loved my own grandmother when she was alive." Mom paused for a couple of beats, and I wondered if she was reminiscing about her childhood and spending time with a loving grandma. "I never in a million years thought you and I would have the same strained mother-daughter relation-ship. Yet here we are." Sobs leaked through from the other end of the line.

"If this is too much, Mom, we can—"

"Nonsense. I need to grab a tissue. I'll be back in a jiffy." I could tell she'd set the receiver down and heard soft footfalls move away and then back toward the phone. A few moments later, she picked back up and sounded renewed. "Now what's next on your list of questions?"

"Daddy."

"This is an awfully weighty topic, Kacee. Are you sure you don't want to wait until we are in person for this?"

I considered her question, twirling my hair around a finger and tugging, scoring a few stray strands left behind, while Barry snored softly at my feet. I knew facing her would already be difficult and confronting her about the one trusted man in my life whom it now seems may have led me astray in so many aspects felt too heavy. My hand trembled as I held the phone. "I think I'd like to ask some questions now, if that's okay. Then I'm pretty sure I'll have more when I see you." I held my breath for her answer, the quivering overtaking my body.

Three deep breaths and count to ten.

"That's just fine, honey." She paused, thinking about her words. "If you're asking about him leaving, I did not force him to do anything. The truth is, I couldn't force him to do anything, even if I wanted to. Like I told you when you called earlier, it took both of us to screw things up. I won't blame everything on him either. I will tell you he possessed an unhealthy level of control over me. At one point he made some very scary threats, and I reached out to a lawyer. But I couldn't do it. I couldn't leave and break up our family like that. And I didn't force him out either. The one and only time I stood my ground was when it came to you and the custody situation. I was not going to let him have you. I knew what he was capable of." Muted sniffles piped through the receiver as she forged ahead. "It turns out that his status in the community and my past history were used against me. They didn't even see that most of my own mental illness was caused by him. I second guessed every move I made. He threatened me. He used me. I went into a deep depression. I started cutting more. I was doing everything I could just to keep my head above water." I detected a tremor in her voice and reached for my water bottle of vodka close by, gulping thirstily to numb the words and calm my own quivering vocal cords. "I made mistakes. I loved you then, and I love you now. That's the best explanation I can give you."

"Why didn't you try to reach out to me when I was older and explain?" I pleaded, wondering if I was pushing her too much yet unable to help myself from tipping a little more as I tried to make sense of this concept---still new and contradictory in my brain.

"Oh, I did, honey. I did. Your dad intercepted every try. Every phone call. I wrote you letters but you never responded. Did you even get my letters?"

The letters hiding at the bottom of my jewelry box, now gone.

"Ummm… yes, I got them, but I never opened them," I admitted, shame burning away my self-appointed righteousness. "Well, I did open a couple of them," I corrected. "They just seemed weird, Mom. The journals. The therapy-speak. Almost like an attempt to assuage your guilt, if I'm being honest."

"Well," she continued, "that's okay." No offense was too great. As if she was so used to rejection and disappointment that they rolled off her like rain from a Teflon umbrella. "Once you got to be an adult, I'd call, and you refused to answer my calls, texts, or emails. My therapist told me I was only torturing myself and exacerbating my depression. That you'd come around eventually and ask for the truth. It was really her suggestion." She swallowed hard. "Do you know I never believed her?"

"I guess she was right." I smiled. "What's that they say about a cat and curiosity?" We both chuckled a little, trying to lighten the mood. "Look, Mom, I'm just having such a hard time transitioning my idea of you as the evil queen to the heroine. From the time I walked through the door of Aunt Jackie's log cabin, it's like my life story as I knew it flipped. I have so much to process."

Barry moved to rest his head in my lap, hot breath warming

my lap while his slobber wetted my blanket. It all felt oddly reassuring.

"I can't imagine what that must feel like for you." She breathed a heavy breath. "But I assure you I'm no heroine. Just ask anyone." Shame and self-loathing infused her words.

"Are you sorry you married him?" I blurted.

"What?!" Mom said, shock filling her voice.

"Are you sorry you married Dad?"

"I heard you, honey. I just—I just… no. Of course not. Why would you ask me that? How could you even *think* that?"

"If you hadn't married him, you wouldn't have all of this to go through. You'd probably be out practicing nursing again, not dealing with the remnants of his bad treatment, and—"

"And not have you, Kacee? Not having you is not worth trading *any* of that—or anything else for that matter. Honey, I'd do it all over again today if it meant I still got you in the end." She sniffed. "Bottom line is that I'll answer any question you have. Truthfully. But at the end of the day, I don't care about what's in the past. I don't care about your father. I don't care that he hurt me. The *only* thing I care about is you. When I lost you, I lost half of me. And I was afraid it might be forever. Now that we are talking, my longtime wish has been granted. I cannot wait to lay my eyes on you and scoop you up in my arms again."

Tears fell fast, soaking the top of Barry's head and darkening a spot on his fur a dingy white. "That's, um, a lot to say all at once," I tried to mask my emotion with a nervous giggle and hugged Barry tighter. "Thanks for talking to me, Mom. I'm going to go now. We will be out there in the next day or so, okay?"

I knew I couldn't hold it together much longer.

"Okay, honey. And thank you for giving me another chance. I love you, Kacee."

"Goodnight, Mom."

I sat in the darkened room with my thoughts. I wanted to feel lighter. I wanted to throw something at the wall. I wanted to not feel like Krazy Kacee.

CHAPTER 28

Aunt Jackie tiptoed over, having left the room for privacy. "How did it go, Sugar Booger?"

"I'm glad I called her. It was good to hear her voice. We made some headway, I think. I didn't ask for a lot of details, but more surface-level questions. She filled in a lot of details on her own." I turned to face her. "Oh, and by the way, she didn't intend for you to give me the Mammi journals, but I kept that as our little secret."

"I ain't afraid of her!" She exclaimed. "I'm the *big* sister, remember?" Aunt Jackie threw her head back and cackled as if she'd heard the funniest joke. It struck me how odd it was that two sisters could be so different yet come from the exact same parents.

"It feels like we connected for the first time in lots of years. She told me she loved me. I feel a little bad about myself, because I didn't say it back. It's like the words wouldn't form in my mouth."

"It's okay, Sugar. Give it some time. You took a big step. Give yourself some credit and a pat on the back. Like this!" She hollered and raised a hand like she was going to whap me hard on the backside. I jumped and screamed, running away from her in feigned terror. Barry began to bark, and we all ended in an embrace.

An awkward silence fell. Breaking it, I said, "Did I tell you I heard back from the 'thumbs up' guy?" I smiled as the words exited my mouth, and she caught onto the joke.

"Oh, you mean the shoe man? And no, you most certainly did not," she stated, slight indignance infiltrating her tone. "What did he have to say for himself and what's he like?"

"I haven't responded yet."

She shot me a wary look with one raised eyebrow, and I could read her mind. Hear her voice. *You've got to open yourself up, kiddo. Learn to trust again.*

I rose without a word and closed myself back into the stuffy little room, with its strong smell of mothballs and mystery overpowering the air.

In a concerted effort to distract myself, I opened up my laptop, the screensaver littered with random photos of Barry. Formulating a new email to Terry J, I asked for any additional leads on Robert Hernandez. We needed to keep an eye on him, lest he attempt to find Mary and the kids. I also fired off an email to our local attorney regarding the length of time the current restraining order would stand. We wanted to play by the rules. Knowing Robert's whereabouts would ease my mind, at least on that front.

While feeling brave, I whipped out my cell and shot off a quick text to online dating Jason (aka Jpeg) at the number provided. I explained I was away on some family business, but I'd received his message and would love to learn more about him.

Three dots immediately appeared on the screen, followed by, "take the time you need." A smile spread over my face.

Sometimes distractions aren't a bad thing, even if it's a digital pacifier.

Signs of abandonment and isolation wafted out from the dusty old quilt, the boxes of journals, the clothes left untouched for years, and a single pair of rusty tweezers left on the night-stand. I plucked another journal from the beaten cardboard box and began to read. Needing to rescue her yet still skimming anger off the top of a soured childhood.

Before I settled on the words for a proper speech, I needed to at least flip through a sampling of each of these journals. A deep dive into each one, page by page, was an impossible feat, since there was still a lot of ground left to cover. I underestimated her penchant for storytelling. I just wished some of these stories had been told to me face-to-face.

December 2, 1989

I went to the doctor yesterday and confirmed. I'm pregnant! Cautiously optimistic this time, after the miscarriage. I didn't tell Richard until he came home from work last night. I made a super special dinner for him. His face was half question mark and half irritation as he walked into a room filled with candles and a table complete with an actual tablecloth. I prepared a bacon-wrapped meatloaf and homemade mashed potatoes. Dessert was banana pie topped with whipped cream. The fiery look he gave me instantly withered my excitement and he barked, "What in the hell did you do?"

Instead of being grateful, he protested that I'd never made him this nice of a dinner in the middle of the week, so I must be guilty of something. He reached out and yanked me by the left arm, jerking me toward him, fingers leaving wretched imprints in my forearm. Panic-stricken, I blurted out that I was pregnant. He dropped my arm in disgust, looking at me with his mouth agape. His whole face morphed into a wide grin. He told me he wasn't going to do anything and that he was just messing with me. Then he beat his chest like a caveman, proclaiming he had some mighty fine swimmers and telling me of course he couldn't live without me. For a moment my instinct was to roll my eyes. I wonder if I've done the right thing by allowing myself to get pregnant. I told him I was excited, but the threat of him grabbing me lays heavy on my mind. Why is he so suspicious? My friend Sarah always says that "guilty minds are the first to point fingers." I wonder if that's true. Could it be that Richard is doing something he shouldn't? Sometimes his temper gets the best of him. I'm about 4 to 5 weeks along, the doctor said.

April 28, 1990

It's a GIRL! I'm having a girl. I've never ever been happier in my whole life! I prayed and prayed for a girl. I know you're not supposed to do that, but I did. And now God has given her to me. This precious little princess. I know deep down Richard wanted a boy, because every man does. Someone to carry on the family name, especially since he has no brother to do it. But today I'm one big ball of happy. I can't wait to begin buying clothes for this sweet girl. Oh, baby girl, I'm going to give you the best life I know how. I promise you, from this very instant, I will love and protect you until the ends of the earth and the end of time. You are beautiful and wonderful and being formed perfectly in God's image. You are enough. I can't wait to meet you, Sweetheart!

June 16, 1990

You are growing and getting active. It's fun to feel you wiggling in there, baby girl. I don't think I can quite explain this new wonder to your dad. I keep trying, but he doesn't seem as fascinated as me. I mean, how can you not sit and marvel at how mind-boggling this is?!

A human being growing inside of me! And in a few months, she's going to be a marvelous little girl. Already a perfect listener. We talk about all sorts of things, and she loves it when I read to her. Richard says I'm wasting my time reading to my stomach, but I believe she can hear me when I read <u>Brown Bear, Brown Bear, What Do You See</u>? I know it's her favorite book. She moves the most when I read it. This is the definition of early literacy for sure.

July 20, 1990

I'm getting so fat. 13.3 pounds over my highest weight ever. People are just plain rude about it. A lady at the drugstore marched right up to me today, excitement in her eyes and a screaming toddler attached to her hip and said, "Oh honey you are getting out there. When are you due?" Who walks up to a stranger and calls another person fat? It's making me uncomfortable, but I keep telling myself I must gain this weight for the baby. I made the mistake of looking at myself in the full-length mirror tonight. Disgusting. I had to remove it from our room and put it in the guestroom. If I keep watching my body grow, piling on pounds like ants building a prize-winning mound, I'm likely to do something I may regret. Richard doesn't help, making tubby jokes on a daily basis.

August 31, 1990

Kacee Marie Havemeier Robinson burst into the world last night at 8:01 pm! August 30th is her birthday. Kacee is Mother's middle name, and Marie is Richard's mom's middle name. He wanted to honor them both. We agreed on putting Havemeier on her birth certificate to placate Mother, grounding her to the family name. Afterall, he and Mother are thick as thieves. Maybe this will bring a happy meaning to the name for me. And, oh what a little treasure. The labor was excruciating. Richard didn't want me to have any drugs during the process, so I complied. I ripped down there. About two inches, the doctor said, but he sewed me back up. That was the most pain I've ever endured, but I don't care. Kacee is worth every contraction and every stitch. It was the happiest day of my entire life! I don't think I'll ever come down off this cloud. She is simply perfect. Weighing six pounds and five ounces, seventeen inches long. Only tufts of light wispy hair and the tiniest feet you've ever seen. They curl and flatten when you touch them, and they are impossibly warm and soft, so of course I'm touching them all the time. I wonder if she's ticklish. Her cheeks are round and fluffy, looking like God dotted her with a tinge of rouge. Her little fingers are perfect and chubby. All ten of them. I counted. Three times. My heart is so full. To have her on one side and Richard on the other brings me an overpowering sense of bliss and contentment. My life is now complete at this very moment. Finally, our life has begun. Thank you, God. I owe you! Oh, how I love you, Kacee

Marie! For the rest of my life, I will love you more than myself or anyone else.

Choking back a flood of tears, I flipped the diary face down for a moment. I closed my eyes, envisioning Mom holding an infant me to her bare chest, overjoyed. My breast felt full, like the moment a deep breath in bottoms out in your lungs, and for the first time I could remember. I felt it. The sense of pride for being my mother's daughter. The explanation for my odd four-part name explained after years of knock-down-drag-out fights with Mom about it.

"Why did you have to give me such a weird name? It sounds like I've been married or something. Having two grown-up names," I'd barked at her.

"That's what your father and I decided would honor your grandmothers the most," she'd say sheepishly. "When you're older, you'll come to appreciate your family. You'll like that your name is different."

"No, I won't!" I shouted. "It's just another reason for the kids to call me 'Krazy Kacee!' I'm a Havemeier, and they associate that with oil — and with you."

Daddy would giggle, saying nothing to defend her and confirm it was their *joint* decision. He allowed Mom to be the sole verbal punching bag for a confused, hormonal, and angry teenager.

The remainder of that journal was blank and the next journal I picked up appeared newer.

———

My ringing cell phone broke me from my reverie, and I picked it up as soon as I read "TrueU" on the caller ID.

"Okay, first of all, don't panic, Kacee. I recruited Janice to help me, and we have it under control." Of course, my first instinct was to begin panicking. Dottie continued speaking, though not nearly fast enough. "The good news is that we're almost sold out for the conference. Participants don't seem phased at all about the switch from Bower to Lee. The bad news is the caterer backed out." My heart rate increased, the vein in my neck thrumming a soulful tune. I tried my hardest to remain focused on Dottie's words, practicing delegation. "I'm fairly certain Benny's BBQ will be able to swoop in," she continued. "It'll cost us about a dollar more per person, but I don't see many other options and my suggestion is to just absorb that cost. If you have another idea, I'm happy to check it out, of course. I mean, you're the boss." I could hear her good-natured smile through the phone, making her freckles wrinkle across her nose. "I was just fixin' to call Benny back and confirm, since I hadn't heard from you."

A wave of pride washed over me, and I realized I'd managed to make it through her diatribe without one verbal interruption. "You're doing a great job, Dottie. That sounds terrific. Thank you for handling things in my absence. Please pass my thanks along to Janice as well." I could feel her pleasure, even after we'd hung up. I collapsed against the pillows in a heap; a toothy smile on my face and a tiny weight lifted from my shoulders. I'd let go of something and the world didn't end.

CHAPTER 29

As I absorbed Mom's words penned by her own hand, I concluded that public Ruth stood in stark contrast to private Ruth. Placing herself in the impossible position of being singly responsible for the success of other fallible human beings, she saw divorce as a failure and my resulting disdain unbearable.

My phone pinged yet again, and this time the familiar sound revealed a message from the assumed name of Marianne.

MARIANNE: He says they are onto him and it's my fault. If anything happens to him, he will make me pay. And he knows I have friends in high places now. Kacee, I'm worried for both of us.

Dammit, why did she use my name? But then I naively realized he could trace my phone number if he knew who I was. Or maybe he was bluffing. I decided to send off a quick message to Terry J and ask him about police involvement. Although the lack of police action is what got Mary into this mess in the first place.

I hammered out an email to Terry about the situation, finding myself refreshing the inbox seven times before convincing myself he was probably not anxiously awaiting my message with bated breath. I closed the lid of the laptop, trying not to worry about my own safety, and responded to Mary via text.

ME: Take some deep breaths. Be aware of your surroundings. That's my best advice.

Making my way into the chilly kitchen to get myself a glass of Diet Coke over ice, my feet nearly froze on the cold hard floor. I needed something a little stronger to get through the next few entries, but I planned to add vodka in the privacy of my room. Continuing without emotional numbing was no longer an option.

December 1, 1991

He was sorry. Again. In the beginning, he'd leave marks lasting for days in the shapes of handprints and bruises that faded from black to purple to green. The apologies used to flow the following morning, sometimes even with tears or pleadings not to leave him. He loved me. He needed me. After the baby arrived, his mean accelerated down one of those conveyor belts on the fast track to nowhere. All his frustrations accompanying new parent anxiety firmly re-established me as his resident punching bag. Now all apologies have stopped. He just takes what he wants and slings me around like a rag doll, trusting I'll cover for him. I mask my bruises from the world, wearing long sleeves and always leaving the house in full make-up. I try my best to remain busy volunteering outside the home to stay away from him. The library has never been in such great shape. I know he'd never hurt Kacee. He trusts I'll stay for the baby. He knows he's right. I know he's right. I couldn't possibly take care of her myself, and I'd be depriving her of a daddy. It's my own fault anyhow when he hits me. Mother always told me I was too difficult, too hard to please. If I can just learn not to provoke him. I'll do better. For Kacee.

I rocked back on my heels. Not only was my father verbally

abusive to my mother but physically abusive, too. I didn't realize tension had been building years before I came along and had only gotten worse after I was born. Did she stay only to placate him, or did she honestly love him? Did my birth cause tension and provoke him, so her bruises were inadvertently my fault? Pain stabbed through my right eye like a hot steel rod. The headache was back with the vengeance of a scorned woman. I fished around in my purse, fumbling with a Tylenol bottle and dosed out three fat white pills and one small blue one. Flashes of bruises on Mom when she pushed up her sleeves, always explained away. Muffled screams heard from my childhood bedroom. I began to hum, yet it wouldn't drown out the sound. "Oh darling, we were just horsing around." "I'm so clumsy. I fell and hit the edge of the shower." All the things she said to me were hallmarks of abuse, and I'd never questioned any of them. No. I hadn't wanted to think the worst. I didn't know better as a child. You just believe your parents and take their word at face value. And, as a proper lady, Mom knew these were things you only dared to talk about with crossed fingers and knocks on wood.

May 4, 1996

Kacee's now finishing up kindergarten. So busy keeping up with her and her baby book, I've neglected my diary writing. Strange. Documenting life's travels may be important one day when I become famous or something. Ha. Kacee's life is zooming by. I've had a great year volunteering at her school through the PTA, and I've met an outstanding group of mom friends. They even asked me to be vice president next year!

It's a win-win for both of us. I've learned sharing can be a challenge for only children who are used to having everything to themselves. At the beginning of the year, I received several calls that Kacee had hit another child or withheld toys to the point of making another child cry. Her rationale was always the same—"I had it first"—and her follow-

up argument was nothing if not convincing. There have been a few times I had to fight back a giggle or two. I suppose we should have participated in a few more opportunities to socialize or in group activities when she was younger. I thought the church daycare group would be sufficient, but I guess not. Richard didn't even like us going there, so that became more and more infrequent. He prefers we stay home, so I'm at his beck and call.

I'm excited about summer coming up. Kacee wants to go to a couple of summer camps with her friends. I told Richard about the idea this evening. He doesn't understand the benefit of her socializing with other children. (Such as her not smacking fellow first graders).

"I don't like you or her fraternizing with those PTA bitches and their snot-nosed brats," he told me tonight. I assured him he'd never even given our friends a shot—the first time in my adult life I've had girlfriends—but he couldn't have cared less. Well, except for Susan, whom he forbade me from ever seeing without his supervision. I swear he wants to keep us locked up in isolation. He believes every kid needs to play some type of sport. I gently pointed out that dance is a sport, but he disagreed. I told him to ask her himself if she was interested in soccer.

December 14, 1999

We went to the square tonight as a family. Richard agreed to go, and I was so excited. However, he stormed off before we even got a chance to see Santa. Santa ended up having a heart attack. What a disaster!

The vivid memory of Santa collapsing onto a life-size plastic reindeer hit me in the face like a loose board on a wooden porch.

Strands of lights adorned downtown Glendale. Bands played Christmas carols. The familiar smell of Christmas wafted off the fifty-foot Eastern White Pine in the middle of town mixed with caramel corn and peppermint-laced hot cocoa. The tree strained under the weight of giant red and green ornaments, fighting for attention amongst the innumerable delicate strands of silver tinsel.

"Do you want to go see Santa?" Daddy asked, leading me across the square toward the five and dime, his muscular thumb stroking the top of my hand. Once inside, Mom trailed behind, her attention everywhere at once and walking in step as if shielding me from some unseen harm. I examined a My Pretty Ballerina doll, the coolest thing I'd ever seen in my entire life, then wandered off to browse the store, overwhelmed by the infinite possibilities that lay ahead. Aisles of candy, toys, even a woman making milkshakes behind a tall counter in the back and a man with a stained white apron that barely shielded an oversized belly called out orders for fresh-cooked fries. I inhaled the grease and could practically taste the salt; the underside of my tongue sparked to life as I imagined sitting at that counter licking the remnants of salt from my fingers. But even a nine-year-old me knew that my imagination would have to suffice.

I could always tell when the storm began to brew. It'd start with the rise of voices. Dad's fists tightened into balls, and Mom's gaze turned downward, defeated before it had even begun. Tension would bubble quietly under the lid for a few moments. The rattle of that lid as the pressure rose was the warning right before the mess spilled over and covered every surface within shouting distance. When it reached boiling, it was too late. At that point, it was still simmering under the lid.

"She only wants that shit because of those thoughts you put in her head about being perfect."

"I do no such thing. Kacee knows I love her just the way she is," I heard Mom say, knowing she was lying just to avoid another argument with him. I'd never meet her standards; it was painfully clear I'd never be perfect like her. She always insisted I was "enough," but we both knew it was bullshit. I knew I'd never have the perfect figure like her, the rolls in my middle reminded me. I knew I'd never have the thick curly hair like her, my thinner, barely curled-at-the-ends hair reminded me. My feet were too big for my body, and my bunched-up freckles made my face look perpetually dirty. Mom effortlessly maintained the proverbial Southern Belle waif-like figure and the skin of someone who had lived their entire life indoors, submerged in a vat of goat's milk, save the few perfectly placed freckles across her nose.

"Kacee *is* perfect. Unlike you. Get that through your skull right now and stop trying to change her." I could hear and see Daddy was speaking through clenched teeth. I couldn't believe he'd said that to Mom and stood up for me. Sometimes, when Mom would make Daddy yell at her, I'd flatten myself like a pancake and shimmy under my bed. I'd lie there still for as long as I could, but if it went on too long, I couldn't help but start pulling my hairs out of my head and twisting them into teensy little curls. One time I collected a whole pile of random strands and tried gluing them onto a doll, but it ended up feeling sort of creepy. The pain from pulling it out seemed to help quiet my mind, like the little yellow tufts of yarn on the red squares of my patchwork quilt.

There in the store that Christmas, waiting to see Santa, no bed existed under which to hide. No yarn to worry. At first, their volume stayed consistent. The roar in my ears muffled all the words together. I stared up at the white lights decorating the ceiling of the toy store and prayed I'd pass out or go blind, certain I'd read somewhere that stress could make that happen. Then, after some amount of time I never could have guessed, it ended as abruptly as it had begun. Mom hugged me, took my hand, and said, "let's go see Santa." I looked around. It was just me and Mom. Dad was gone. She'd made him leave again, and I worried if he'd come back this time. Even at that age I just knew it was her fault and I couldn't blame him for fleeing her. But I knew he'd always come back for me. He'd told me as much.

"Kacee Girl, if your mother ever pushes me so far away and I'm forced to leave, I'll find a way to get you. I'll find a way for us to be together. Always," he'd said, staring at me with his steel eyes in a way I knew he meant it, unblinking and serious. He'd told me so many times we'd always be together. It was him and me against the world.

I searched through the crowd, catching a glimpse of his navy-blue sweater by the exit door, his steely eyes glared back at Mom. I could still smell a hint of his woodsy soap and faint smell of whiskey and smoke. Two paces ahead of me, she was moving as if he'd never even been there at all. She secured our place in line to see the Jolly Old Guy, but as I'd soon find out would be a common theme throughout my life, we don't always get what we want—or need.

Reindeer toppled along with Santa, and elves began clearing the area along with screams and scampering employees. Santa's untimely demise was of course to blame for why I didn't get the one lousy item written on my list that year. *I just wanted them to stop fighting. I wanted her to stop making him yell and just be a* **normal** *mom. For once. I wanted peace. For Christmas, at the age of nine, I only wanted my family back. No toys. Just my family.* Santa died and took my belief in fairy tales with him.

I remember seeing that look of pure hatred directed at my mom and realizing things were getting bad. How is it possible I'd forgotten that look? It's like it was erased from my memory.

I kept reading, almost as if searching for a truth I knew but had forgotten.

Was it all my fault? What if I could have changed things?

My eyes scanned more entries.

January 12, 2000

I wish I knew what to say to him these days to make him happy. Does he not think Kacee might wonder why I keep coming up with new bruises? While getting ready this morning, I was trying to make conversation and inquired about his job, specifically his research. He flew into a rage and took that as me accusing him of cheating on me. I didn't have time to say anything before his hand shot out toward my face, a hot palm print across my cheek the only sign his mood had changed.

A white flash of pain radiated through my head, and I stepped back without saying a word. I realize I'm numb to some of his tactics, but he knows I'm a ride or die wife. He'll never let me leave with Kacee and he knows I'll stay in the hell he's created. And I will if it means I can be here to protect my daughter. Unless he kills me first.

I laid the journal face down on the fetid bedspread and pulled my own familiar quilt up over my shoulders, the soft fabric caressing my warm cheeks. I toyed with the yellow tuft of yarn and buried my face in Barry's neck. He licked my cheek as if he could sense my wrestling match with history and only he could signal the end of the round. After a few giant hugs, I convinced him to join me in the kitchen and closed the door behind us, his oversized feet padding closely behind with thump-thump-thump-thumps. I needed some lemonade, and Aunt Jackie knew just how to make it.

"Hey kiddo. I'll bet I know what you're here for. Looks like a lemonade kinda break."

"How'd you know? I wasn't sure you were back yet, but I thought I heard the front door."

Slumping at the table in my red and black checkered flannel pajama bottoms and gray V-neck tee despite the middle of the afternoon, I watched Aunt Jackie gingerly pull the amber-tinted highball glasses from the second shelf of the cabinet. Watching her fill each with ice, life felt familiar for the first time in a long time. Slowed down, non-threatening, and low stress. Perched at the table, I felt like I was that same elementary school girl coming here after school, hair in pigtails held in place with the help of matching ponytail holders with teeny bows attached to the ends.

"Sometimes your favorite person in the whole daggum world just knows! Tell me I am… don'tcha break my heart now." She held me in a tight grip around the waist, her boisterous voice emanating from her soft, cushiony body. Barry nuzzled her hand in approval, shamelessly soliciting a pet, then plopped his hefty body beside my chair and began gnawing on Ted the purple monkey.

"You *know* you are, Aunt Jackie. You always have been. Now let me go so I can breathe," I giggled, wrestling out of her grip.

A Cheshire Cat grin spread across her face. Oh, how my love for Aunt Jackie used to cause bickering between Mom and her. Mom never understood the bond the two of us shared. Aunt Jackie had the best qualities ever; those of loving grandparents, the big sister I never had, and a side of loosely structured rules not unlike a cool babysitter I'd heard some of my friends at school talking about.

Aunt Jackie sashayed to the refrigerator and pulled out the sugar-laden liquid gold, pouring two big glasses and cutting fresh slices of lemons for the side. She grabbed three sugar cookies to go with each drink, and one more for her new best friend, Barry. He seemed to appreciate her bakery skills the most. We convened in the squeaky green chairs at the end of the table.

"Find what you were looking for, Darlin'?"

"To be honest, I really didn't know what to expect when I started reading. It's like I've opened the hood of Mom's life and I'm peering down into a jumble of crossed wires. I thought I wanted to know, but now I'm not sure. Part of me wishes I'd left the car parked on the side of the road with the hood closed. Each journal feels like playing with fire. I'm already burning, and I haven't even gotten to the divorce yet."

"Has anyone ever told you just how much you look like your momma? Between your long hair and blushing cheeks, you're a dead ringer. You have that same dance she had in her eyes when she spoke of her passions when she was young. And that messy bun of spun gold you wear everywhere… it's just like hers. People must tell you that all the time."

I grinned at her attempt to draw another parallel between Mom and me. "Not lately. Have I mentioned I haven't solidified my speech yet? I'm gonna do a little more tonight and try to turn in early. At least it's coming together in my head."

All she could manage was, "Good Lord willing and the creek don't rise." She smiled and held up her glass of lemonade in a one-woman toast.

She stood and kissed the thick pile of hair that I'd tied in a messy bun. I pushed a few escaped curls out of my face and leaned back with a sigh.

CHAPTER 30

Billowy, gray clouds of warm breath puffed out into the frigid morning with every efforted exhale. Barry loped along beside me, tethered by his leash, yet paying little attention to his restraint. One quick walk around the expansive neighborhood and then we were off to the activities of the day. Trotting as if he had free rein of the road, my breathing settled to a comfortable pace. By the time we crossed Eighth Street, my heart raced, though not from the exercise. Palms sweaty as the leash slipped in my fingers, my eyes darted about. Something was wrong. We were being watched. Barry and I rounded the corner by the red bricked house with the clapboard white porch. I'd admired this house every time I came to visit Aunt Jackie. Towering ivory plantation-style columns flanked with sky pencil hollies, a circular brick driveway, and a tall cedar mailbox. A sudden noise clattered from the south side of the property, piercing the otherwise silent morning. My head snapped, and Barry dug in his paws, his eyes trained on an invisible target. I spooked and pulled at his leash, palms still slippery with sweat, to reroute him, and all the while I couldn't shake the eerie feeling that other pairs of eyes were on me.

I might be developing paranoia. Is that an early sign of mental illness? It seemed like everything odd made me question my sanity, especially since arriving back in Glendale. The shorter the distance between me and Mom, the more I realize we may not be that different after all.

I want to ask Aunt Jackie about Mom's mental illness, but I'm terrified to learn the truth. What if it's hereditary and these are the warning signs?

Aunt Jackie stood ready to meet us at the door, the house filled with the distinct aroma of coffee brewing.

"Welcome back. Have a nice walk?"

"We sure did," I lied. Afraid to admit the entire truth.

She bent down to pet Barry, now sprawled on a red mat beneath her feet. "Looks like you tuckered this boy plum out. The cats are over there with a bee in their bonnet 'cause he's taken over their nap mat. Don't look like he's movin' anytime soon though," she chuckled.

Aunt Jackie poured up two cups of steaming black gold and set them on the table along with a sugar bowl and fresh creamer.

My phone began playing its familiar jingle. "Hello?"

Terry J, the private investigator, was calling. Palming the iPhone, I barely uttered a greeting before he began rattling off words, his matter of fact and steady cadence chocked full of courtesy and information, tinted with a hint of wariness. "Kacee, I have some answers for you. Is now a good time, or did you want me to put this in an email? I'll be honest, I'd feel better just telling you now." The teensy hairs on the back of my neck stood at attention.

"No email necessary. Please go ahead," I assured him.

"I've found your guy—the husband. Looks like he's staying in a run-down motel called Motel Sunrise."

The breath went out of me as I felt the heat simultaneously drain from my face. Aunt Jackie must have seen something she didn't like, since she mouthed the word "what?" I waved my hand dismissively and redirected my attention back to the phone conversation.

"That's about twenty minutes up the road," I said. "From me, I mean. Wait, of course you know that. S-sorry," I added with a slight stutter.

"Precisely," he said. "That's why I wanted you to have the information. You need to watch your back, Kacee. I'm not sure it's Mary he's in pursuit of. At least not *just* Mary. It seems you may also be on his list. I can't figure out the motive, though… aside from you helping Mary. Anything else I should know about?"

"What was that last text about? Did you figure it out?" I asked.

He said he had not yet been able to locate the exact motive or even if Robert was making a legitimate threat, but he believed any threats should be considered valid unless proven otherwise.

"This is the first you've heard from him? Through Mary?" he asked.

"I did receive an email warning me to back off a couple of days ago, but I ignored it. I've got so much going on down here with my mother and all."

I heard the audible sigh and frustration infiltrate his voice, yet he refrained from chastising. "Go ahead and forward that to me, watch your step, and if you get any more signs—however small—call me right away."

"Oh, there is one thing. I don't know if this is significant or not, but I was walking my dog this morning, and he kept redirecting me, almost as if he were leading me away from something. And I'll be honest, Terry, I was a bit spooked, too. Like eyes were on me." Untying my shoes to free my sweaty feet, I continued feeling Aunt Jackie's attention on me as she pretended not to eavesdrop. "Also, a couple days ago, I was in town and had a very strong feeling of being watched then, too. I thought I was just being paranoid, but maybe… maybe not." My body felt heavy. My throat was closing.

"This is good. We're gonna get some professional eyes on you, Kacee. How are you always landing yourself into these situations?" He chuckled as the words left his mouth, although I know it was a serious question. "And you're gonna owe me for this one for a long time!"

"If I didn't, you'd be out of a job. So there. And thanks for looking out for me, my friend." The line went dead, and I turned to see Aunt Jackie, cushioned hip propped against the kitchen cabinet, white-knuckling the edge of the countertop. She raised a single eyebrow at me, signaling her expectation for me to relay details of the conversation for which she'd been unashamedly eavesdropping.

"It's just stuff for work, I promise." I lied. She saw through my lie easily and stared me down until I relented. "Ok, fine. Sometimes one spouse gets upset with another spouse, but I'm the one they want to come after, since I'm the one that owns the place. I've got it handled… I promise."

She proceeded to tell me about a man that came by Henry's house two days before looking for me while I'd run out on an errand. He'd told her about it, but he dismissed the idea. My body felt stiff. I asked what he looked like, but she hadn't seen him. Only Henry. I flung open the door and made a beeline to Henry's front porch, rapping on the door.

"Well hello there, young lady."

Breathlessly, I asked if he remembered the man who came inquiring about me.

"Shore do," he said. "Odd duck, he was."

"What did he say? What did he look like?" I chirped.

Henry tugged at a strap of his overalls, shifting his weight from foot to foot as he thought about it. "Nothing too special really. Come to think about it, I didn't even see a truck or nothing. It's like he come outta nowhere. He was a pretty big guy. Dark hair, tan. Didn't talk like he was from these parts."

I slid my hand through my hair, forcibly willing my breathing to slow.

"Can you remember specifically what he asked you, Henry?" Not wanting to sound too panicked, I added, "Anything is helpful, really."

Henry gazed off toward the road as he thought about the question. A long pause was followed by, "the only thing I can recall is he asked if I'd seen the likes of you and called you by name." A smirk spread across Henry's face, and he added, "call it watching too many of them copper shows or what not, but I asked him who wanted to know."

"And then what happened?" I felt like jumping at him to speed the story along. Clawing my way to the end. I knew I had to be patient.

"That's it."

"What do you *mean* that's it?"

"That's it. He shrugged once he realized I wasn't going to give him no more information and started walking back toward the road. Honestly, I thought it was strange, but people are strange. So I shut the door and that was that," he said.

"Thanks, Henry," was all I could muster. I could tell he was beating himself up, and guilt set in. I reached up and hugged him. He'd been through so much with the loss of his wife. I motioned for us to sit on his porch swing, and he obliged. We sat in silence, swinging gently, watching the grass blow and the trucks in the distance kick up the clouds of dust from the gravel road. Frogs trilled and crickets chirped. I thought how easy they had it out here. Their only responsibility was to exist.

"It's all right. Don't you worry." I placed my hand on his shoulder, ensuring I laid no blame with him. "It was probably nothing after all." I knew it was more than nothing, but no sense in worrying sweet Henry. There weren't many folks more pure in the world than Henry. And certainly not anyone who cared more for my dear Aunt Jackie.

Turns out sometimes lying to yourself and the people you love comes easy when you know it's for the best. I considered it a family trait.

CHAPTER 31

September 28, 2000

Susan called today. We haven't been able to chat in a while, so it was fun to catch up. She phoned to tell me she was pregnant. I am so happy for her and James. I hated missing the wedding, but Richard forbade me to go without him. And he wasn't going, because he didn't want to go. I am fortunate to have such an understanding friend. I felt safe to talk freely on the phone, only because Richard wasn't home to eavesdrop. I wanted to tell Susan all that had been going on with him. From the cheating to his attempts at convincing his coworker, Molly, that we have an open marriage. His steadily increasing binge drinking is just the cherry on top of the shit sundae that is my life these days. But I didn't want to spoil Susan's news, so when she asked about how things were going with Richard, I just said, "Fine. Everything's fine." I've gotten used to stifling and filtering the real me. I've become afraid to speak out of turn for fear of punishment. My girlfriends have been ripped away from me, one by one. Susan is "too bossy and demanding." Even Jackie is "too nosey." He wants to keep me all to himself, that way no one can report any suspicions. I feel so isolated.

We agreed to meet for lunch soon, but I think both of us know it will be longer than that. Getting permission to leave by myself isn't *easy these days. Plus, I'm growing uncomfortable leaving Kacee with Richard. I worry about what could happen to her if he passed out or got angry and mistook her for me.*

I need to take a break.

I deemed this a milk and peanut butter night. Somehow a spoonful of crunchy peanut butter and a glass of milk always does the trick when I can't sleep. A quirky stunt Mom used when I was a little girl. She used to tell me it was the perfect combination to ward off monsters. From the age of six, when insomnia or a bad nightmare would set in, Mom would come into my bedroom armed with a tall glass of plain milk and a giant spoonful of extra crunchy peanut butter. She swore the monsters didn't mind smooth peanut butter, but crunchy peanut butter was a monster's ultimate nemesis. At six, this seemed perfectly plausible. Be it psychological or having some nutritive properties, it has worked my entire life, and I needed it to keep working its magic as I faced some old monster battles over the next few days.

Jackie was right. I'd already learned so much about both of my parents by reading Mom's journals, maybe more than I ever anticipated. Definitely more than I bargained for and certainly enough to make me feel like I'd walked through the last several years with blinders on.

Apparently, marriage wasn't what she'd thought it would be. So much of it was make-believe. The flowers and pictures of the fancy wedding, long gone. She'd focused on the good and tried her best while blocking out the bad. Life was always playing two simultaneous movies in her head, and she never knew which one was real. She'd continued that double life for so long. The happy wife hooked arm in arm with Daddy as he paraded her around in silky red dresses, exploiting her waif-like figure at important dinner dates. Yet, he somehow never thought twice about fracturing that same arm as he twisted it in anger, forcing her to lie to me and everyone else about an accident while lifting patients at the hospital. But I knew my mom, and I knew she needed me. I might be the only one able to understand her. After all, I'm her only daughter, and I owe it to her to at least try. I'm going to do everything in my power—the powers SHE bestowed upon me—not to let him win this fight. To reclaim her good name. And to let her know I chose wrong. I was a child at the time, but I'd chosen wrong, nonetheless. After a lifetime of spite-colored glasses, I was seeing life through her eyes, and I wanted to be there for her. I'd only hoped it wasn't too late.

Mom always said, "if we learn from our mistakes, it's not a lesson lost." At the time, I saw her as a monster and as a result, refused to listen to any words of wisdom she had for me. But I was ready to listen.

CHAPTER 32

'd texted Breanna to ask if we could reschedule our coffee for the next day, allowing me to get through some more journals and better plan my visit with Mom.

I texted briefly again with Jason, a good distraction, and way out of my comfort zone. I must admit he seemed terribly charming, though I felt like he's holding something back. He was raised by his mom after his dad abandoned them around the age of seven. He was an only child and thankful for it, saying he's comfortable being alone or with other people, but he didn't rely on others for his happiness. All features to which I could relate.

We once did a study in college surrounding Only Child Syndrome and E. W. Bohannon's work on the subject, which dates back to the 1800s. Many such findings have since been debunked, yet only children are undoubtedly unique in many ways when it comes to how they approach relationships, independence, and a level of perceived perfectionism. In short, we tend to view the world differently from children born into families with multiple children. As I learned more about Jason, I found much of myself reflected back and wasn't sure if this was good or bad.

He clearly held his mother on a pedestal, as he spoke of her in flattery and flowery language. He grew up in Arkansas until the age of about sixteen, at which time he and his mother moved to Trenton.

We still hadn't gotten to the point of the conversation where he shared how he ended up in a teensy, out of the way, population one-thousand-and-nothing town like Trenton, where he practiced law.

He was thirty-two with no kids and had never been married. At first, I thought this suspicious then paused once I realized any finger pointing would render four angled back at me. Sometimes I forget my own age and path in life. Now in my mid-thirties I find that I think of myself as my mother's age. She warned me that I'd do this.

During our conversations, Jason stated his favorite color to be purple, and his favorite movie as Chevy Chase's *Vacation* (the original).

All promising attributes in my book.

Perhaps being in Glendale and opening up new possibilities and avenues was making me feel off kilter, but I'd yet to receive an actual photo of Jason. I found this a bit concerning and I told him so. I inquired about the two shoes on his profile picture, and his explanation was this: "I don't believe in judging a book by its cover. I've found too many folks around here do just that. Also, if I ever get married, I think I'd prefer inscripted shoes to wedding bands."

Oh, he might have melted my heart, even if he turns out to be a three-foot ogre with four hairs and a horrific case of pustulous acne.

As I buzzed back through the kitchen, dressed in jeans and a button-down flannel accenting a red ribbed tank, my blonde hair hung loose in curls down my back. It was 9:30 a.m., and Aunt Jackie inquired with surprise impregnating her voice, "Where are you off to, looking all spiffy early this morning?"

I told her my plans to meet Breanna at Coffee Beans and how I'd asked to move the meeting. Then perhaps we could go to

Mom's facility as soon as I returned, to which she grinned, then promptly frowned.

"What is it?"

"It's just, well, I'm not sure things are going to work out with your mom on that schedule, but you should go ahead and meet your friend."

"Why not?" I asked, alarm and disappointment fighting for the front seat of my emotion train.

"Let's discuss it when you get back," she said. "Enjoy your time with your friend," she uttered with a forced smile and a kiss on my cheek. "I think it's important to this entire discovery that y'all talk out your differences, Sug. You girls owe it to each other. I love you, darlin'. Now git on outta here." She swatted me on the backside, sending a rush of air up my shirt, and I scurried out the front door.

———

I walked into the familiar coffee shop, brightly lit with patrons lining the bar top counter and filling nearly every booth. The black and white mottled tile floor looked crisp despite its age and in contrast to the worn red vinyl booths. It held a 1950s feel, including the jukebox standing in the corner. Mr. Mandy, the owner and long-time Glendale resident, opened Coffee Beans back in the early 1980s, just a couple of blocks off the square. I'd heard his son Randall came back from college to help him run it along with his family, as he was getting on up in age. When I walked in, I saw Mr. Mandy's hand shoot up in greeting as if I was a long-lost customer, and he plastered a big toothy grin across his face. The aroma of coffee and bacon nearly knocked me over as it filled my nostrils. Random neon signs hung on the walls, signaling "eat here" and "better together," giving the restaurant a cheery atmosphere.

I waved back to Mr. Mandy and immediately spotted Breanna wearing a navy-blue shift dress and stuffed in a booth mid-way back in the restaurant. She waved both hands wildly to get my attention, in case I hadn't noticed her.

"Thanks for being so flexible with the time," I began, sliding into the booth, the sound of clanging dishes alight around us.

She extended an arm in greeting and acceptance. "How have you been?"

"Well, I thought I was doing okay until the inevitable resurfacing of my past." I let out a halfhearted chuckle so as not to seem too serious as the waitress came by to pour coffee into the white ceramic mug she plopped in front of me with a thud.

"What about you? Your daughter is so adorable. Are you married?"

Breanna's eyes stared down at the table and she spun around an empty sugar packet like a helicopter blade. Shame. "I tried to marry her biological father," she said. "It just didn't work out." The curtness in her answer told me she did not wish to discuss it further. "What about you?" Her eyes rose to meet mine, infected with curiosity. She picked at her fingers, and I noticed her cuticles looked as if they'd been bitten to the nubs, a nervous habit she'd had her entire life.

"Heavens no!" I exclaimed. "I can't even hold down a real boyfriend. I work all the time at TrueU."

"What have you done since returning to Glendale?"

"I've been sifting through Mom's journals, and I'd like to visit her and tie up a few loose ends before her celebration. I think it'll help me finish the speech. To shift those last puzzle pieces into place." My fingers trembled as I lifted the cup to my lips. "We are supposed to go when I get back from here." I paused, "Although something must have happened with scheduling. As I walked out the door, Aunt Jackie said we may not be able to keep the appointment with her after all. It shouldn't be this difficult to visit my own mother. I mean, I guess I sound like a hypocrite saying that when I'm the one who's been away for all these years and came here demanding to see her on my timeline, but still..." Nervous chatter overtook all available air space, and I could feel myself getting amped up. I twirled a rogue strand of hair around my index finger, yanking hard.

A little girl in the booth behind us began bouncing on the seat, jostling me with each harrumph as her hiney hit the bench. Her mother, stationed across the table from her, begged, "Sadie, stop doing that. You're jiggling the nice lady behind you." Sadie was clearly having too much fun filling the time between ordering, sipping her chocolate milk, and waiting for her pancakes to be delivered to heed her mother's warning. Her mother was too tired to argue and gave up without a fight, resolving herself to texting on her phone while my seat popped up and down every few seconds until Sadie's breakfast and her mother's coffee arrived at the table.

My foot began dancing the rhumba right there in the booth, and I reached into my purse to fish out a Xanax, washing it down with a quick jolt of coffee.

Breanna paused, then began again. "Part of the reason I wanted to meet with you today," she said, hanging her head, then snapping it up to make eye contact with me, "is that I've missed you. I also think you deserve to know why I said the things I did about your father. It's not going to be pretty, and you aren't going to like it. But I'm going to lay it all out there. What you do with the information is your business." She spit the words out all at once.

My stomach dropped to my feet, pulled up into my throat and rushed back to its original location, all in a matter of a nanosecond. My voice cracked as I looked Breanna square in the eyes, "Oh, and why is that?"

She stared at her half-empty coffee cup, circling the rim with her index finger. I watched the waitresses bustle about, carrying trays of cups, forks, and a sky-high stack of empty plates stained with blotches of ketchup and jelly. A plate crashed to the ground, shattering behind me, and I jumped six inches off the poorly padded, red booth seat, wondering if I'd popped Sadie a tiny bit.

"I've played this conversation over and over in my mind a thousand times. It never has a good resolution and there's never an easier way to tell it, so I can only hope you will listen to me with an open mind and know I have no ulterior motive in sharing it. I lost you, my best friend. I've raised Maya all on my own and been shunned by much of Glendale for having a child out of wedlock. The only other person to whom I've told this story is your mother. Well, and a detective. That was shortly after you decided to break off permanent ties with her *and* me." She took a long, ragged breath. "I guess what I'm saying is I have nothing else to lose. I only want the opportunity to be honest with you, once and for all. All I know is that you were told I was spreading horrible false rumors about him, and this was sufficient cause to erase both me and your mom from your life."

"That's true," I nodded in affirmation. "Dad and I had some deep conversations, and he told me the crux of it, but it was, of course, his version of the truth. He told me you'd accused him of stealing drugs from the hospital and doing inappropriate things with women. Mom backed you up, and y'all rallied other townspeople against him. He said if I continued even a tiny bit of communication with either of you, it would look like I supported your behavior. They'd drag me into an investigation and make it worse for us. He advised me to think carefully about the type of publicity brought to TrueU as well and swore that you accused him falsely because you needed attention and were in pursuit of money to support Maya. That you were sore over the fact we didn't talk much anymore and that I'd moved out to Plantation to start a career while you were here saddled with a baby since you went and got yourself knocked up." Thinking for a moment and pausing a beat, I added, "knocked up was his phrase, not mine," as if this helped soothe the situation.

My memories ran wild and took me to a place I swore I'd never visit again. The last thing I needed in my life was more drama, ushered in by false tales being told about my dad by those with an axe to grind. He may not have been the best dad, but he was not a criminal. But I was here in this place, so I might as well hear her out.

Signaling to the waitress for a coffee refill, I blurted, "just spit it out already. We're sitting here, so go ahead and tell me your story." My hands encircled the handle of the coffee cup, trying to absorb its warmth.

Drawing in a careful, deep breath, she said. "Your dad molested me, Kacee. And not just once, but on multiple occasions. When we were kids. I tried so many times to bring it up to you, but—"

My face burned. Not a slow burn, but a Texas third-degree sunburn kind of hot. "Just wait a minute. You're telling me my father, one of the only adults that even bothered to give you the time of day, tried to have sex with you?" I looked over my shoulder, mindful of little Sadie and the words coming out of my mouth, but my voice wouldn't quieten. *Three* deep breaths and count to ten. 1, 2, 3...it wasn't working this time. Not even a little.

Gathering every ounce of patience I owned and self-talking just like Margaret taught me, I tried to speak as a sound resembling an injured whale escaped. I tried again. "Look, Bre," I said, "I no longer think he's perfect as I once did, and I'm trying to be sensitive to your perception of this situation. But you're honestly trying to tell me that my father abused you? This doesn't make sense. And I'm going to be completely up front with you. If it's Havemeier money you're after, you're barking up the wrong tree. I renounced that side of the family a few years back. I'm sure Mom is still holding out hope and putting some money aside for me, because Mammi would have insisted. But I can't touch it. Er, I'm not *going* to touch their money." I slammed my napkin down on the table a little harder than I'd meant to, splashing coffee and sending silverware clattering to the ground. Rooting with haste in my wallet, I tossed down a twenty-dollar bill and resumed my rant, standing. "I can't do this right now. I just can't." I felt my face fall with disappointment. "And to think

I gave you the benefit of the doubt by showing up here today." Indignantly I added, "to think we were once best friends."

I stormed out of the restaurant, never looking back, even when the door slammed against the jamb. Calling Daddy was my first instinct, but I wasn't going to do that. At least not yet.

I plopped down in my car and buckled my seatbelt to the dinging of my cell phone. A text message from Breanna. "He's currently being investigated on another charge of molestation of a minor. If you don't believe me, at least maybe you'll believe that. Look it up. Here's the number of the detective in charge of the case."

I recognized the number immediately. Detective Amanda Bower.

CHAPTER 33

drove to nearby Heron Park, idling in my car a few moments before venturing out into the brisk air. The leaves on the overarching oaks were turning yellow and starting to fall, making cascading messy piles on the hardening ground. The park looked vacant, save for an older couple holding hands and walking at a leisurely pace and a young mom pushing a small boy bundled up like a bubble-wrapped Christmas gift in a navy and slate accented stroller.

I needed space to think. Environmental expanse tended to free up room for my jumbled brain to wander without limitations, or at least that's how I thought of it. I tied my paisley scarf around my neck and buttoned up my coat, careful to cover my ears, walking with no destination in mind. The icy breeze blew my hair as I listened to the little bubble-wrapped boy giggle, and I thought of the small pleasures in life. How quickly those fade as the evils of adulting sneak into our lives, strangling out the happy moments as a boa constrictor squeezes the life out of its prey until it breathes no more.

I slowed my gait and perched on a nearby bench, its wood faded to an ugly gray from years of weathering.

Breanna and I had been as close as sisters. For the sake of all the Mary Hernandezes of the world seen every day in my job, I owed it to Breanna to hear her out. If not, I'm no better than the person I'd accused my mother of being before landing in Glendale. A bona fide hypocrite. I came here for the truth, and I needed to get it. I needed to hear all sides before forming my own conclusions. This is what I did for a living, after all. I had acted childish in the face of hurt. I phoned Breanna, and she picked up on the first ring.

"Would you be willing to drive over to the park?" I blurted, fingering the anchor around my neck. "I need to hear your side of the story. Something inside me is unsettled by not understanding the root cause of this whole saga. I need to hear it. No matter how brutal it's going to be."

"Okay, fine." She conceded. "I'll be there in ten."

Eleven minutes later by my watch, she walked up the pebbled path, and it struck me how much she looked like her mother. She even walked like her, when her mom was sober that is.

How many folks in this town say I remind them of my mom, besides Aunt Jackie, of course?

She sat beside me, shuffling her feet back and forth across the loose dirt underneath the bench, watching the dirt shift as her gaze remained down.

"I'm sorry for running out of the coffee shop."

Breanna's eyes pivoted toward my face. She reached out and took my hand.

"When I spoke to your mom a few years back," she began, "she told me Richard's behavior had become erratic to a point of alarm during the last five or so years of their marriage. She said his drinking had gone so far beyond what anyone saw, except for her. She tried to shield you as much as she could but knew you heard the fighting and wondered how much of the bruising you'd noticed."

"What else did she say?"

"She worried you wouldn't understand that her coming

between the two of you was for your protection—from him." I inhaled at her words, the air making a hissing sound as it passed through my parted lips and clenched teeth.

She continued, biting the top of her finger. "She requested a second meeting with me. Much like you, it was too much to process at first glance. I tried to tell my own mother after the first incident, but she got so mad at me that I never told another soul, except you a couple years ago."

"You *never* told me all of this."

"You weren't ready to listen, Kacee. I tried to contact you, remember? I tried and tried calling and texting. You wouldn't answer. You kept saying your dad told you not to speak to me because of all the supposed lies."

"Oh. That." I looked toward the dirt in shame, regretful I'd listened to him on most everything about most everyone in my life. I was starting to doubt my own judgment more than ever before.

"Once Maya arrived, the nightmares returned. I could no longer suppress them. I began seeing a counselor, and she helped me sort through the memories---one by one."

My eyes focused on a rusty spot under the edge of the see-saw. If I cocked my eyes to the left and slid halfway down the bench, with the back bar resting above my shoulder blades, it looked like a Mickey Mouse head. It should have been *me* that Mom felt she could open up to and not my best friend. I felt oddly envious, though I knew it to be the wrong reaction. I picked at a scar on my left forearm with my index finger, reddening the raised reminder of pain.

We sat with linked hands as tears streamed down her face. "We spent more time at your dad's place once we got into high school, because he'd buy us liquor. The only rule was we had to include him in our partying. Remember?" Her large eyes pleaded with mine, implored me to recall the same memories she was stirring, the outside world whizzing by and mine frozen in time. I nodded. "At first it was fun, but after a while it just felt weird. By that time, you were hooked on drinking and used it as a tool to gain popularity." My mind flipped for a brief moment of silence as two young girls about the age of nine or ten roller-bladed along the hills without a care in the world. I paused, recalling that feeling… before life got complicated. "All our friends knew your dad's house was a party place."

Breanna sighed, memories overtaking her and stacking thoughts into folders. "You once told me, after consuming a large amount of alcohol, that you made some sort of pact with him. I questioned you as to details, in a nonchalant teenage BFF manner. You disclosed that he would be your primary *go to* parent. It seemed a bit childish, you admitted, but said your dad needed it. That y'all had signed an actual agreement. Do you remember any of this?"

The agreement. The pact. A dull knife tore at my soul at its mention. It created our special bond. My head ached at the details. The stabling light resurfaced, the room spun, and I felt my vision go blurry, eyelids fluttering.

"Are you okay, Kacee? Kac?"

Breanna's hands squeezed my shoulders, and I blinked up to look at her. "What?" I asked in confusion.

"You zoned out."

"I did? That's odd. Yes. Yes, I'm fine. I haven't been sleeping well," I retorted, knowing full well I was not fine. Horrible nightmare snippets of repressed memories bubbled to the surface, and I pushed them down.

Breanna didn't understand. Couldn't understand about our pact. The pact.

Daddy needed me. No matter what happened, I had to trust him. His happiness depended on me. He was a good person. Deep down, at least. It was more important to him that he remained needed and the favorite parent. Mom would be fine. Everybody knew that.

"I rode my bike over to your dad's house one Tuesday afternoon after school. You were going to meet me there but had a choir meeting and were running late. I knocked on the door and Mr. Robinson ushered me inside and made me a soda."

"As he moved closer, I could tell he'd already started drinking even though it was three o'clock in the afternoon. The truth is, I'd grown accustomed to such behavior because of my mom." Looking ashamed, she hugged her bag close to her.

"He began talking about a lady he had been dating. They'd fought over stories of their exes and how she just didn't understand him. How women his own age found it hard to unravel his intense level of complication; all he wanted was to love his family and be free to be himself. I told him the concept didn't appear difficult to grasp. He moved toward me and put his hand on my thigh, squeezing it in a playful manner. 'If *you* get it, why can't a girl my own age get it?' I shrugged it off and asked if he had any chips. By the time we found snacks, you were home. I never mentioned the incident. You'd invested too much in making him the leading luminary and your mother the Machiavellian mercenary of your life story. The commitment was too strong, too ingrained. Mr. Robinson spent years convincing you of the horrendous things your mom did in their marriage, during their divorce, and while parenting you. And I could deal with a few inappropriate comments made by a crass middle-aged man who'd had a few too many beers if it meant getting to keep my best friend. You were the only person I had in my life."

She bit at her nails, the old familiar comfort of bleeding cuticles, fiddling with her fingernails for distraction, nibbling and tearing, nibbling and tearing.

A blinding pain shot through my skull. Flashes of light pierced my brain as if a tiny little monster was trying to break out.

"Over time, it seemed like he popped up more and more. You and I were sixteen and well into our sophomore years of high school. Without real parents of my own, I found myself confiding in your dad about not fitting in at high school one night at a sleepover, after you'd dozed off watching a movie. He was kind, listening like I was the only person in the world. I cried, and he hugged me. In retrospect, it was more than a fatherly hug. It lasted a little too long; he held me a little too close; he ran his hand down my back a bit too… seductively." Breanna shivered when she said the last bit, and I found myself doing the same. I was listening intently, even though I was horror struck. "At the time, I was just a teen, and I guess I just wanted someone to love me."

I stood and paced through my confusion. Were Mom and I out school supply shopping while he was luring Breanna into something more sinister? Did Dad hit Mom when I left for school? Why wasn't I there to protect my best friend and my mom? Why didn't I know I needed to? Confusion slid away as searing guilt burned in my chest.

She continued. "About a month or so after that, I got sick at school with a migraine headache, worse than my usual variety. I tried calling my mother, but she didn't answer. Chances are, she was passed out somewhere since it was after two in the afternoon. My dad was out of town, of course. I assumed your mom was prob'ly at the hospital when I got her answering machine. I called your dad to see if he might be available. He answered, and I asked if he could come and pick me up and take me home so I could take my medicine. He showed up at the school within ten minutes. Instead of driving me home, he drove me to his house. Said he had the same prescription there, and I could rest uninterrupted while having someone to keep an eye on me. I felt so awful that I didn't care where I landed if I got the drugs I needed and was able to sleep off the throbbing in my brain. He was a doctor, after all. The drive seemed extra bumpy and impossibly bright that day, and the pain was shooting like a hot coal being forced from one side of my head to the other. The truck rolled to a stop, then he lifted me like a ragdoll and carried me through the front door and into your room, reappearing with two white pills and a glass of water. I gulped them down. The last thing I remember is your dad flipping off my Jellies and covering me up with a purple woolly blanket.

"I woke with a startle, your dad perched beside me on the bed, rubbing my back. He said he was checking in on me, because I had been asleep for a while. I remained in a headache medicine daze and remember turning over and pulling the purple blanket up to my chin. The details get fuzzy here, but I can recall him whispering, 'I can make your headache better; just relax.' Your dad put his hands under the sheets and had his way with me."

"*Stop it!!*" I yelled, then covered my mouth, embarrassed by my reaction. "I didn't mean to snap. It's just that I find it hard to believe that he'd do that to you. My best friend." Backpedaling, I said, "I mean to anyone, but *especially* to you."

She reached out with two hands, steadying my shoulders. "I know you don't want to hear this, Kac. But you need to hear it. You need to know what kind of man he truly is. I have a feeling you may even have something buried way down deep, begging to come out."

I whispered, almost to myself, "You've got no idea what is bottled up down there." My body stiffened, steeling against any further intrusion into my mind.

I stood to leave but stumbled from emotional paralysis. She grabbed my arm, whirling me around. "You will listen to me. You will hear all the horrid details, because someone needs to make you believe he was not the good guy. People around here think you're fragile like your mom. Afraid you'll break. I know better about both of you. I know how strong you both are. So, you *will* listen," she yelled. Fire punctuated her words, matching the heat in her face. "He raped me, Kacee. I tried to move him off, but I couldn't. He overpowered me and what's worse, he enjoyed it. He sat at the bottom corner of the bed and pleasured himself. My limbs refused to obey me, and my ears pounded out the marching band's Friday night halftime show. I felt him slide my panties on and wriggle my pants back up my legs before I drifted off into a deep sleep. By the time I woke up, you were standing in the room asking if I was feeling better. I spent the next several days wondering if it was a dream. After all, he was a well-respected doctor. But let's just say, it wasn't the last time."

I broke away from her grip with a force, sending the contents of my purse sailing. Lipstick, wallet, and cell phone lay splayed across the green grass of Heron Park. A gentleman walking his dachshund and two ladies in their twenties nestled their toddlers for a quick escape, eyeing me with apprehension. I'd seen that look before and in the not-so-distant past. People in this very same town used to look at my mom the exact same way, with skepticism and wariness looming in their eyes. I could read their thoughts as their brains yelled, "she's crazy." The only difference was the target, and I was horrified.

"I'm not trying to upset you, Kac. I'm letting you know what happened to me. Remember our 'blood sisters contract'?" I shook my head at the naivete of our youth. The idea that a piece of paper and a tiny drop of blood could ward off all the lies and problems of the world. "I'm coming clean," she said. "I still have my notebook paper with our prints on it."

She still had hers, too?

"Look, Kac," she began. Her hands balled in a fist and the veins in her neck protruded as she clenched her jaw. "I tried forgetting about it. I made sure I wasn't alone with your dad for a while after that. I figured I'd just fix the problem myself. But it kept happening until he started dating Laura on a regular basis and I fell out of the picture. He never apologized or acknowledged the situation again. It was like he had some sort of alter ego."

I sat in horror, staring at Breanna. I knew I was supposed to say something, yet my mouth felt glued shut and my tongue five sizes too big. I reached over and grabbed her hand. I thought I might vomit. Breanna's story reached under my skin, clawing my insides. My head pounded to the point of nausea, and I rummaged through my purse for the water bottle filled with vodka, finding it and taking a long satisfying gulp.

"If it's really true, why didn't you just tell me? I could have confronted him."

"You wouldn't have. You'd just take his side. You always did."

"You don't know that. You never gave me the chance." Tears streamed from my face, and I turned away from her.

"Didn't you see how terrified I was, Kacee?" A hurtful anger shot from Breanna's eyes. "I was embarrassed, scared, and couldn't risk losing you. Besides, I blamed myself. Surely I did something wrong to cause him to act this way."

"And the others? Are there others making the same allegations? I'm assuming you reported this. I know that's why you called me. And I assume all of this has to do with why Dad so abruptly insisted I cut Mom out of my life for good a few years back."

"I've been in counseling my whole damn life because of him. I finally mustered up the courage to report the events to the authorities. 'Course there's no evidence, so it's all about taking statements and giving forensic interviews. It's a 'he said, she said' situation like so many other sexual abuse cases. Apparently, they found enough evidence to question at least one more victim. I don't know the details. Confidentiality stuff, ya know. The deciding factor came with Maya. To think he may have done this to other girls and, if not reported, may assault a child like Maya someday. That's too much. I think if you allow yourself to dig deep enough into your childhood, you might discover something that will help you see the truth." She paused for a moment. "Or you can keep living a lie as his puppet for the next thirty years. Making your mom out to be the evil queen. It's up to you. I hope you do some soul searching. The only question is how much you're willing to risk setting it free." She stood up and gathered her things. "I've got to go pick up Maya. She began walking away, but swung around, her body angled toward me, hand on her hip.

"Kacee?" she called. "One more thing. Remember this quote by Gene Kelly: 'I may be rancid butter, but I'm on your side of the bread.' I mean that, whether you believe it or not. I've always had your back." She paused, pivoting on one foot. "And thank you for sending the book. It meant a lot to know you still thought of me. Even if it was an interesting choice."

Fingering my anchor necklace, I sucked in a shallow breath that felt like it was suffocating me. "What book?"

"The Count of Monte Cristo." I got it in the mail a week or so ago. I knew it was yours, because you always put your initials in the bottom left corner of the back flap. Purple pencil. You've done that since we were kids." She waved goodbye, and I stood with my feet cemented to the ground.

Whoever sent that book—my book—is likely the same person who rummaged through my apartment. Why *The Count of Monte Cristo*? It was the ultimate story of betrayal.

CHAPTER 34

drove back to Aunt Jackie's but instead of taking a direct route found myself winding down the road to the Havemeier homestead. The last time I visited, my world was different. Solid. I could identify my circle of trust—Mammi and Daddy.

Everything had come undone. The Havemeier Grand House, once lavish and luxurious, cowered in shame. Trim that once glimmered pristine white now shone yellowed and peeling, porch rails rusting. Fire Nandia bushes that had once accented red and Mountain Laurel bushes bursting perfect purple splashes of color now piled together in overgrown heaps of muted greens and browns, strangling out their vibrance. How easily the shine can be worn off anything once the ugly truth is unearthed. All Mammi ever wanted was to keep up appearances, both on the inside and the outside. Her best feature, her most valued asset, now lay in pitiful ruins. Her princess heiress in a mental institution, the other one living in a modest home with half a dozen cats. Her favorite son-in-law, an accused predator. Her beloved granddaughter now questioning every damn lesson she'd ever taught her. I reached into the glovebox with an unsteady hand and pulled out the rarely used tissues. What was once a powerhouse of clout and (perceived) perfection now stood choking on years of neglect.

I contemplated driving over to Daddy's house on my way back to Aunt Jackie's. For all I knew, he could have up and moved in the last year and not told me. I altered my course and drove northeast toward Roxbury Lane, past the towering sycamores and the ancient red barn with the tin roof that had nearly rusted through in several spots. I drove past Mr. York's old homeplace and past the Berry's farm. I got so far as Farm to Market Road 2551, three miles from the turn-off to go to Daddy's, before the voice in my head begged me to redirect course. I couldn't trust myself alone with him, especially if he did all those things to Mom and Breanna. If he lied to me and made me believe he was someone he was not—my entire life. He continued to show up as the leading actor of my own night-mares. All those things were unforgivable, and I was already working through how to redeem myself with one parent.

I turned my little white car around, rattling doors still rattling. Deciding to make a pitstop at Lenny's gas station for a fountain Diet Coke and a bag of potato chips before heading back to Aunt Jackie's, I fed all my vices before reaching my soft spot to land. Most of them, anyway.

When I returned to her house, I walked through the heavy front door, letting it close with a thud. I flopped down onto the couch in all its creaking protest, and bathed in Barry's kisses and the otherwise silence of the house. Aunt Jackie trudged in from the back bedroom, startling me. Her face was puffy, and I could tell she'd been crying. Henry followed, nodding in my direction but not uttering a word. He made himself at home in the kitchen, stirring a cup of aromatic coffee while positioning himself at the green table to give us a little privacy. Startled at her unusual show of emotion, I put my hand on my aunt's shoulder and gave it a gentle squeeze.

"What's the matter?"

"Oh, I'm all right. How'd it go with your friend?" She inquired in a voice a quarter its normal strength.

"Terrible, actually. She told me some stories about how Dad molested her when we were kids. She seemed sincere, but I don't even know what to believe anymore. I think the whole damn world has gone crazy, if you wanna know the truth. I'd begun to think maybe she and I could rekindle some sort of friendship, and maybe we can. I just never expected this for sure." Barry crawled up beside me, laying his head in my lap and easing my anxiety with a single lick.

The cat-shaped phone on the wall jangled, and Jackie rolled her eyes from the interruption, holding up a finger and ambling over to lift the receiver.

"Hello?" Aunt Jackie answered, her forehead squeezed into a tight frown. "I see. Yes, yes, I suppose you are right. I just wanted to… never mind. I've said my piece. It's just a bit of a surprise. I mean, how did… No… that's all." Her face contorted into the makings of an ugly cry, sucking up tears and swallowing hard. "Yes, thank you for calling."

"Who was that?" I questioned, as if it were any of my business.

"Let's talk about it in a little while, okay?" She set her chilled hand over mine, patting it and ending with a lengthy squeeze before releasing her grip. Henry ambled in from the back room, never too far from her side these days. Maybe this is how it always was with these two since Ethel died. Aunt Jackie says, *just friends*, but I'm not sure I believe the sentiment.

Her eyes met Henry's in a knowing way only couples seem to speak to each other—talking without saying words. I wondered what was being whispered in the silence between them, barely concealing a thin layer of truth and begging to be peeled back. Henry offered a quick nod and a sad grin, and she turned her attention back to me, giving the arm of the sofa a little tap with her open palm. Dark circles rimmed her eyes, and she forced a smile as she instructed, "Now continue what you were saying."

"Are you sure you're okay? Want to talk about it?"

She shot me a sharp look telling me we *would* finish the conversation we started. Aunt Jackie was not one to start a new thing before another was tidied up. I nodded and continued, "Well, I guess I was just surprised to learn you knew any of the stuff with Breanna and didn't tell me, is what I was saying," trying to curb the sharpness in my tone.

"Your mom told me a little about it before she was admitted the last time. If you ask me, the stress of all the reports and detective work is one reason she landed back where she is," she said flatly.

My head spun and my meager breakfast lurched up. "If you knew this, why wouldn't you tell me?" I asked in an accusatory tone, punctuated with splayed hands.

"It wasn't my place. Not my story to tell."

Aunt Jackie looked at me through glazed eyes. "And yes, she was very much involved. She wanted to help, as usual. After Breanna told her and she recovered from the initial shock, she did everything she could to help her. The police put your momma through the ringer. I offered to go with her down to the station each time, but she wanted to go alone. Told me she vomited twice while she was there; once on a detective." Aunt Jackie giggled a little and so did I, picturing the scene. "I know that embarrassed the living daylights out of your momma, but lordy can you imagine the face of that detective? Especially since she said he was a big 'ol burly man? I mean, who puts a little 'ol tiny thing like your momma, talkin' 'bout this sorta thing with a man anyhow? Told me the next one they got her was a woman. 'Bout her same age, so she felt a right more comfortable. Serves 'em right if you ask me."

"What did they ask her? What did Mom have to do with what happened to Breanna?"

"They asked her all sorts of things, Kac. All sorts of personal things. I remember her coming back to the house, collapsing in the red recliner, and recounting the interview with me. She was absolutely broken."

When Aunt Jackie rose, a guttural sound escaped her pursed lips before she disappeared from the room. She reappeared with a singular journal, one with a bright red and white checked cover. "This is the last journal your mom gave me. I'll bet she's detailed some of her interviews here."

I sat by Aunt Jackie, squeezing Barry off the couch with an apologetic kiss on the nose so we could both fit, and I flipped through the first few pages. He flopped at my feet, laying on top of my toes, refusing to leave my presence. They detailed times when I left for college and first moved away to Plantation. Those were difficult days for Mom. Even though I wasn't the best daughter, she still knew I was close by. After a few pages, I found what I was looking for. She wrote about Breanna coming to her house and telling her about Daddy, and then the subsequent interrogation.

October 29, 2021

I had an interview with the police today. It went something like this. "Ms. Robinson, I want to talk a little about your home life with Richard, both immediately preceding the divorce and around the time of Breanna's reported molestation. Can you do that for me?"

It felt like they were trying to pry me open like an oyster, scraping through my insides with their grubby fingers, looking for an invisible pearl that was long ago stolen.

The detective asked if Richard and I have a history of fighting.

Who doesn't have arguments with their spouse? She made me feel as if I could have done more... could have done anything to stop him. There were things I'd never told another soul. I told her of fights between the two of us. How sometimes I used myself as a human shield to protect Kacee from Richard's wrath. Sure, he'd be sorry the next day after he sobered up. Truly, genuinely sorry. But it wouldn't take long before it happened again. I relayed the underage drinking he allowed at his house after the divorce. My suspicions were confirmed by Breanna. I'll forever blame myself for not being more diligent and investigating my gut feeling. I told her how weekends at Richard's were followed by a full week of deprogramming; Kacee continually returned volatile and resentful. Lashing out at me once she got to be a teenager. Sometimes full-blown verbal attacks, screaming strings of "I hate you" at me. Richard had no rules at his house. Zero. Zilch. Well, except for the unspoken rule that the world revolves around him. His malignant narcissism and hedonism remained so thick the sharpest of knives couldn't carve out a single slice of decency.

Then the detective dropped the bomb of all questions. "Ms. Robinson, did your ex-husband ever take advantage of you in a sexual fashion?"

I told her there were lots of times I didn't want to, but we were married. It wasn't rape or anything. The detective then grasped my hand and said, "I want to be clear. No still means no even if you are married, Ms. Robinson."

I was not prepared for this statement. I felt a bubbly kind of shift in my stomach like bees flying around in a tizzy inside me and thought I might be sick again. I'd justified this answer a million times in my head. I had yelled and screamed at him at the top of my lungs when no one else was listening, biting pillows during the act to stifle my sobs, melting like a snow cone in Texas heat. I'd berated myself for allowing it to happen and attempted to regain control of the situation and of my world through food. The familiar ghost haunting my soul again until I'd picked up the shiny razor blade, shredding my arm in neat lines. The blood flowed a crimson river, and the release calmed my mind—if only for that moment. I needed to silence Mother's voice. Something had to overpower my mental pain, and cutting was the only thing I'd found that could make me forget. Make me feel something different.

I told no one. Now this detective—this perfect stranger—was directly asking me the questions I had avoided for so long. It was none of her goddamned business. No. I wouldn't tell her. But what if it could help Breanna? What if it might save Kacee? So, I took a sip of the room temperature water she'd placed on the table in front of me in the cloudy glass, dabbed my tear-stained face with the already-dampened and mascara-blotted tissue, and boldly stated, "My own husband raped me on a regular basis. Generally, after he'd been drinking." I slumped back in my chair and let out a sigh heavy enough to fill a small tank.

I prayed no follow-up questions would be asked of me, and I guess the detective must be awful spiritual since none came. She squared up her papers and thanked me for being honest. She was much easier to talk to than that pot-bellied, balding guy smelling of onion rings and stale coffee they put me with the first time around.

Paraphrasing a lifetime of love for my daughter into a thirty-minute conversation made it appear so insignificant. I told the detective about the slow build of resentment following the divorce and how that was fostered and festered by Richard. How my sweet baby, just a child of twelve, was fed horrible lies about her mother abandoning them both. How Kacee was led to believe that it was me---her mother who "caused" the divorce. How she was merely a bargaining chip, lost in an abyss I'd created, nothing more than a pawn in a sick game of revenge. Richard never missed a chance to shine a spotlight on my mental health struggles, often telling Kacee she should live with him.

Aunt Jackie and I both raised our heads from the journal at the same time, silence filling the room. The revelations had taken a lot out of both of us.

"By the way," Aunt Jackie began with direct eye contact that said she meant business, "that female detective was none other than your very own Detective Amanda Bower. That's why I teetered at the mention of her name when we spoke the other night."

My heart stopped beating for a full thirty seconds, a thick taste of betrayal hung in the air. "Detective Bower has known about this all along? She knows Mom? Why wouldn't she tell me? In all the years I've known her..." My voice trailed, feeling like a fly caught in an unsuspecting web.

"I s'pose that's not how this red tape works, if I'm being honest. There was a bigger picture." She paused in reverent thought, hands flat on the table in full surrender. "Let me ask you a question, kiddo… did your momma ever mention to you people were accusing your father of these terrible things?"

I shook my head. A response I suspected she anticipated. A part of me wondered why, yet I knew Mom was so desperate at that point to save any morsel of our own relationship that she knew bad-mouthing Daddy would only drive a bigger wedge into our troubled relationship.

"Your momma told me she tried to call you over and over after this happened, but you wouldn't return her calls. She said she wrote you letter after letter. Does any of this ring a bell?"

"Yes. She even mentioned the letters when we spoke on the phone. But she didn't tell me why. Or how important they were," I implored.

I thought about those letters, sitting in the bottom drawer of my jewelry box with Mammi's beloved jewels, sealed and unopened, save for those lone two with journal entries only now making sense. And now they were mysteriously missing.

What if I'd opened them? Would I have even believed her?

Pain stabbed against my left temple. The letters were gone the night Barry and I searched the jewelry box. I know I hadn't moved them. Tiny specs of light danced across my field of vision like fireworks.

Three deep breaths and count to ten.

Pushing through the physical pain in my head, I asked, "so, what IS the end of the story? Was he cleared of all charges, I'm guessing, since he still lives here in Glendale? I thought about driving by his house today but then thought better of it." I avoided telling Aunt Jackie about the strong whiff of his scent after leaving Ms. Annamae's shop. She'd likely try to kill him herself.

"As far as I know, the investigation is still pending, Kac. I know they called your momma in to ask her more questions two or three different times. They didn't seem to have strong enough cases." I sat in silence. Fire alarms sounded in my head, and my headache was suddenly uncontrollable, throbbing. I clenched my fists.

She added, "although if he did what he's accused of, I'll hunt him down, *Gunsmoke* style."

"Aunt Jackie!" I exclaimed.

A dry yet serious voice chimed in from the other room. "And I'll bring the ammunition." I'd forgotten Henry was still there. *So much for minding his own business.*

"I'm just telling you the truth, kid," she said, proving my earlier theory.

"I came over for some brownies. I'll be next door if y'all need me," Henry blurted, as he ambled past the two of us without another word, patting Aunt Jackie on the back lovingly as he walked past.

The light flashes shot through my right eye and straight up toward the ceiling, as if something was trying to escape from the tippy top of my head, my eyelids dancing to hold in my thoughts.

"Are you all right, Sug?" Aunt Jackie asked.

"Oh, I'll be fine. Just these darn headaches. I think I'm gonna have to break down and go to the doctor."

A fleeting image of Daddy standing over me, yelling, popped into my brain. I was lying in bed, and he was screaming at me. His face contorted into the same expression that appeared in my nightmares, each one ending in a sweaty, foul-smelling embrace. No, no, no. I fear I'm living up to my Krazy Kacee nickname.

As we sat listening to the cuckoo clock tick out the minutes, an impulsive thought blipped into my mind. "Let's go ask her right now." I swallowed hard, reaching for a pill to calm the pain, yet determined in my thought. "You said you were going to alert the staff to adjust her medication for a visit. I'm ready to see her. Or as ready as I'm ever going to be. I want to ask her about this. Do you think she can handle it?"

Following me back to the bedroom where I began changing into jeans and a decent shirt for our upcoming visit to Mom, Aunt Jackie perched on the edge of the bed, balancing half of her weight on one foot. Her eyes desperately tried to conceal the depths of her emotions, but I knew her too well. "Hold on," she said softly. "The phone call. That was your mom's place."

CHAPTER 35

Aunt Jackie relayed the conversation she'd just had in a near monotone voice, as if she'd been rehearsing the message for hours but had forgotten any manner of inflection. When she'd finished, we sat together in stunned silence. I'd prepared to go see Mom that day, but I'd never expected it to be under those circumstances. We clung to one another, the only thing that felt real in the moment. Mom had been through so many hills and valleys over the years. Those had become the norm, yet nothing felt normal anymore.

Aunt Jackie pushed herself off the bed, brushed her fingers through her thick hair and scooped up Trixie, who'd begun encircling her feet.

"They said they'd call when we had the green light to come. So that's something," she said with a smile meant to reassure. I forced the upturn of my lips, then buried my face in my pillow as Aunt Jackie told me she'd be going to lie down for a while.

"Try to get some rest, Sugar," she called over her shoulder, cat in tow, as her footsteps and swallowed sobs echoed down the wooden hallway floors.

I tossed and turned for the next several hours, Aunt Jackie's words repeating in my head like a record player left to play long after the room had emptied. I must have finally drifted off around three or four, but never felt as if I'd slept at all.

But by nine o'clock the next morning, I could no longer ignore my restlessness. I'd tossed the sheets into such a tangle and scattered journals from one end of the room to the other, trying to stay confined so as not to wake Aunt Jackie. Barry was whining and something besides words clawed from the inside of me to get out.

I pattered toward the kitchen to brew some fresh coffee extra strong, my sock feet remaining quiet while Barry's nails click-click-clicked a rhythmic staccato, meeting Aunt Jackie in the hall-way. "Did anyone call by chance?" I asked with anticipation.

"Actually, Sugar Pie," she began, a pained sense of victory in her voice, "they called this morning. I explained the special circumstances with the award ceremony planned and all. We can go *today*. You can spend all the time you want… or need, with her. Just tell me when you're ready."

"Okay… just a few more finishing touches on this thing and I'll be ready." I closed the door behind me, handing Barry a fresh bone.

May 1, 2002

Kacee walked into my bedroom today while I was crying. I cannot believe I allowed her to see me in such a disheveled state! I am supposed to be her rock, and I can't manage to keep from crying around her. She asked me what was wrong, and I told her I wasn't feeling well. I had to laugh, because her next question was, "Mommy, is it your woman time of the month?" That seemed like a plausible explanation, so I asked how she knew. She said they had been learning about that at school, and it was common for women to get emotional during their menstrual cycle. Not even eleven yet! I hugged her so tight and asked her if she could possibly know how much I loved her. She nodded, blonde ringlets dancing about her beautiful, innocent face. I love her more than anything and told her to always remember that.

Molly caught up with me at the hospital today. I was cordial. She came at me, assaulting me with her words and asking me what the hell I was trying to pull. She said Richard told her about my refusal for a threesome with her and that is why he started going out with Melissa. What? My head went dizzy. A threesome? As in sex with two other people? He's philandering with another woman now? I slid to the floor of the hospital to keep from fainting. She glared at me, disgusted. I didn't even know how to process what she'd said and certainly couldn't speak to it. After a minute or so, Molly realized I lay innocent of the accusation, and I saw genuine pity in her eyes, bordering on the flavor Mother used to dish out to me. It made me sick.

A singular word crossed her lips. "Bastard."

She told me Richard had informed her they were breaking up because she wanted a threesome. She had never had one before, and she mentioned that trying it would be fun. He agreed but said he would only do it if his wife liked the other woman. He told Molly I didn't agree to her. He had been telling Molly all along we had an open marriage. He was free to sleep with other women, and I was free to sleep with other men. Is that even a marriage? With how many other people has he shared this information? My life and what's left of my reputation are crumbling before my eyes, and I don't know what to do. I have lost all control. Every shred of it, if I even had any to begin with. Molly hoisted herself up, steadying using the wall, when it became clear I had nothing more to say to her and walked away. She walked away from me with her shoulders slumped in shame and embarrassment. Good.

My head felt hot. And heavy. Reading of my parents' sexual trysts wasn't at the top of my list, yet it deepened my understanding of what my mother was dealing with in her relationship to my father. I clutched my legs, holding tightly to myself. It was becoming a familiar pose.

May 2, 2002

As soon as Richard returned home last night, I told him we were going to talk. Like it or not. I'll admit I was afraid, but this wasn't something I was willing to let go. He was simultaneously trashing our marriage, our family, my reputation, and my career. A ludicrous rumor like this would undoubtedly get out to Kacee's circle of friends' parents before long and affect her too. I confronted him with what Molly told me. He told me she was a crazy bitch and not to listen to her. Feeling bold, I sassed back that there was only room for one crazy bitch here, and I was the resident expert. He was not going to get away with whoring his wife out to whomever he pleased. If he wanted to go sleeping around with other women, he needed to find a new plan. I have never spoken to Richard like that.

I reminded him that Molly wasn't such a crazy bitch when he was hanging out with her 24/7 and "working late" with her multiple nights a week. He slammed his open palm against the kitchen countertop, making the wine glasses jump and creating an awful clatter, telling me I was only trying to nail him with something else to make him look bad.

I told him I never WANTED to believe her, but at some point, I had to stop playing the part of the fool.

He went into the kitchen and grabbed a beer. His answer to all conflict was to numb it. I snatched the beer from his hand. I know it was stupid, but I was furious. He grabbed it back and slammed it on the ground, glass shattering everywhere. Aghast, all I could think of was Kacee. As if on cue, she came out of her bedroom holding tight to a dingy Bob the Unicorn and asked what was going on. Seeing both of us standing there, she shook her head. Richard went running to her, saying her mom was being crazy again and broke a plate in anger over nothing. He, of course, got to be the hero and the one to soothe her back to sleep. By the time he came out of the room, I'd cleaned everything up and was too tired to talk about it, likely by design. I feel like I'm at my wit's end, defeated, and deflated from asking about going to counseling together and being told by him I'm the only one with a problem to fix. Evelyn told me it won't work if he isn't willing to come. I'm losing hope.

I'm brought back to the present by more flashes of light. The blinding agony of these buried memories were clawing their way back to the forefront of my mind, one at a time.

I'll never forget the sound of the shattering bottles—nearly every night.

September 9, 2002

He threatened to kill me tonight. Actually kill me. I suggested a date night last week. At first, Richard guffawed at the idea. Later, he came back and said he would agree to it. I really felt like this was progress. When I arrived home from my shift, he'd already taken Kacee to Mother's house. I walked upstairs where he was watching the Cincinnati Reds on television, surrounded by an impressive collection of empty beer bottles. Disappointment filled me. I knew I shouldn't even bother to confront him. I did it anyway. Stupid.

I reminded him of our date night and only asked if he was going to get ready. He looked at me with malice in his eyes and told me no. He shouldn't have to take his own damn wife out on dates, he reasoned. Either he cares about the marriage or he doesn't. And if he doesn't care, he should, because we have a twelve-year-old little girl who is counting on us caring. She's betting on having two parents for a very long time.

He grabbed my wrists, his large, husky hand swallowing both of mine in one grasp, threatening to toss me through the window upstairs and enjoy watching me fall to my death. He told me he could make it look like an accident. I slept in the closet, door locked overnight, fearful he might just make good on this promise. It has to stop…for me and for my sweet Kacee. I've endured the name calling, turned the other way when he's been unfaithful, had sex forced upon me, and pretended to be content with raising our daughter alone. I've bought makeup to conceal my bruises and even popped my own collarbone back in place after he fractured it. I've covered up for him for too many years, tried to be the best wife and mother I know how to be. It's never good enough. It's never going to be good enough. I'm never going to be good enough. If he can make these types of threats toward me, it's possible he could follow through on such things with her, and I can't take that chance. Tomorrow I'm contacting an attorney. Against everything I believe in, I will explore my options and hope God forgives me. Mother was right all along. I can't keep a marriage together.

Jackie says Mother shoved religion so far down our throats when we were younger that she feels like she's belching up onion rings fried in old grease from Boltin' Bob's on the corner when she crosses through the church doors. For me, I feel like it's all I've got right now. For me and for Kacee. God, please help Kacee, even if you can't help me.

It was more than I could bear. I cinched my long sleeves toward my elbows to carefully examine each of my scars, then collapsed on the floor, emotionally exhausted. If I squinted to look closely into my memory, Mom's arms came into view. Yellow bruises at bedtime. Purple marks on her neck. Sadness in her eyes.

I grabbed my quilt, rubbing the squares. Slammed doors and broken glass burst through the edges of my memories.

Dad blamed Mom's mental issues and anger problems. Mom had just stared at me in sad silence during every lie-filled explanation and every hug he gave me afterwards as he ushered me back to bed. After all, he was there to protect me. Wasn't he? I needed him to love me, to approve of me. Perhaps I knew deep down Mom would always love me no matter what. But Dad… Dad's love was conditional. The pact. Something more just out of reach of my memory. I couldn't clutch it. Not yet. Not while the yelling echoed in my ears, loud as Mammi's cowbell calling me to supper.

The headache cracked my skull as flashes of light flitted like fireflies before my eyes, just before my vision went black and I sank into the nightmare.

Barry nudged my hand and whined. I realized I was trembling. Did I faint?

Shaking my head at the horror, I pressed on. My father threatened my mother's life. I never knew Mom had to hide in my closet. He left the marriage before the divorce. *He* forced *her* out. I should have paid attention once I grew older and she wanted to talk to me. I shut Mom out just like I'd shut out

Breanna. It'll have to wait till after Mom's celebration, but it's time to face the truth. All these loose ends need tying up into miniature slipknots.

Mom detailed being served with divorce papers as she exited the church house, three months after the closet event. I raked at my memories, knowing an event so significant would surely be buried in there somewhere, even if suppressed. Nothing. Questions swirled like a Texas tornado until I landed on an image, one of Mom and Deacon Smith standing in the small grassy patch near the parking lot of the tiny white building. He handed her a folder and she shook her head with vigor, a scowl littered her face decorated with three coats of mascara and one solid slathering of red lipstick. I thought I remembered her wiping away a rare tear with a tissue pulled from her Bible. Hands to her hips, she hung her head in apparent defeat and snatched the folder from him as I approached, calling, "Momma?" She placed a hand on the small of my back.

"What is *that*?" I'd asked.

"This?" She hesitated. "Oh, um, just some papers for a committee meeting," she'd said, face flushed in my mind's eye. I hadn't noticed as a child, but I could see it so clearly looking back. This must have been the moment she learned Daddy wanted a divorce.

He filed, because he wanted to proclaim some unspoken authority over her. He left her powerless. Oh, how she fought for me and for the marriage. Dad left her with no other option. She *was* trying to protect me.

November 1, 2002

Richard didn't think I'd wait up for him last night, since I had an early shift. I waited. I didn't care that he was drunk. Somehow these papers he so cruelly served me in front of God and everyone have lowered my inhibitions. I was ready for the fight. He came at me with,

"I know you already met with an attorney, and I wasn't going to stand here and let you steamroll me." The only people I told were Susan and Maria, another nurse. Maria and I have been friends and coworkers for about ten years. And I know Susan would never say anything to him. Would Maria? Maybe she's the latest flavor of the month. This seems like the least of my problems right now, and I find myself not caring. Not even a little.

I told him that I did meet with an attorney, but I couldn't bring myself to break the family apart. How is he okay with this? He damn well better know I will fight for Kacee. If he thinks I won't, he's about a half a bubble off plumb. That child will be safe and in a stable home with me. She won't be raised by an abusive drunk. I may have been his punching bag for all these years, but I'll be damned if she's going to be next.

I suggested we at least settle this out of court. There was no reason for mudslinging. If he is dead set on divorcing me, let's at least be civil about this. For Kacee. I knew what he was after as soon as he said he'd be civil if I would agree to pay him $50,000 a year in spousal support, plus child support, and give him primary custody. By the way, he wanted the house too. I should have guessed. This was all about money. My family's money. That's why he married me in the first place. It isn't like he's dead broke—he's a surgeon for goodness sake! This is going to be an ugly fight, as I will never agree to give him Kacee. He'll have to step over my cold, dead body before I'll hand over my precious child to him. She is not the pulley-bone. If he doesn't want me anymore, that's his prerogative. He's NOT taking my reason for living. He might not be familiar with this side of me, but there's an "old kind of crazy" associated with the Havemeier name, and if he wants to fight me over this baby girl, he's about to see it. I'm about to show him precisely what that means. The worst is yet to come, because we have to tell Kacee we are divorcing.

I held Mom's journal in my trembling hands, remembering that fateful night when they told me I was destined to be a child of divorce. It was shortly after my twelfth birthday. Every ounce of bitterness, anger, and sadness was relived on the page.

Dashing up those stairs. My Heelys heavy on each step. *Clop. Clop. Clop.* My legs couldn't carry me fast enough. I wished those shoes would roll me away from this nightmare. My life was over. I hated them both. Somewhere in my soul I knew it was coming. I watched Mom and Dad fighting, yelling, ignoring each other. All the questions swirled in my mind like some awful Slurpee combination mixed on a dare. Waiting to know my awful, hateful fate. Realizing all my friends would soon know, too.

Her face unable to mask her concern, Aunt Jackie inquired, "So, how're you feeling about everything with your mom? What can I do to help?"

"I've just read Mom's recap of the moment they told me about the divorce. That was a tough one to digest—like reliving it all again." I tasted the bitterness seeping through my teeth and heard their long-ago voices raised at one another, me buried under the bright purple blanket tossed across my bed, shivering as I cuddled with Bob the Unicorn, and praying they'd change their minds, knowing they wouldn't. Afraid of what would happen to me, who'd determine my fate, and if I'd have to switch schools. I didn't want to give the neighbors another reason to call my mom horrible names or toss their pitying looks my way. Their volatile volleying voices from downstairs hummed a familiar tune, yet this time venom colored Mom's words. Her anger grew in volume, and I could tell she was pointing an accusatory finger toward my dad. Eventually, they took turns knocking on my locked door, begging me to come out and talk, both feeling the sting of betrayal at my refusal. I felt as if keeping the wooden barrier between me and the two of them remained the only control in my life in that moment. I was too young to know how to deal with this threat of change and cook it into anything except vitriol and resentment.

I allowed the divorce to splay me open, to damage me and ultimately brand me like prized cattle. I allowed the stigma to define me—causing me to avoid human contact. Steering clear of anything other than surface-level relationships, afraid to rely on anyone but me. I'd already disappointed myself, so bringing anyone else into the picture was a recipe for disaster. But I was starting to understand that was the nature of life. Families are complicated and sometimes deeply flawed. Messy. Maybe I could rise above the ashes, the strong woman my momma always wanted me to be. All along, I was loved. I was loved so deeply and unequivocally by her. I *was* enough.

"I remember, Sugar," Aunt Jackie said. "I remember it all." She dragged the stray wooden chair leaning against the wall to the edge of the bed, its legs scraping the floors, and she lowered herself into it as she placed one rough hand on my leg. "I wish I could take it away for you. All the hurt. I wish I could bottle it all up and throw it out back for the cows to eat."

After the yelling came the ugly aftermath. The court proceedings. The division of property. The perpetual tug-of-war that lasted six months before everything was finalized. I never knew what went on in court. I guess I never cared that much, other than I didn't want to live with either of them. I was mad at both---more Mom than Daddy. Mom kept the house. Dad moved into his apartment. I stayed with Mom most of the time, and I went to Dad's every other weekend. Mom, of course, made me a calendar so I would know when I would be at which house.

Dad told me he heard Mom say countless times how much of a burden I was and how she wished she never had me. How I interfered with her career. I thought back to the instances when I'd overheard Mom comment to her friends, "It's tough to juggle a kid and a career." Perhaps that's what she meant. When I caught her on the bed crying; maybe that's why she was depressed with such frequency. Was she fed up with me? He told me she *never* wanted me in the first place.

It was like hovering above my mother and being unable to reach down and grab her out of this horrible nightmare I created. For twenty years I lived with the despair of depression while sinking into an abyss of anxiety.

How would I ever be able to make this up to her?

I met Jackie's waiting gaze, and she moved toward me with arms outstretched; I collapsed into her comforting embrace. Reliving these memories was worse than I imagined.

This may be the toughest day I've experienced in all my thirty-four years.

CHAPTER 36

After nearly an hour had passed, Aunt Jackie peeked her head into my room, papers and journals strewn about, and I noticed her hair and makeup was already half done. "Are you just about ready, Sweetie?"

"Almost. Give me a few more minutes, ok? I need a second to finish this last journal, then I think I'll be all set." My gaze adrift, I searched for the right answer. "I'm close to where I need to be; I want the speech to be as perfect as I can make it. Then a quick shower and change."

"That's fine, Sugar. Just don't make it too long. Your mother does not like to be kept waiting, you know." She gave me a wink, and honey dripped from her lips.

I needed time to process all I had learned. Picking up the journal, I ran my finger along the page as I continued to read about my father tricking Mom into being hospitalized, likely so he could use it in court (or at least the court of Glendale public opinion) against her. Everyone in the town labeling her as crazy for the early attempt on her own life. I scanned up the page to her and Jackie cleaning out the old house. Oh, how she adored that house. Her whole life had centered around me, yet, at the time, I could only see the satellites. I couldn't believe I had ever trusted him. *Loved* him. *Worshipped* him. And all he'd ever be was a cheating, abusive, lying, manipulative monster. My father was alive and well, but with each page I flipped, he'd begun dying. As in slow motion, one thing I believed about him after another turned to dust until all that was left was hot burning rage. By the time I'd read the last page, he was dead to me.

I jumped into the shower and let the scalding water wash over me as I counted chipping yellow tiles along the walls. One, two, three. A thin layer of mud-colored mold lined the grout, likely from years of inattentiveness and living in the country with its simpler lifestyle. I hoped the hot liquid would cleanse some of the filth I read before it seeped to my core. I hoped the steam would allow me to breathe again.

Water dripped onto the faded blue bathmat as Barry waited from his perch where he'd watched me through the steamed glass to ensure I wouldn't somehow drown myself in the shower, head tilting with each soaped body part and oblivious to the concept of privacy. I pulled a waiting dry towel and wrapped it around my dripping body. I used one of the unwritten pages of her own journal and the spare nub of a pencil I found wedged in Aunt Jackie's cabinet to finish writing. The words flowed like the water, free and clear.

"Kacee?" Aunt Jackie's voice called again, tinted with frustration.

"Five minutes and I'm coming." I scribbled a few more notes, haphazardly applied a coat of mascara, my dress, and darted out of the room.

Pausing at the front door, I ducked back to grab my anchor necklace. I could count on one hand the number of times I'd removed that necklace since the day I'd first put it on.

"Close your eyes and turn around, Kacee Girl," he'd said. It was my thirteenth birthday, and this was Daddy's special present to me. "It's an anchor. Do you know what that means?"

I'd shaken my head, eyes pleading with him to impart his infinite wisdom.

"Anchors are symbols of hope. A wise man once said, 'Hope is being able to see that there is light despite all of the darkness.' Remember this, baby girl. When things go bad, when you have to be home with your mom, anytime you can't be with me, you just rub this anchor and feel me with you. I'm always with you."

I nodded and hugged him.

Back then, he was my anchor, my world. For twenty years, I'd continued to wear that necklace every day.

I glared at the metal with contempt, turning it over in my hands. It seemed to burn like a lit match—hot, bright, then nothing. I set it back down on the dresser. *Not today, Dad. It's Mom's turn.*

I bolted out of the room and bumped smack into Aunt Jackie, Barry loped close behind. He came to an abrupt stop as we collided, she and I laughing at our clumsiness at just the right time. The mood lifted.

"Well, don't you look pretty as a peach?" she complimented.

"Thanks, Aunt Jackie. I'm not feeling so pretty right now." I tugged at the sash on my crimson dress, concerned it might not fit quite right. *All that chocolate ice cream from Cookie's.*

"You can do this, Sugar Plum. Stay strong. Your momma's been waiting, and I'll be right by your side from the moment we walk in until the time we leave."

"I'm going to hold you to that." I stepped back and finally got a chance to really look at her. She looked lovely. Delicate. "I don't think I've ever seen you wear pink, Aunt Jackie. It looks great on you."

"I feel a little off kilter, but I wanted Ruth to see me looking daring. Tell you the truth, it makes me feel a li'l bit spunky." Her girlish giggle made me smile.

Ready for Mom's visit and the ceremony to follow, I announced the speech had practically written itself. I grabbed my black satchel hanging listlessly on a brass hook near the front door. I turned my back to Aunt Jackie to mask the quick swallow of vodka straight out of the bottle. We loaded ourselves into the truck, Aunt Jackie trying to make small talk and dispel the pervasive heaviness in the air.

"Kacee, I want to prepare you. Your mother is quite a bit thinner than the last time you saw her. Her health has taken a definite toll on her, and she dropped to *well* under a hundred pounds. With everything going on, I want you to be as prepared as possible when you see her."

Nearly numb, I shook my head with slow motion precision while twisting the Kleenex I'd thankfully pulled from the box on the way out the door. I was equal parts anxious about the speech *and* seeing Mom, so I only really heard half of what Aunt Jackie was saying. I gently dabbed at the tears on deck waiting to fall, while trying to maintain the last quivering scraps of composure that had been threatening to abandon me without warning. As my rising panic began to set in, I finally shattered like Mammi's fine China on her tile floor and pivoted to face Aunt Jackie.

"What will I say to her?" I pleaded in a voice that sounded as broken as I felt. "I've replayed this moment a thousand times in my head, but I know nothing is going to come out right. I was her greatest joy in life and yet ended up as her biggest source of pain. I'm such a disgrace to her."

"First of all, your momma is now, has always been, and always will be proud of you, Peanut. Just for *being you*. You've never disgraced her for even one minute of your life. Second, speak your heart. Though everything's changed, nothing's changed—your mom has always been a better listener than a talker. Remember there is not one thing you could ever do or say to make your momma love you any less than she did the day you were born. Just talk to her, Kacee. It's all she's wanted for so long. Tell her what's on your heart, Sweetie. That'll be more than enough."

Silence crowded the space in the old truck as we tooled down County Road 827. I stared pensively out the passenger window, mulling over what lay ahead as I made a feeble attempt to fix my mascara in the rearview mirror of the truck. Clouds of road dust surrounded us, temporarily blinding me to the craters in the bumpy road, surprising the old, rugged tires as we bounced up and down along the rough terrain. Tiny rocks and specks of gravel sprayed from the treads of the trucks heading in the opposite direction, glancing off our windshield in fits of rage as they passed, angry at the sudden disturbance. I wondered if there wasn't an odd parallel to be found in that stretch of dirt road. Mom's journals stirred up their own dust storm in wake of otherwise bumpy, yet steady, potholed paths, the likes of which had certainly changed my outlook on so much of my past. Sometimes it only takes one little rock to get it all started.

CHAPTER 37

Home is the place where you can drive and not think, where you navigate by feeling. It's not a conscious decision, and I didn't recognize it until Aunt Jackie's truck rolled into Glendale town proper. I could get around this town with my eyes blindfolded, after being spun around for hours. Memories came flooding back to me like scenes from my favorite movie. I knew exactly how far away we were from my childhood home, judging by Johnson's big red barn and the sight of Adam's Body Shop. As soon as we hit town, my nose picked up the scent of Avery's BBQ like a bloodhound to its kill. I'd bet anyone ten dollars we were within walking distance of Haskell Road; home of the best sliced beef sandwiches this side of Dallas.

I might have tried running away from some of the people here, but my roots were planted firmly in the town's soil, sprouting beautiful flowers and weeds alike. I never realized the importance of those roots until I tried severing them. Turns out sometimes they grow back if you don't get them all, like the ones buried way down deep on that old oak tree out back of Mammi and Pappi's property. The arms of grace waiting, no matter how long I've been gone. I reached into my bag in search of a little blue calming pill. Fingers wrapped around it, I suddenly let go.

No more numbing of my feelings. Today, I wanted to explore all the feels—good and bad— that sprouted. The pill hit the bottom of my purse with a nearly imperceptible sound, and I took a long swig of my Diet Coke. Just straight Diet Coke.

Here we go.

We pulled up to the big majestic white building, and my legs felt leaden with each red, high-heeled step, coercing them to keep advancing. Aunt Jackie hooked my arm, and we made it through the large heavy glass doors, met by scores of friends and familiar faces in attendance for the event. Ms. Annamae Armstrong and Mrs. Henrietta Haygood didn't let me make it so far as three steps inside the threshold before grabbing me up and burying me in their oversized bosoms, smothering me with overwhelming smells of dry parchment and rosewater, tinged with hints of menthol. Edna McIntyre squeezed my hand, thanking me multiple times for coming to give the speech, as she kept repeating, *"so* proud of you!" I eyed Susan from a distance. She smiled a soft smile and raised her hand in a wave, wiggling her fingers. I politely thanked folks for coming and broke away from their crushing embraces so I could breathe again.

I lumbered my way to the front where I spotted Mom, as beautiful, as ever. Her hair was noticeably thinner, although it hung in white-rooted, golden curls just above her shoulders. Red lipstick perfectly accentuated her thin lips, as if she'd come straight from the beauty salon. Donned in a fancy red dress paired with her favorite ruby necklace—a gift from Mammi—all eyes rested on her, an emaciated figure of beauty. She didn't look sick or "crazy." She just looked like my mom. My mom who'd been awaiting the return of her prodigal daughter for a very long time. I tenderly grasped her hand, cold to the touch, and held on tight. Time seemed to stop; the air sucked out of the room like a vacuum. My breath hitched, my stomach flipped, and my heart opened.

Stooping over the dark walnut casket smelling of freshly cut red roses laid atop, I slid my fingers across my mother's breathless face, knelt next to her, and spoke directly to her for the first time in many years. "I have so much to tell you. It wasn't supposed to be like this," I sniveled, shoving the hard sobs down deep into my gut. "I'm so sorry for not believing you, Momma. I was supposed to get a chance to tell you how great you are and how I've realized what you endured for me. I *never knew*. Your words, your very own journals are what brought me back." My stomach tightened like the laces of a shoe, and I felt eyes staring. Gawking. I didn't care. I blurred them out. It was just me and Mom now. It was finally our time. I stood before her and everything I'd been holding in poured out.

"I think somewhere deep inside of me I knew, but I was too stubborn to allow you to tell me," I whispered to the woman who'd waited in vain to hear these words. "I foolishly clung to the promise I made to Dad, and he let us both down. I'd never have known if not for your journals. I regret that decision with every fiber of my being. I'm going to tell the truth now. I'm going to tell this whole damn town who you were and who you will always be to me. I hope that brings you some peace." My fist over my eyes, voice raised in agony and tears, "God, why did it have to be this way? I hope you know how much I love you. I've always loved you."

As I rose and turned, Aunt Jackie grabbed me, enfolding me in her arms. Overcome, my body shook, and I couldn't control the weeping that racked me to the core. It had finally become a reality. Mom was gone, but not without her baby knowing the truth in the end, even if it all felt too late.

"Wait," I urged Aunt Jackie. "I brought something for Mom to take with her. To keep her company and to keep her safe." I reached into the black bag and pulled out Bob the Unicorn, nestling him gently beside her. Bob sported the drab gray color of passing time, his single horn slightly off center from multiple attempts at reattachment and years of love. Bob was my companion in life. Before Barry, he was my one and only true confidante. I didn't need him anymore, but Mom might. It was important to me that she take him with her into the next life, if there was such a place.

"Okay. I'm ready now," I declared, looking up at my aunt in hopes she wouldn't see through the facade of confidence. She guided me to the front row, one arm around my shoulder and legs wobbling like a newborn calf learning to walk. In a way, I guess I was being reborn that day, rebirthed into the truth.

After the service began, I rose to speak, and the entire audience fell silent. The room spun on an axis, and my mouth went dry. Big dollops of sweat formed across my forehead, cascading down my cheeks.

Stop staring at me.

I needed a minute. I wouldn't let them focus on the crazy. I closed my eyes for a moment to regroup. I would show the world what a devoted mother Mom was and how I was determined to live out her prophecies. I would be brave for her.

Three deep breaths and count to ten.

Approaching the microphone in silence, save for the *click-click-clicking* of my heels, the air felt stagnant. Smelling of pine and flowers, moisture from the threat of rain seeped into the building and overtook the room. Gloom fell like a bag of sugar on each shoulder as I neared the podium and the first words. Standing a little too close, it popped with my breath. I backed up and tried again. "Hello," I said, testing the waters. "I'm Kacee." A muttering settled over the room as my words echoed across it. "I feel differently today than I did the day I was asked to give this speech about my mother." I began. "As odd as it sounds, on that day I wasn't sure I knew my mom the way a daughter my age should. I wasn't sure I even wanted to know her. We'd been through so much and were at odds for so long, and I blamed Mom for the lion's share of my troubles. Thanks to my rock, my dear Aunt Jackie, I have begun to grasp the complexities and wonder of Ruth Havemeier Robinson. I only wish I'd done so ten or twenty years ago. Or at least in time to say 'thank you' for her innumerable sacrifices and most importantly for *always* loving me. Even the times I was abhorrent and unlovable."

I shifted in my uncomfortable shoes, an attempt to keep blood flowing. "But wishing only makes us lose pennies. I don't have kids, so I can't stand up here and profess any sort of prophetic parental advice. What I know now from watching others and from reading Mom's journals, is that most parents start off with a grand vision, an unshakable drive to love and nurture their child the best way they know how. To give their children a better life than the one they had. They want their children to be better than they are—in some form or another—and have their own definition of 'better.'" Attendees began to nod, slowly and then with more vigor.

I was connecting. I was making a difference. Just like my mom.

"Every parent uses their own experience to guide them while parenting, either because of it or in spite of it. I think my mom used both. I think it's a mother's ultimate goal to see her child grow up happy, healthy, and independent. In that, my mom certainly succeeded. I suppose these last several years she's probably second guessed herself lots of times as to whether or not she made me *too* independent. I'd tell her she didn't. I made myself a little too stubborn and unwieldy." A muffled laughter spread through the room.

"My mother was there for me. I just didn't reciprocate that favor, nor did I appreciate the fact that she remained there for me, despite my little horrible self, at times. Most teenagers want to learn to fly without the strings their parents know they still need, the guidance from someone who has walked in their shoes. The one thing she continually told me growing up is that I was 'enough'. It took me a while—years—to fully understand the gravity of those words. To be honest, I still have moments where I must repeat her words to myself, when my own self-doubt creeps in. When I can't find her measure of enough and must remind myself that my heart was all that counted. Mom wanted to make sure I knew I could rely on myself, just as I was. I'm not perfect, but I'm *enough*. She didn't want me to second guess my decisions, be it in a relationship or through my own self-image. She wanted me to hear her voice way down deep, in the quiet of my soul that I am 'enough.' Even all these years while I tried blocking out her voice, I continue to hear it."

I forced myself to take a breath and glance at my speech notes. The room was packed with folks that loved Mom and knew the great things she did for so many people.

Why did I choose to miss out on so much?

"In retrospect, I also think it's important to look at the goal of being a good daughter. One which I did not accomplish, but a point I want to make to all of you coming to honor Mom today. My mother was a healer. Not only in her profession, but I'd venture to say she went above and beyond to help many of you when you were in need. She consistently put others before herself. She was a servant. Y'all were honoring her for that very thing. I have now stepped into a role of facilitating healing in my career as a social worker, perhaps unconsciously imitating her. I think it is only fair to honor her name by learning from me and my failures. Daughters (and sons), it is your job to treat your mothers with respect, no matter their age. Moms make mistakes. They are human. Allow them to be human. Allow them to say something or do something they shouldn't. Love them anyway. Afford them as many 'take backs' as they afforded you growing up, and you *know* that was a lot." An awkward chuckle rippled through the crowd. "Don't let anyone, and I mean *anyone* talk you out of having a relationship with your mom. Even your other parent. She had not done anything horrible enough to deserve me deserting her like I did. I let one person's opinion start an isolation process that would last the better part of twenty years, the last several of which was a complete shut out; no contact at all whatsoever." My voice hitched at the words. "She didn't merit that. I expected perfection from a fallible human being. When she couldn't produce it, I penalized her in the severest of fashions. I took away the one thing…the one person with whom she wanted a relationship. Me. Yet she provided unmerited favor and grace to this ungrateful little girl. She kept loving me and still wanted a relationship with me."

Turning my attention away from the crowd and toward my mom as if she was the only person in the room, I spoke directly to the woman who had gifted me the strength I needed to get this far in life. "Somewhere in the back of my mind I thought you'd always be there, Mom. Time would be on my side. Maybe I'd consider it after this project or that big decision." Looking out toward the people crowded into the pews, I implored, "Let me tell you something, friends. Time is not infinite for one person. *Any* one person. Heal your broken relationships now. As Maya Angelou once said, 'Do the best you can until you know better. Then when you know better, do better.' I have told you all, so you can 'do better.' Learning from each other is how we grow. I know she would blame me for none of this. That's who she was. That's who she *still* is. Ruth Joy Havemeier Robinson will continue to live on in me. Thank you all for coming to celebrate my mother. Mom, I love you. *You* have *always* been enough."

For the first time in years, I felt the arms of my mother. I hoped she was smiling at me. I longed to think she was proud.

My foot hit the final descending step of the stage as my eyes locked with those of Breanna Rangle in the back row of the church. She tried to give me an encouraging smile, tears rolling down her face. Though I'd been the worst friend to her when she needed me the most and rejected her because of her accusations against my father, she'd shown up to Mom's funeral. She lifted up a book, and I saw it was *The Count of Monte Cristo.* She nodded her head at me in affirmation. My eyes blurred, and clarity raced forward in my mind.

It was never about the Havemeier fortune. It was my turn to make good on the blood promise.

Without thinking, I swiveled my body and climbed back up the steps, ascending to the microphone.

"One more thing," I said. The microphone screeched, and I

stepped back, trying again. "This is highly unconventional, but since you all are here, I want to say it. Since Mom is here, I must set the record straight. Once and for all."

I need you to hear me, Mom. Please be listening. You always listened. It was me who couldn't hear.

I squinted my eyes, steeling myself for impact. "I was sexually molested by my father as a child. Dr. Richard Robinson, whom you all have known and loved for years, is a monster." An audible gasp radiated from the guests, followed by a low hum of voices. "This whole damn town wanted to make Mom out to be the one belonging in the nuthouse, because that's how he orchestrated it. If you must know, she was prone to some mental instability due to childhood issues. But he was the abuser. He abused both of us in ways unimaginable to most and undeserving to all. We were both too scared to talk about it, not even to each other. I think we felt as if we were protecting the other from our unspoken tragedies. It took the bravery of an extremely good friend to help me decide to tell my story. I wanted Mom to know. I'm sorry for not telling you sooner, Mom. I'm sorry for everything! I don't know what I'm going to do without you!"

I saw Breanna rushing toward me up the center aisle. And then it was black.

CHAPTER 38

"They're waiting for me at the gravesite. I have to go," I pleaded.

Aunt Jackie and Breanna, haloed by bright lights, stood over me, peering down their noses in stoic anticipation. I laid swathed in paper thin sheets amidst an uncomfortable and unfamiliar bed, connected to obnoxious beeping machines.

"Where are we? What's happening?" I implored, tendrils of panic creeping in.

"It's okay, Sugar," Aunt Jackie soothed. "You collapsed, and we brought you to the hospital."

Standing across the stale, bleach-filled room was Detective Bower, dressed in black slacks and a black blazer, a hint of pink peeking out from beneath the collar. The tiniest of heels dotted her feet and, for the first time ever, I noticed she wore a splash of makeup. Rose pinched her cheeks, gloss glimmered her lips, and were those false eyelashes or just good mascara? Confused by the scene, I asked, "Did you go to the service?" She nodded her head a hearty yes. Her eyes were stoic. "Mighty fine service, Kacee."

"Wait, have you been following me? Why did you—? What is the—? Is that why you wouldn't do the conference?" Pieces snapping into place like a long-lost jigsaw puzzle. "Do you drive a gray truck?"

"It's complicated," she replied. "But I do not drive a gray truck. Has someone been following you in a gray truck?"

"I don't know. Maybe. I think so." I admitted. "This is all too much."

"The case against your father has some pretty far-reaching effects and doesn't involve only you and Breanna. There's a third victim that has come forward as well. I knew it was just a matter of time before you were able to admit it. I had too many leads informing me the relationship between you and your dad was, say…" She placed her finger against her pronounced cheekbone, brushing her Shirley Temple black hair and searching for the right word, "inappropriate on his part," she finished. She propped her arm against the wall, leaning into it, the other planted on her hip, drawing attention to her firearm. "Edna McIntyre and I have been friends for a great long while. We were college sorority sisters. Don't you dare laugh." The detective pointed her finger at me in a halfhearted joking manner, an attempt at lightening the mood.

I smiled a weak grin. The thought of the brave detective and Edna, of all people, flaunting around as young college sorority girls flashed across my mind's eye.

"From what I hear, your momma deserved that darn award three times over. If anyone's ever deserved the Outstanding Lifetime Achievement in Glendale Community Service, it's your mom. Man, I read the bio that Edna wrote—volunteering at food pantries, starting a non-profit for children's literacy, and the crazy number of hours she gave to your school district. That's impressive. I wish she hadn't been so sick. When we started planning it, she was doing great. And then she took a pretty steep downturn and, well—" Her voice trailed off quietly, not knowing how to finish the sentence.

"She was such a good person, and all I could see was the bad. Criticize her. Just like everyone else in her life," I sobbed.

The nurse walked in to check my blood pressure and replace a bag of fluids. She smiled with a look of pity in her eyes. The walls were so… white. My anxiety began to rise, and my breathing sharpened. I examined the room for clues. Sharps bag. No visitor limit. Quick check of my arms—no restraints. Painted hallway walls. All clues of a traditional hospital and not a psych ward. I settled into the thin and noisy yet somehow lumpy mattress. Afraid to ask the question, though educated enough to draw on context clues, I felt safe here. Surrounded by those who care about me, homing back in on the conversation.

Detective Bower continued. "You were fed a bunch of lies, Kacee. Don't be so hard on yourself. When I met with your mom, I could tell you were her absolute pride and joy. The worry and concern she put into you was genuine, as I suspect most things were in her life. I had an inkling you'd come back for something important to your mom. After knowing you for so many years, I picked up on that same character trait in you. I also knew your dad would get wind of your homecoming. A reunion he couldn't risk without some sort of intervening." She hung her head in dismay, eyes searching the ground for answers. "I s'pose we never saw *this* coming. When she passed so suddenly—nobody ever expected her demise to be a heart attack after all she'd been through—we worked with officials at the hospital and coroner's office to expedite things and hold the funeral at the same time the celebration was scheduled, on account of everybody being here already and all. Your dad never showed, though he had you followed. I'm so sorry for what you went through, kiddo."

"I knew the timing of the award was off, but I couldn't quite put my finger on it," I admitted, voice in a whisper. "I thought it odd to be scheduling her ceremony when she was sick and all. I just can't...I just can't believe she's gone. And my dad…"

My skin prickled, as a thought convulsed. "Wait! So the person Terry and I spoke about… we thought it was about Mary… but you're saying it was about Daddy?"

"They might actually be related, honey. It's quite a spider's web," the detective said.

Coldness seeped through my veins as the nurse injected yet another liquid through the IV in my arm. I shivered. "After Breanna came to visit me and Dad several years back, Dad said I had to cut ties immediately with her and Mom. He said they were conjuring up a scheme to implicate him in a criminal drug ring, and that Mom was sneaky enough to make it work. Since they'd both worked at the hospital, he made the whole thing sound plausible. He paraded that stupid pact I signed when I was younger in front of my face, reminding me that I had chosen him and not Mom. Truth is, I know this sounds ridiculous, but I blocked out a lot of the sexual abuse because of that pact. I'd see it in snippets in my mind: dreams, visions. Nightmares. But I'd second guess myself, thinking I was going nuts and not wanting to speak of it for obvious reasons. I suppose I suppressed it my whole life. It would ruin the image I had of him. Or at least my subconscious wanted to forget it all and retain the image I had as a little girl. In retrospect, that's why I lashed out at Breanna so sharply. At that moment, my memory began to trigger. It became real.

"He was trying to defend his status while creating distance between me and Mom. He'd brought in a counselor friend of his from the hospital who told me how detrimental Mom's reputation could be to the agency. He told me her past suicide attempts and association with psychoses could destroy the entire reputation of TrueU. It sounds ridiculous now. I feel stupid and regret it all. I guess the best explanation looking back on it is that I was brainwashed by him." I cupped my hand over my mouth in shame of what I'd just said.

"Sweetie, you were under the influence of one of the best manipulators this side of the Rio Grande," Aunt Jackie reassured me, giving her leg a hearty slap. "I've watched it too many times with your mother. I can't explain it, but I know it's some sort of vile, wretched gift. Or curse. What I can say for sure is your momma never blamed you. Not for one minute of one day. She was so proud of you. You cleared her good name today, too. And I know she's singin' with the angels and beaming down right now. Probably saying, 'that's my girl!'"

I smiled at Aunt Jackie, never wanting to believe something more than that very thing.

"If there is a heaven, I'm certain Mom is up there running the place and recruiting volunteers. List by list. That's for sure."

Detective Bower thirstily chugged her coffee. "Your dad wasn't completely off base there either about the criminal drug ring, honey. He *is* being investigated for stealing drugs from the hospital. Seems he utilized painkillers and hypnotics as part of his 'seduction' plan." She made air quotes with her fingers and pulled an associated puckered scowl with her lips. "And used them as grooming tactics for himself. He had a whole crew working for him on the drug side, we think. That's where Mary Hernandez's husband comes in. Authorities are collaborating on that as we speak."

They were working together? I swept back to the words of Terry J when he warned me to be careful and look out for myself. It was no coincidence I was targeted. Did my father and Robert know each other? The words wouldn't come, yet the spiderwebs of depravity began to connect.

My head felt fuzzy. I was certain it wasn't a side effect of the anti-nausea medicine dripping into the tube connected to my arm; I closed my eyes and listened to the sound of the good detective's voice. "Working at the hospital, it seems he utilized his sources and had several affairs with different nurses, sweet talking them into smuggling out drugs. 'Course they thought he needed them for personal use. Nonetheless, this snake stretches long and gets awfully tangled, with your dad holding it by the head. I think he got bit this time." Detective Bower chimed in, looking satisfied with the final words.

My nerves frayed like a rat gnawing the last braid of a rope. I'd lost my mother, who I felt I'd only gotten to know through her journals. At least we'd been able to speak those two brief times on the phone. That was something. Then I'd admitted in a public forum to childhood sexual molestation by my father. Now to learn that the same man whom I idolized for most of my life may soon be a convicted felon on other counts. This was too much for one day.

"Was one of them named Molly?" I offered, surprising myself at the utterance.

"Excuse me?" Detective Bower and Aunt Jackie chimed in unison.

"A nurse. Was one of them named Molly?" I cleared my throat and shifted in the bed, attempting to sit a little straighter and prop myself up on the flat pillows afforded me. "I'm asking, because Mom suspected he was having an affair with a nurse named Molly. Could her journals help?"

The detective's eyes lit up like a child who'd just been promised free jellybeans for life.

My mind pendulum swung back to the passing figure I saw outside of the agency last month. Then again in town. My walk with Barry. The strong familiar woodsy peat smell. The smokey overture. The grey truck.

Could that actually have been my father? Was he following me? I gasped at the thought he may have been *in* my house.

Unintentionally, my thoughts seeped through my brain and spilled out of my mouth, though it seemed nobody had an answer just yet aside from the certainty that I was being followed. My heart raced.

"Settle down, Kacee. What is it?" Detective Bower questioned.

"The book!" Breanna shrieked. "Did you ever report the break-in?"

"What break-in, Kacee?" Detective Bower questioned. A darkness filled her eyes.

"About a month ago I had a break-in. Er, I guess it was technically a break-in." Realizing the foolishness of my statement and my failure to report it, I continued to explain. "I thought I was going a little nutty one night, because I would have sworn two photos sitting on my mantle were switched in their frames. The next thing I know, one of my bookshelves is all messed up, like a dang tornado came through but only touched down on one shelf of one bookcase. The singular thing I found missing in the whole house was one book. One simple book...well and Mom's letters. I didn't report it, because the last thing I want is to be the next Crazy Robinson. No need to offer backup to the childhood nickname of Krazy Kacee, right?" I paused on my rant, keeping eyes locked with Breanna for encouragement. She nodded, motioning and urging me to go on. "Anyway, how would someone even get up to my house on the second floor, mess up a shelf, and take one book. I reasoned it out myself, writing the bookshelf mess off to Barry and the idea that perhaps I loaned the book out and just didn't remember." I added, "when you've lied to yourself your entire life about something so big, this is hardly notable."

"But the book was none other than *The Count of Monte Cristo*, Kac! The ultimate novel of power and vengeance. Think about it!" Breanna shrieked, as if she'd personally ripped off the mask to expose the true identity of the monster at the end of Scooby Doo. Always a little on the dramatic side, she waved her hands wildly through the air.

She did have a valid point.

Breanna rose to her feet. "Then the bastard mailed it to *me*, knowing how he violated me. Thinking the way he intimidated me when I was younger would last my whole damn life. Pleased with himself he'd torn apart our friendship. Counting on the fact nothing or no one would ever be able to convince you to turn against the almighty Richard Robinson. Plus, did you ever locate those letters your mom wrote you?"

"I haven't been back to Plantation. But what if y'all searched his place and found them..." I gestured to Detective Bower.

The letters. What if Breanna was right? It had to be Richard who stole the book and mailed it to Breanna. What if he had been inside my apartment, rummaging through my items, looking for the letters my mom sent me? He was trying to send me a message...a warning of sorts. Is it possible he's been under my nose for the last several months, lingering one step behind me and watching me?

Goosebumps prickled my arms.

I couldn't focus. The beeping machine began going haywire, and the nurse rushed in, needle in hand.

"Just to settle you down, Sweetie," she cooed.

"Wait, Detective Bower... does this mean you can do the Stop the Abuse conference now?" I smiled.

And then I was out. Whatever was in that needle did the trick.

CHAPTER 39

The following weeks and months were met with forensic interviews, fact finding, and a pile of legal proceedings. I moved through the days in a self-preserved anesthetized state, feeling as little as possible. Richard faced two different types of charges, one being multiple counts of sexual molestation of a minor and the other for taking controlled substances from a hospital and administering them to minors. Both felonies. The officials were reviewing camera footage and gathering documentation from nurses. I felt if we could manage to send him to prison for a very long time, Mom would be pleased with me. I could breathe again. My childhood guilt for disobeying him and sense of betrayal were at odds with my logical brain. I longed to turn it off, but some patterns cannot be erased, despite how horrid it looked to outsiders. My own guilt over those feelings ate me from the inside out.

I smoothed my black suit, smiling to myself with the red scarf accent I'd chosen for the occasion. I needed a little extra gumption for the day. I'd never stepped foot into a real courtroom before, and this was certainly not the way I'd thought it would happen. I always figured it would be something a little tamer… like jury duty. The attorney tried her best to prepare me for the lineup. We ran through mock questioning, and I'd practiced giving my testimony at home in front of the mirror. My goal was to be able to stand strong and speak without blubbering. So far, I hadn't successfully made it through. Not even once. The attorney said some emotion is good for our case; it shows I'm not calloused. However, I know a huge chasm exists between "some emotion" and the level of uncontrolled rage and sadness I experienced each time I recounted my story.

I anticipated half the town to show up for his arraignment, as Glendale had begun fracturing over the issue. Some had labelled me as Ruth's crazy daughter, trying to get attention by bringing false accusations against this "good man." Others believed me, having been caught on the wrong side of Richard's fly traps.

Applying long overdue lipstick, I tried positive self-talk, a technique gleaned from Margaret. My wish was that, by dressing in the armor of a proper lady as Mom had taught me, she would be there with me in spirit, supporting me with her strength. I inhaled deeply as I exited the ladies' room and proceeded toward the courtroom to take my seat next to my attorney.

My father entered with his attorney in tow. I could feel his presence even before I spotted him. I shivered and goose bumps covered my body, running down my thin spine. He'd aged ten years since I'd last seen him. Gray hairs threaded through his otherwise thick black mop of hair and stippled into his well-kept beard. Sitting behind that defense table was not the person I called Daddy. In his place sat a smug man wearing an expensive suit intended to conceal his unforgivable transgressions. He'd grown paunchy in the middle, softness that didn't extend to his heart. He looked at me and smiled a smile morphing into a sinister smirk.

Surely, he still loved me. Or was this another one of his tactics to keep me from divulging all I knew? How could I ever be sure or trust him again? I can't. I won't. I need to stay strong.

I looked back at Aunt Jackie, sitting in the row immediately behind me, her face full of unadulterated hate. The tension between the three of us hung thick in the air as he looked side-eyed back over his shoulder, having the gall to leer our way. Onlookers gasped at his audacity, few residing in the standing-room-only courtroom in support of Richard.

Seems the tables have turned in the court of public opinion.

I hoped Mom was looking down to see herself as the revered parent and Dad being touted as the crazy one. The irony of the situation brought a certain level of pleasure to me. I wondered if she'd appreciate or scold me for mentioning it.

He'd stolen my childhood and broken my mother. It had only been nineteen months since the last time I saw him. I thought I was mad at him then, but I'd suppressed the real anger. The real hurt. Embers smoldered at the base of my stomach, leaving me scorched like the black residue from a wild grass fire. I'd never felt true hate before that moment, but I was pretty certain that's what I was feeling. Experts and songwriters often say that hate and love are two of the strongest emotions we can feel and aren't opposites, but rather separated by a thin line. On this day, I understood that sentiment.

"The state calls Miss Kacee Robinson to the stand," came the call in a booming voice.

His betrayal of my entire childhood piled up as I made my way to the stand, growing more enraged with each step. I wondered if my strength could withstand the storm. If there was ever a time for me to be brave, for me to channel my inner Ruth Havemeier Robinson, it was at this moment. I stared at him through seething eyes from the stand. He flashed a soft smile at me, trying to crack my clear chisel-faced anger.

Not this time, Dad. Not this time.

"Miss Robinson," the prosecutor began, "Is it true that you made a public declaration at your mother's funeral that your father sexually abused you as a child?"

I swallowed hard. "Yes."

"I know this must be terribly difficult for you to be here

today. Is it also true that you and your father made some type of a pact after your parents divorced?"

"Yes, that is true."

Now came the tough questions. "Could you elaborate on that pact a little, Miss Robinson? So, the court can learn more about what the alleged pact consisted of?"

Voice trembling, "the truth is, there were hints of inappropriateness from a young age, looking back." Tears threatened my eyes. "He always did my math homework with me from the time I was small. I remember tickle fights afterwards, his hands finding their way up my shirt after Mom left for volunteering. And I was only eight or nine." My brain lit on fire as I continued. "Cuddling too close. Touching too much. Setting himself up to be the only trusted adult in my life. But everything began to unravel at a rapid pace when he and Mom divorced. It took me a while to figure it out, to see past the lies and the manipulation. When I say a while, I mean long into my adult years. Mom was the gatekeeper. She kept him under control and covered for him. This meant I ended up blaming her for even more things." I shifted my weight in the hard wooden witness stand chair.

"The pact came into play following a rare yet fun week spent with my aunt and my grandmother. We'd gone on a little girls' trip down to Elkstown, where we enjoyed tons of shopping, eating in independent cafés, and my Mammi even attempted swimming, which was way out of her comfort zone. I made the grave mistake of telling my father all about it. Shortly thereafter, he produced the pact." I used air quotes when I said the words to ensure the court knew this was his term for the contract and not mine. "I believe it was to ensure he would remain the favorite parent. He told me the mouth sex, as he called it, was the only way to make the pact official and binding. Without our special bond, it would be another piece of paper, he'd told me." My heart hammered in my chest, and I thought it might break loose. "I believed it to be my job to take care of him now that Mom had abandoned him, abandoned us both, as he explained.

Turns out this one act had more impact than I had concluded early in my life. I assumed the role of caretaker as an only child and grew accustomed to being the main support for both, in one form or another from quite a young age.

"He even had the nerve to ask me, 'You don't want to lose both parents, do you?' Who asks that of a child? I remember being so frightened and thinking I'd do anything. Anything. My world had already fallen apart. I couldn't lose my Daddy."

I tearfully told the court what it felt like, as a fourteen-year-old, to have my own father's body weight laying on top of me. To smell him in a different way. His smoky, woodsy man smell. To hear him breathing as only a man in the throes of passion draws breath. Him trying to somehow create a sick moment of intimacy by kissing me, his tongue entering my mouth and confusing my senses. My own mind willing any other thought I could possibly conjure— *puppies, new clothes, Disney World*. The feeling of him entering me and the physical shock it sent through my body. The pain as my hymen burst open, not knowing what had happened but feeling as if I had split into two pieces. I just wanted it to be over. My confusion as I watched and felt in horror the thick mixture of semen and blood trail down my leg, helpless for answers as to what it all meant. Was I dying? Would I be pregnant? Visions still burned into my brain of him discarding my body after having sex with me. Leaving my barely teenage self all alone, questions swirling in my head. Never offering answers or explanations. I'm not sure he was capable of doing so, as that would approximate a sick form of parenting. No, he was off justifying his actions already, indulging in a post-coital cigarette, while I prayed in futility to a God I'd already abandoned that it would never happen again. I was left to deal with my own private anger when it did. Every. Single. Time.

"Over time, my mind went blank. I pushed those moments so far back I wasn't even aware of them. They would haunt me in dreams. A bunch of hazy images and smells would visit, and I would startle awake. My gut churning in disgust for thinking of my father in a sexual way. But when I read my mom's diaries and when my best friend told me he had done it to her, too, the dam I'd maintained for so long to protect myself broke wide open. Memories flooded in, even as I tried to deny them to myself. I remembered every single time my dad told me it was time. The acrid stench of his alcohol-laced breath. The pain of the intercourse, the pain, the pain. The pain. Going home afterwards and blaming myself for the shorts I wore, for the new bra I bought, for curling my hair.

"I'd almost convinced myself there was actually something wrong with me for not being able to form a normal intimate relationship, yet not quite ever being able to put my finger on what that was. The incision he made was so large, I caved into myself." I pivoted to face him. He stared at me, disinterested as if watching a B-rated television series. "I almost fell for it, Dad," I said. He stared back at me with glazed eyes, looking right through me—cartoonishly evil. "I can see now it was all about control," I ranted to the people sitting silent, aghast, in the courtroom.

"You're damn right it's about control! Somebody had to control you, to parent you," Richard sprang to life, slamming his open palms against the defense table and bursting out of his seat. I watched his wide-eyed lawyer tug at his tailored suit coat and whisper, "sit down," through gritted teeth. Ignoring the request, he continued. "I may not have done everything right, little miss prissy pants. But I damn sure didn't do anything inappropriate. You're up there all high and mighty, twisting my words. Just like the good little clone of your fucking mother that..."

"Order! Order!" The judge banged his gavel. "Mr. Griffin, if you cannot control your client and his outbursts, I will be more than happy to do it for you. You will not receive another warning from this bench. Do you understand me?" He looked powerful from up there on that pedestal, robed in black, and I couldn't help but wonder if my father's abuse made him feel the same way. Maybe that's why he'd done it. He needed to feel as if he was ruling over something, or someone, important. Making the decisions. Banging the gavel.

"Yes, Your Honor, I understand." Richard's attorney acknowledged, with a stern glance given to my father and whispered words of warning. Richard sat sulking in his forced silence, arms crossed across his chest.

"Ms. Robinson, you may continue," the judge instructed, with a nod and a sympathetic look in my direction.

"My mother was never the one *wanting control*. As you can see, my father has issues." I looked his way, staring dead in his eyes, fueled by his reprimand. He wasn't getting his way this time, and my face broke into a coy smile. Feeling uneasy, I glanced at Aunt Jackie. Through tears, she gave me a thumbs up, indicating I was doing just fine.

Three deep breaths and count to ten.

"Issues of control, and one thing he couldn't obtain was utter mind control over my independent mother—at least not when it came to me. So, he broke her trying to get it. When it didn't work, he broke me." I shifted in the witness stand seat, thinking carefully. "But look at me now, Richard. I didn't stay broken." I looked at him and smiled, more of a smirk, perhaps. A release of emotion followed, and I pronounced, "I guess I really did turn out to be a lot more like her than you ever realized."

I wondered what he was thinking as I sat behind the tiny wooden partition separating us, looked him straight in his cold, unwavering eyes, and declared, "You've hurt me for the last time, asshole. I've had enough; this is it. In fact, I've had enough for both me and for Mom, because like she used to tell me, and you could never see… I was *always* enough just as I was. I never needed your approval or your abuse to prove anything. And I sure as hell don't need it now. But I hope *you* get everything you deserve."

———

A month after my hearing, the verdict came in. Unanimous. Guilty on all counts. And a few days after that, the judge ruled he would serve two fifteen-year consecutive terms for sexual assault of a minor, one thirty-four-year term for aggravated sexual assault of a minor, two ten-year terms for possession of child pornography, and one year for stealing drugs from a hospital and administering them to a minor. In total, he would be locked up for eighty-five years without parole.

CHAPTER 40

Back in Plantation, I submerged myself in my work, attempting to block out the last several months.

I vacillated between my mix-matched apartment and the office, operating from a perspective of rote muscle memory. One Monday morning, as I left my residence, about two weeks after the hearing, I noticed Jeb stepping out of his door.

"Haven't seen you in a while," I called. Startled by my voice, he pivoted on his foot to face me, brief eye contact made. I shifted back toward my door, bending to gather my bags.

"Have a nice day," came a deep baritone voice in response. I felt so victorious I fist pumped into the air once his back was turned. He spoke. Jeb spoke. I drove to work with a renewed spirit and faith in the now-debunked idea that people can't change.

Almost the minute I arrived at the office and greeted Dottie with a "good morning," I sat at my desk and found my phone chiming with a text.

JASON: If you don't want to talk to me, it's okay. I felt a connection with you, and I want to make sure you're alright.

It had been weeks since I last communicated with Jason,

bordering a month. Ignoring the last several text messages seemed wrong, though I convinced myself it was more wrong of me to plop someone smack into the middle of my crazy life.

I turned the phone over and over in my hands. The device felt heavy and hot. The last thing I needed was a commitment. Someone else to worry about. Heck, I'd just cleared the slate, unwillingly and voluntarily, of the responsibilities of other people. Being alone was definitely the right choice. *Wasn't it?*

On the other hand, it seemed unfair to continue to disregard this man who'd been so kind. So patient. So *interested*. As I watched the cat's tail click off the minutes, I thought how I'd felt uncharacteristically comfortable sharing with a perfect stranger whom I'd yet to even meet for coffee. I began to type.

ME: I'm sorry. You deserve much more. I've been through a court case with my father, and my mother passed away. You seem very nice. I'm just in over my head.

There. Closure. The 'what could have been' niggled at my heart, but it was the right thing to do. I bent down to retrieve a file folder from my bottom desk drawer and hefted the thick width of it onto my already cluttered desk.

JASON: Could I interest you in a coffee?

What part of my reply isn't he understanding? And why was I even entertaining the idea of going?

Before I could stop them, my fingers began to type.

ME: Sure.

JASON: How about I come your way and meet you at Brewster's Corner around six this evening? I'll be wearing purple.

The only possible response I could grant was a simple, "see you there."

The remainder of the day, my mind wandered. What if he's super short? Or unusually large like an overinflated balloon? I chided myself for such vain thoughts, yet reminded myself I was only human. At five forty that afternoon, I shut down my computer and tucked away the stray files lying scattered on my desk.

"Where're you going all gussied up? Got a hot date?" Dottie joked, as I strode by the front desk on my way out the door, unusually early and even more unusually in full make-up.

"Actually, I do." I smiled.

"Hold up! Whaaaaaaat? And you didn't tell me?" She leaned back, and I could tell I caught her off guard as she pressed her hand against her chest in a feigned heart attack.

"Well, it just sorta happened. And if by some snowball's chance in Hell this works out, I have to take back every bad thing I said about you and Janice and that online dating thing." I giggled.

"You go, girl. Call me later and tell me all about it. I'm gonna text Janice right now!" she squealed, clapping her hands together and fishing for her cell phone from her bag.

Fluffing my hair in the rearview mirror and haphazardly dotting on red lip gloss, I made my way into the coffee shop, trying not to look like a lost child. Scouting for gentlemen in purple, I heard my name before I spotted him. A bass voice sang out, "Kacee?" I turned to spot a handsome man with toffee brown skin and horn-rimmed glasses. He towered above me at about six feet tall and sported an amethyst button up shirt and black slacks coupled with shiny sleek wingtips.

"Jason?"

He had a humble expression on his face, one that made him look shy even though he didn't strike me as a bashful man.

"Yeah, I know I'm not what you expected. Um. Which is… a Converse shoe, obviously," he joked. I chortled, my chest squeezing a little. This beautiful man felt apologetic for who he was.

"No, you're not what I expected," I said. "I expected someone three feet shorter than me. Or someone bursting out of his shirt around the tummy area." We both released the laugh that stress had held hostage.

We each got our coffees, me a double espresso, him a plain house (no sugar, no cream), and located a small table slightly out of the main traffic pattern in hopes to drown out at least some of the buzzing chatter.

"Thanks for suggesting we meet," I said. "I don't want to pull you into my family drama, though. It's such a mess. I mean I'm not even ready for a relationship. I haven't even *been* in a relationship with anyone besides Barry in years. Barry's my dog, by the way."

"Whoa slow down, sister! Who said we were in a relationship? Just because you've finally seen me and know how dashingly handsome and irresistible I am in person, don't go thinking we can jump right into an engagement!" His quick wit and humor were truly infectious.

"I have an obvious question for you," I said, bringing the conversation back to seriousness.

"Okay, shoot."

"Why didn't you tell me you were Black? You know interracial dating is a bit out of the ordinary around here."

He thought for a moment, his lips pursed together. "Why didn't you tell me you were abnormally short?" He smiled, his broad shoulders shrugging with his retort, face slightly blushing. "Look, I know it's not the same thing. I also know what it's like to be judged by the color of my skin. It's happened all my life. I'm not ashamed of who I am or trying to hide it from anyone. I just wanted you to know me for me. *Then* you can decide whether you like me or not. Don't make that decision based on my height or my skin or my hair." He thought for a moment and lowered his voice to a whisper, leaning in. "It would be perfectly reasonable to make the decision based on someone's shoe choice, however," he remarked with a smirk.

I couldn't help but feel the flip of my stomach. The overused butterflies. A handsome man with a deep appreciation for good shoes.

The sun shone through the window and highlighted his face. I'd never dated anyone of a different race before. I could hear Mammi now. Hell, I could hear half the town of Glendale and most of Plantation. Annamae Armstrong would throw a fit. Or wag her Confederate flag at me. These parts of Texas hadn't progressed along with the rest of the world. Who knows if they ever would. But why did I have to stay stuck there, just because I'm surrounded by outdated ideals and stereotypes? If I chose to stick to such principles, I'd be no better than to be sucked into those judging me by Richard and the others who spread rumors about my mother.

"Tell me more about your family," I said. "What made you move to Trenton with your mom?"

CHAPTER 41

"So how do you feel after all of this? It's been quite a journey," Margaret asked, peering at me over her new designer reading glasses.

I was back in therapy sifting through the dust that had settled around me in the wake of my discoveries. "I'm still sorting it out, I guess you could say. I feel relief and guilt and happiness all at the same time. It sure wasn't what I expected to find. But I guess life never is."

I thought all I'd wanted were answers. A way to help me figure out my childhood, the divorce, my mother's behavior. I'd thought if I could dig up the facts, I'd be able to piece myself together. I got those on my journey back to Glendale, most of them penned in Mom's own hand. I even clawed my way through repressed memories of sexual abuse and sent Richard to jail. This should be a relief, yet a twinge of guilt lingers. Heck, my best friend and I reunited as a result of this crazy, mixed-up journey.

Mary and I had also been in contact after the trial. The authorities were poking into Robert's involvement and turns out he may be brought up on some accessory charges. We talked through pursuing the violation of her restraining orders. I encouraged her to try for sure. He committed a crime. It is, sadly, so tough to make those things hold up in court. One of the many misgivings of the justice system, in my opinion. On the bright side, his pending charges have made it easier for her to pursue divorce. Harassing her and the kids has gone down on his priority list as protecting himself has risen to the top.

I pondered Margaret's complicated question, in light of all that had taken place since our last in-person visit.

"I thought I'd feel more… I don't even know how to say it," I whispered in frustration, fingers raking the length of my hair.

"Satisfied?" Margaret suggested, her large eyes and round face staring back at me in patient observation.

"*Exactly!*" I said emphatically. "I should feel more satisfied at this point in my life. I mean my heavens; I solved my own childhood mystery. I was the prize witness for putting a child molester away, one who just happened to abuse me, my mother, *and* my best friend. I've buried my other parent." I laughed an inappropriate laugh. "I've always wanted to start over. Well, this shittastic predicament we're in now certainly lends itself to reinventing myself better than one I've ever seen, don'tcha think?" Out of breath and feeling hot steamy tears leak out of my eyes, I slumped back in the chair.

She reached behind and grabbed a tissue, holding it out as compassion filled her eyes. "You've dealt with a lot since you first decided to visit Glendale. That's for sure. I know it was way more than you bargained for. Truth is most family issues usually are. Now I know you don't want to hear this, Kacee, but some of these feelings you're having now are long overdue. You lived in denial for so long about the types of abuse you saw and endured. Both of those deeply affected your development. And they will continue to affect you."

"So you're saying that I'm cursed for the rest of my life because my biological father is Richard Robinson?"

"No. Not at all. What I'm saying is that you've got to accept the past *and* how it has shaped you and your future relationships." She paused a moment and prepared for a rebuttal as she began, "Now I know you are going to tell me Barry is all you need and you aren't cut out for the petty dating scene, blah, blah, blah, but you never know when the right moment—"

"Well, as a matter of fact, I have been talking with a really nice guy." Through my sniffles emerged a wry grin.

"And you've held out on me all this time?" Margaret exclaimed, slapping her leg and her mouth falling wide open. "Let's hear it!"

"His name is Jason, and we met on that crazy online thing I chastised Dottie and Janice for putting me on. I don't know… one day I decided to hop on there and answer his messages. Aunt Jackie and I were horsing around and needed a little pick me up." I could hardly contain the fluttering in the floor of my stomach. "I didn't even know what he looked like for the first several months we talked. Isn't that crazy?"

Margaret smiled in a knowing way, listening with sparkling eyes and intensity as I continued my story. A light rain pelted the window outside. *Tap. Tap. Tap.*

Pursing my lips and thinking, I rephrased. "We share so many common passions. A general overall theme of making the world a better place. We are both only children, who grew up in less-than-ideal homes. Though I suppose there isn't such a thing, is there?" I shifted my weight as the rhetorical question hung in the air. "He's an attorney building a small practice about an hour outside of here in Trenton."

"I sense hesitation in your voice and feel a giant 'but' coming up. What is it, Kacee?"

"Well, it came as more of a surprise than anything. I haven't told my friends yet, because I don't think it should matter. In an ideal world, that is. Yet you and I both know we live far and away from any sort of quintessential existence. He's Black."

Margaret grabbed for her cup of water, as an apparent tickle in her throat launched her into a coughing fit. I could envision the words of wisdom swirling above her head, yet I knew I'd caught her completely off guard. She averted her eyes, focusing on the parquet floor littered with a day's worth of Texas dirt. I wondered if she was silently counting and breathing the way she'd taught me.

"Kacee, if you are happy in the place where you are, do not let anyone rob you of that happiness. You speak of this young man's skin color as if it is a handicap, a burden. And you're partly right. To a lot of folks in this town, it will be just that, a reason for judgment. He should know that, and you have an obligation to let him in on what he's getting into if the two of you continue to develop this relationship. However, I've got the right mind to tell you, Sugar, that if he's living in Trenton, he already knows. I'll bet he throws his hands up when he's pulled over by a police officer without being asked. I'll bet he's used to being stared at and watching middle-aged white women with coiffed hair pull their small children close to them under the presumption he may hurt them if he goes out for a stroll after dark—all as a byproduct of the color of the skin he was born with. I'll bet he knows what it's like to be Black in a small southern town where not many things change." She tilted her head and folded her hands in her lap as she stared pointedly at Kacee. "The question is— Do you? And are you prepared to learn? That's a heavy question and a conversation I'd suggest you have."

I felt as if Margaret had taken a pin to my big news balloon, deflating it with one prick. Why are these things I'd never considered before? Look at how Mammi treated people of color. It wasn't that long ago. I was willing to learn and wanted to continue getting to know Jason for himself. He'd told me the first time we met in person the reason for his profile picture. He doesn't like assumptions to color people's first impressions without getting to know him first. That truth hit hard.

Crossing and uncrossing her legs, Margaret said, "I'm not trying to minimize the fact that you are getting back out there and engaging in life again. Gives me such comfort, honey. I am so proud of you."

"Thank you. I do have a question, though. Nearly every night Richard haunts my dreams. I hear his voice. I just want to know when I will get rid of him. Once and for all," I clamored.

"You won't, Kacee," Margaret calmly replied. "He is part of you. Forever. That's not the answer you want, but it's the hard truth. You can either use that to fuel the fire of good inside you that already burns, or you can keep him around as a crutch in your closet and blame every bad thing that happens on him. Play the victim. Your choice. *All* the choices are yours at this point. You are free to love him or hate him. And you might find yourself doing both at once. Stop feeling guilty for it. And stop punishing yourself. There are no more consequences to feelings or actions by or to him. You disarmed him, Kacee. You've usurped his power. And now it is *all* yours. You are in charge of your own self. Just you. To quote your mom, you are enough."

Her words kicked me in the chest. It was a concept I'd never considered, yet it made so much sense. I'd beat myself up every time I missed him, if only the good parts of him, the few that remained. I'd penalized myself, if only in my mind, for not getting to Mom sooner. For listening to him for so long and believing his mind games. For destroying my friendship with Breanna. For moving away and leaving Mom to deal with all of it on her own. For so many things.

"The best you can do for yourself is to stop trying to deny your past, honey. Don't let it consume you but acknowledge it's there. It will affect how you relate to your friends, your aunt, maybe even the grocery store clerk. It will most decidedly affect any intimate relationships in your future. But it also empowers you to relate to your clients in a unique way. It's nothing to be ashamed of. In fact, our past experiences make us who we are today. And what I see is an incredibly strong, independent young woman. I never met your momma or your Aunt Jackie but sounds to me like you mighta got some of those traits from them. And I think you hit the jackpot there." The corners of her mouth turned up, and she scribbled something on the notepad beside her.

"I'm pretty sure you are right. Did I tell you we are officially renaming TrueU Agency?" She raised an eyebrow, curious. "It will now be known as The Ruth Joy Center for Wellness."

A wide smile spread over her reddened cheeks as she pressed her hands together in a silent clap. "That's a wonderful idea!"

I still needed approval in many areas, something I knew I needed to work on, but Margaret's enthusiasm warmed me, nonetheless.

Time was up, but she took my hand in hers. "I know you are busy right now. I encourage you to come back at least in the next couple weeks, if you can. This is hard work. I want to leave you with a thought. Maya Angelou once said, 'I can be changed by what happens to me, but I refuse to be reduced by it.' Think about that, Kacee."

"I will," I smiled. "And we must be destined for each other."

A question mark formed through her furrowed brow.

"I quoted Maya Angelou in my mother's eulogy. She's one of my favorite authors. Which means you just gained credibility points," I quipped, half joking. She grinned. "See you soon, Margaret. I promise. And thank you."

CHAPTER 42

I emerged a different person in the months and years following my mother's death. It's been almost two years now, and there are still tiny pieces of the investigation that aren't wrapped up. It seems Richard's evil tunneled underground for miles. Aunt Jackie and I now talk via cell phones. I bought her one last Christmas, and basic lessons are a part of our weekly conversations. It's fun to feel like I'm helping *her* for once.

I've decided that Mom ultimately died from a broken heart. She was perhaps the strongest woman I know, and I will always blame myself for not listening earlier. Aunt Jackie concedes Mom is proud of me for vindicating her name, and I sure hope so. I take small comfort in the knowledge Richard can't hurt anyone else on the outside now.

I can't help but think how, once again, evil prevailed in a life that did nothing but uphold faith in her God. To say it's unfair would be cliché, yet I find myself wanting to scream it from the top of my roof some days. Instead, I silently pledge to Mom that I'll carry out her legacy. I'll try to understand her faith and uphold as many of her principles as I can without compromising my own.

It turns out Mom left me an obscene amount of money, despite my childhood wretchedness. That included her interest in the Havemeier Oil business. One thing's for certain, I'd never seen so many zeros before sitting down with the estate attorney. I still haven't decided what I want to do with it all. I suppose knowing I have access to all this money doesn't make me feel much different than I did before. I continue to live like a self-proclaimed penny pincher—except I got out of that cramped apartment and purchased a house in Plantation for Barry and me. He has a giant backyard to run around in, and Aunt Jackie is helping me start a little garden. I'm thinking of adding on to the newly renamed agency. It's funny that I went so long not talking to Mom and now it's that same silence I can't stand.

After renaming TrueU, I finally found the slogan I've been searching for all these years: "You are enough." I had an artist paint the phrase on the wall with big loopy brush strokes. In bright red, of course.

Last year, I admitted to Aunt Jackie that I have a problem with prescription drugs and alcohol. Dottie, of all people, confronted me. A ballsy move, if you ask me. I'd mixed up appointments several days in a row, and Dottie was growing tired of taking the blame with clients. She's known for quite some time, watching me retrieve secret stashes of liquor to wash down hidden pills. At first, I was angry, but as I allowed time to settle and reflect on Richard, I appreciated the direct confrontation.

Mary is all settled in the townhome I'd messaged her about. She checks in from time to time, and I am so proud of her for restarting a good life for her and the kids. She works as a hairdresser and arranges school pick-ups and drop offs like a champ. Mary took the initiative to file for divorce. She and I worked together with Jason to get Robert served without revealing her current home address. Surprisingly, he signed the paperwork, including the proposed settlement, with no qualms. He's still under investigation for his part in the drug transportation.

"I think he knows he's sunk," she told me during a recent conversation. "I only know how thankful I am to you for saving me from that situation," she spoke through tears. "My children are happy to come home now. My oldest made the comment a few weeks after we moved to the new place, 'Mom, it's nice to call a place home where there's no tension. To not wonder who's going to be hit each night. To know nobody will be screaming at me while I'm trying to study for a test or just go for a walk.'" She'd paused then told me that he'd actually thanked her for divorcing their dad, something she never thought she'd hear. The kids were so relieved to be released from the constant anxiety.

Such positive interaction was precisely the mission statement of The Ruth Joy Center for Wellness. Infusing women with the confidence to take care of themselves and their families.

Aunt Jackie is still in her log cabin with her cats. I go visit her and Breanna more often. I bring Barry along, and we sit at her same old green table, planning to solve the next great world problem. We even go to church when I visit, in Mom's honor.

Detective Bower is gearing up for this year's Stop the Abuse, though Detective Lee will be our secondary speaker since she did such a great job the year Mom died. They make an excellent team, and ticket sales continue to soar, bringing in increased donations for TrueU.

Today is Richard's 58th birthday. I can't help but wonder if he regrets what he did or if he never thinks about it. If he ever thinks about me, the girl he once touted to be his pride and joy.

I dialed Breanna.

"Hey there."

"Hey yourself," she said.

"Would you like to go grab coffee this morning?" I asked. "I'm driving into Glendale to visit Mom and Aunt Jackie."

"In honor or in spite of Richard's birthday?" she questioned. Her words caught me off guard.

"I, uh, I guess sort of in spite of. I can't quit thinking about him today, and I knew you could relate. How in the world did you remember it was Richard's birthday today?"

She paused for a moment. I could hear her fishing for the right words. "His birthday falls exactly one month to the day after my mom's. We never celebrated hers, but do you remember your dad always wanted a big party for his?" Apparently choosing her question with painstaking care, she continued, "Did it ever bother you that the only 'friends' at that party were your friends and the moms of your friends? I've thought about this a lot. I s'pose it doesn't matter too much now, given the situation, and maybe it ain't even my place to say it. But I'll bet there's no party he's enjoying today," she said with a satisfied tone.

"I think you're right about that. And he has us to thank." I felt her smiling along with me, even through the phone. "How is your mom doing today?" I asked.

"Today is a good day," she replied with a somber tone. "Having Maya around lifts her spirits, so we try visiting as often as we can. The dementia diagnosis threw her for a loop... all of us, really. I know it's only going to get worse, and I think that's what scares us both. You know, it almost seems like a cruel joke," she paused. "We both blamed our moms for so much of our broken childhoods when we were growing up that we never got to know them. We weren't mature enough to think through the *whys*. *Why* did they act the way they did? I didn't know people drank to numb pain from twenty years prior, yet that's what my mom was doing. I thought she was just being a shitty parent. And the same with you. You finally understand your mom's motives and reasoning behind her parenting and thought processes. You lost your mom physically and now I've started losing mine mentally." We audibly sighed in unison.

"I suppose that's the part of 'life's not fair.' I don't like it, though. Not one bit." She lamented.

"That makes two of us. I'm headed that way in just a few,

and I'll phone you when I get there. Maybe meet at Coffee Beans? Seems we could both use a hug today."

"Sure," Breanna clipped. "Oh, and Kacee?"

"Yeah?"

"For all we've been through, I'm sure glad we have each other to wade through this crazy life again." I felt the warmth of her smile pour through the line. "See you in a few." And with that, she was off the phone.

I'm trying to focus more on me and my future life versus the past. Not forget about my history, but rather forage my future. Attempting to lean on Margaret's advice and growing right along with our now-weekly sessions.

Jason and I have been on nineteen official dates so far and a few dozen unofficial ones. He likes country music, big dogs, ice cream, and doesn't mind a little bit of instability in my life. I've introduced him to Aunt Jackie and Henry. I could tell Henry had an inappropriate comment hiding up his sleeve, but he was pleasant, and Aunt Jackie's quick backhand kept him at bay. She's happy to see me happy. Jason also enjoys helping out at the agency, which is nice. He's even offered to consult on a few of my tougher cases. Dottie says he's "hot," and falls all over herself when he comes into the office. We do get our fair share of looks from townspeople, but I figure I'm still under Mom's quota. I suppose we were both unfairly judged, and this old world could use a few more Havemeiers doing the right thing. I'm not rushing into anything, but it sure is nice to have a two-legged companion.

CHAPTER 43

Each time I'm in Glendale, I drive out to the cemetery to visit Mom's grave. The rows upon rows of gray stones stand in perfect symmetry and reverence, in stark contrast to the bustling life on the adjacent main road. I try to find a new headstone each time I'm out there and imagine who that person might have been in life—a teacher, a congressman, maybe just someone's sweet grandmother. It helps me to believe their spirits stay connected to this earth by being thought of.

The wave of grass makes a gentle whoosh with the wind, and if I listen close, I can hear the leaves hit the ground as they fall from the giant red oaks. Not even the birds are singing today. As I approach Mom's marker, I notice a molasses-colored bunny with a stark white fluffy tail scampering between the gravestones. I sit down next to Mom, and the bunny perches himself at a nearby grave to watch. Eavesdropping. I'm an interloper in the sanctuary of his home, his beady eyes darting about yet not far from my whereabouts.

"I brought you some flowers, Mom. White hydrangeas, your favorite. I keep going back to Richard's prison sentence and wondering where the turning point started. I mean, eighty-five years without parole, and I wonder if it even phases him. It's not exactly atonement, but I guess it's as close as we're gonna get. For now, at least." A giggle spilled out of my gut from nowhere. "Do you remember reading Dr. Seuss to me when I was little? You were always reading me something." *Oh, The Places You'll Go* has always been one of my favorites. Here I am venting about all this stuff that's gone wrong, and the words chimed on autopilot, as if whisked out of a dark catacomb of secret memories in my brain.

I splayed the flowers out evenly in the concrete vase attached to her headstone, arranging them the best I knew how. "I guess we did go through our share of 'bang-ups and hang ups.' Like in that story, huh, Mom? Especially you. I knew you were strong, but I had no idea what you lived with—and through—all those years. I don't think I could have withstood that level of self-sacrifice." An old Chevy sedan meandered down the row of gravestones, parking a good distance from where I was perched, a family of three piling out of the car with fresh flowers and fresh tears.

"I'm sorry, Mom, that I didn't tell you about Richard. I should have. And I wish like hell you had told someone what he was doing to you. Maybe Susan. It sounds like you two were going through a lot of the same stuff at the same time and each of you was afraid to speak up. She was great at painting it all roses, but I've learned James hit her. I don't know if you knew that or not." Pausing for a beat to breathe, I then resumed. "Speaking of Susan, she came by Aunt Jackie's the other day. I've enjoyed getting to know her. The first time she walked into my office, I was surprised. I guess I can see why you'd want her on your side, even as a little girl." I chuckled to myself.

"It's all so unfair. How could one man be allowed to shatter so many lives?" No answer.

I touched the stone, rubbing it for good luck. "I close my eyes, and I see his face. Once I admitted it out loud it made it true, and now I can't unsee what happened. Why didn't that sovereign power of yours keep this from happening? I was just a little girl, and I'm so angry with your God. I don't want to be. But I am. I've been angry ever since you dragged me to church, and I had to listen to the preachers and watch all those other people look down on us. I don't know how you got past all of that and managed to not only find peace again but trust and love in this God that doled out such a joker of a life card to you. I know you aren't going to come up out of that grave and tell me. I sure wish there was a way to make that happen. I s'pose that's only happened once. After three days, wasn't it? See, Mom... I listened in church after all." I smiled to myself. "If you can help me out somehow, I'd really appreciate it. I'm still going to see Margaret, and that's going alright. I feel like I'm working through a lot, but I can't understand the spiritual side. Maybe with more time I'll get there." I sat with my hands in my lap, wringing them and ignoring the cold dirt clinging to my back-side. "I miss you and feel like I can at least stop running now. I even met a boy. I think you'd like him. He's finally teaching me how to trust. And he wants to take me to church, too." Giving the flowers one last touch, I knew they wouldn't stay pretty in the elements. I turned back to the grave and kissed the hard stone. "I love you, Mom. See you soon."

I paused for a moment, the heel of my tall brown boots digging into the soft earth. "Oh, and I sure hope you've found 'the bright places where Boom Bands are playing.'"

Who knows, maybe there is an afterlife. Maybe if I can learn to trust again, I can find that thing called *faith* she touted her whole life. She said her god never gave up on anyone.

In the middle of it all, I remember thinking I was lost. Unidentified. If every player in my life had failed to be who I'd made them out to be, then I had no identity. My foundation had crumbled. As time continues to pass, I realize that couldn't be farther from the truth. We all create our own versions of the truth —both for ourselves and other people. We are only responsible for our own selves, and letting others define us is an act of weak-ness. I am no more or no less Kacee Robinson because of the actions of Mom or Richard. I can be shaped by those actions, but each day I'm responsible for laying a new foundation for myself.

As I turned to leave, I glanced at the bunny, scurrying away and seemingly satisfied with the discussion. Soft on the outside, yet quick in speed; his ability to change direction lying only within himself and no outside force. Bunnies have vision spanning three hundred and sixty degrees and are known to be fiercely independent; I found his presence ironic at the least. "Watch over her, buddy," I said. "She's pretty darn special."

The little rabbit paused and stared with his dark eyes and twitchy nose. Some of the most awful experiences in life open doors to beauty we never knew existed. Or perhaps the world's definition of beauty obscured my eyes from the true wonder within.

Ruth Havemeier Robinson was a true wonder. Taking a person at face value is the most foolish action we take as individuals---one of life's great conundrums. Thanks, Mom. It turns out we were both always enough.

The issues dealt with by the characters in the pages of THE MEASURE OF ENOUGH are real. Domestic violence, sexual abuse, mental illness, and eating disorders are a few of the subjects most notably experienced by Ruth and Kacee. If you or someone you love is struggling with one of these concerns, please consider utilizing resources below. Otherwise, please take a moment to educate yourself as to the rampant prevalence of these topics in our society today. Be an advocate. Let your voice be heard.

Domestic violence

Domestic violence, also known as intimate partner violence, is a serious, preventable problem that is a wide-spread problem in our country and around the world. Domestic violence is governed by the willful intimidation, physical assault, battery, sexual assault, or other abusive behavior as part of a systematic pattern of power and control perpetrated by one intimate partner against another. It can occur among heterosexual or same-sex couples and does not require sexual intimacy. It includes physical violence, sexual violence, threats, and emotional/psychological abuse. The frequency and severity of domestic violence varies dramatically.

· In the United States, an average of 32 people are physically abused by intimate partners every minute.

· On a typical day, domestic violence hotlines nationwide receive over 20,000 calls.

· 19% of intimate partner violence involves a weapon.

· 1 in 5 women and 1 in 59 men in the United States are raped during her/his lifetime.

· 1 in 3 female murder victims and 1 in 20 male murder victims are killed by intimate partners.

· Women between the ages of 25 and 34 are the most vulnerable to domestic violence, with almost half of the population of women encountering at least one incident of sexual violence, physical violence, or stalking by an intimate partner during their lifetime.

·   Each year, 10 million children are exposed to domestic violence, which the Centers for Disease Control declared a "serious, preventable, public health problem."

·   According to The Center for Women and Families, of the 1 in 15 kids exposed to domestic violence, a heartbreaking 90% are eyewitnesses who will feel the effect of it for their entire lives.

·   Only 34% of people who are injured by intimate partners receive medical care for their injuries.

·   Intimate partner victimization is correlated with a higher rate of depression and suicidal behaviors.

·   Between 21-60% of victims of intimate partner violence lose their jobs due to reasons stemming from abuse.

·   The cycle continues as 1 in 5 high school female students report being physically or sexually abused by a partner.

- 60% of children in the United States are eyewitnesses to domestic abuse against a parent.

*Center for Disease Control and Prevention

**National Coalition Against Domestic Violence

***Break the Cycle 2024

National Domestic Violence Hotline at 1-800-799-7233 or 9-1-1.

Eating Disorders

Eating disorders are defined by the National Eating Disorder Association as follows:

Eating disorders are serious but treatable mental and physical illnesses that can affect people of every age, sex, gender, race, ethnicity, and socioeconomic group. National surveys estimate that 20 million women and ten million men in America will have an eating disorder at some point in their lives. Obsessions with food, body weight, and shape may also signal an eating disorder. Common eating disorders include binge eating disorder, bulimia nervosa, and, less common but very serious, anorexia nervosa.

· Eating disorders have the highest mortality rate of any mental illness.

· Eating disorders affect all ages and ethnic groups.

· Every 62 minutes at least one person dies as a direct result of an eating disorder,

The National Eating Disorder Helpline is 1-800-931-2237

*National Eating Disorder Association

**National Association of Anorexia Nervosa and Associated Disorders

Anxiety Disorders

The wide variety of **anxiety disorders** differ by the objects or situations that induce them but share features of excessive anxiety and related behavioral disturbances. Anxiety disorders can interfere with daily activities such as job performance, school, work, and relationships.

—National Institute of Mental Health

· An estimated 19.1% of U.S. adults had any anxiety disorder in the past year.

· Past year prevalence of any anxiety disorder was higher for females (23.4%) than for males (14.3%).

· An estimated 31.9% of adolescents have some type of anxiety disorder.

· Of adolescents with any anxiety disorder, an estimated 8.3% have severe impairment (DSM- IV criteria used to determine impairment).

· The prevalence of any anxiety disorder among adolescents was higher for females (30.8%) than for males (26.1%).

*National Suicide Prevention Hotline 1-800-273-8255

Sexual Abuse

Sexual abuse of a child is defined as, "conduct harmful to a child's mental, emotional, or physical welfare, including conduct that constitutes the offense of indecency with a child, sexual assault, or aggravated sexual assault; failure to make a reasonable effort to prevent sexual conduct harmful to a child; compelling or encouraging the child to engage in sexual conduct; and causing, permitting, encouraging, engaging in, or allowing the photographing, filming or depicting of the child if the person knew or should have known that the resulting photograph, film, or depiction of the child is obscene or pornographic." Definition taken from Texas State Family Code, Section 261.001

·   Adults can also encounter sexual abuse, which should be taken seriously as well.

·   1 in 5 women and 1 in 71 men will be raped at some point in their lives.

·   51.1% of female victims of rape reported being raped by an intimate partner and 40.8% by an acquaintance.

·   52.4% of male victims report being raped by an acquaintance and 15.1% by a stranger.

·   91% of victims of rape and sexual assault are female, and 9 percent are male.

·   In eight out of ten cases of rape, the victim knew the perpetrator.

·   Annually, rape costs the U.S. more than any other crime ($127 billion), followed by assault ($93 billion), murder ($71 billion), and drunk driving, including fatalities ($61 billion).

·   81% of women and 35% of men report significant short- or long-term impacts such as Post-Traumatic Stress Disorder (PTSD).

·   Health care is 16% higher for women who were sexually abused as children and 36% higher for women who were physically and sexually abused as children.

·   1 in 4 girls and 1 in 6 boys will be sexually abused before they turn 18 years old.

·   30% of women were between the ages of 11 and 17 at the time of their first completed rape.

·   12.3% of women were age 10 or younger at the time of their first completed rape victimization.

·   27.8% of men were age 10 or younger at the time of their first completed rape victimization.

·   More than one third of women who report being raped before age 18 also experience rape as an adult.

·   96% of people who sexually abuse children are male, and 76.8% of people who sexually abuse children are adults.

·   34% of people who sexually abuse a child are family members of the child.

·   Only 12% of children raped EVER report the rape to authorities.

*Contact local authorities.

*National Sexual Violence Resource Center, 2018

If you or someone you know is struggling with one of these issues, please use the above resources or seek professional help. You can always call 9-1-1 in the event of an imminent threat. Domestic violence and sexual violence for both adults and children, is a real issue. They are some of the most underreported crimes, causing some of the most damaging and long-lasting devastation. Mental health is a problem often swept under the rug in our society. Speak out. Get help. Encourage your loved ones to do so. They are the brave ones. Don't walk through this alone. YOU ARE ENOUGH.

If you enjoyed THE MEASURE OF ENOUGH, I'd be honored if you'd tell a friend or coworker. Share your experience. And sign up to be on my mailing list for upcoming news, future book launches, and promotions at https://www.deonnakay.com/newsletter. Thank you for reading and see you in the pages!

ACKNOWLEDGMENTS

A huge thank you to you, the reader! I hope you enjoyed THE MEASURE OF ENOUGH. This project has truly been a labor of love for so many reasons. Although a work of fiction, I have personally struggled with some of the heavy issues depicted in these pages, so it was important to discuss them. Please take time to thumb through the Final Remarks section for information and resources.

I must thank a few folks for their undying support throughout this journey. First up is my most amazing little mini-me, cheerleader, and the one who always believes in me, even when my belief in myself falters. A huge thank you to my daughter, Hope. Your wisdom is beyond your years, kiddo! I love you beyond words.

To my dad who instilled in me a love of writing and my sister who taught me how to read long before any formalized education- thank you! Thank you to my dad, sister, and brother (in law) for continuing to ask about the book and knowing that it would eventually be published, even if it took a few years. Your support means everything.

Thank you to my late mother and guardian angel, who believed in me when I began penning this book nearly six years ago and during every single phase of my life.

Thank you to Mrs. Wynne, my very favorite English teacher. She taught me (a long time ago in middle school) a respect for writing and a love for language that I've never lost, along with the knowledge of how to correct your mistakes with a good red pen.

A big thank you to my MANY supportive friends who've continued to keep up with my progress on this work, beta read for me, offer input, and listen to me blow off steam about the joys and struggles of writing a book.

To my writing partner and writing bestie, Jess Ames. I'd never have made it this far without your critiques, many sleepless nights of guidance, and words of encouragement. We were in the depths of this thing together, sometimes wondering if it had a bottom!

Thank you to my book coach, developmental editor, and all the other hats she wears, Monica Cox. You are simply amazing, friend.

To my girls at the Women's Fiction Writers Association. This is the group that keeps me sane, or as sane as I get, most days of writing. When things get too hairy, this is the group that knows, and I'm so lucky to have found these ladies.

It takes a village, and I am blessed to have the best one.